"Gibson is the Raymond Chandler of the digital age, *noir* master of the Web. [*Idoru* is] written with crackling style and hurtles forward with the speed of a bullet train. Moreover, it's filled with delicious little tidbits where Gibson plays with the obsessions of trash culture and carries them to their post-millennial extreme."

—*NEW YORK DAILY NEWS*

"Gibson remains, like Chandler, an intoxicating stylist . . . Clever and provocative scenery . . . vivid, slangy prose. Chia is one of his most winning creations."

—*NEW YORK TIMES BOOK REVIEW*

"Spooky . . . [*Idoru* is] a sharp satire on the uses and abuses of technology and has much to tell us about the dangerous path science has laid out for us."

—*BALTIMORE SUN*

"Gibson's trademark mix of high-tech pyrotechnics and dark psychological comedy is in evidence throughout *Idoru,* and his characters are as compelling as ever. Gibson's novel should come with a warning label: *Objects in the novel may be closer than they appear.*"

—*TIME OUT*

"His most exhilarating work to date. Another great achievement for Gibson. Once again, his take on the future shows him weaving a great, surreal thriller out of imagination and invention."

—*BOOKPAGE*

"An enthralling ride . . . Rollercoaster prose and dazzling prediction."

—*THE RECORD* (Hackensack, NJ)

"Offers a vision that will tantalize anyone interested in the inevitable tsunami of digital information that is aimed directly at us."

—*PHILADELPHIA CITY PAPER*

"Highly approachable, engaging, and persuasive."

—*KIRKUS REVIEWS* (starred review)

"Gibson remains on the cutting edge . . . [*Idoru*] resonates with startling realism as it presents a future not unlike the present, part hell and part paradise."

—*BOOKLIST*

21st century Tokyo, after the millennial quake.
Is something different here, in the very nature of reality?
Or is it that something violently *new* is about to happen...

Colin Laney is here looking for work. He is an intuitive fisher for patterns of information, the "signature" an individual creates simply by going about the business of living. But Laney knows how to sift for the dangerous bits. Which makes him useful—to certain people.

Chia McKenzie is here on a rescue mission. She's fourteen. Her idol is the singer Rez, of the band Lo/Rez. When the Seattle chapter of the Lo/Rez fan club decided that he might be in trouble in Tokyo, they sent Chia to check it out.

Rei Toei is the idoru*—the beautiful, entirely virtual media star adored by all Japan. Rez has declared that he will marry her. This is the rumor that has brought Chia to Tokyo. True or not, the* idoru *and the powerful interests surrounding her are enough to put all their lives in danger.*

"*Idoru* is a prophecy, a prayer for information baths that never drown the supplicant. It is also a text on paper, beautifully written, dense with metaphors that open the eyes to the new, dreamlike, intensely imagined, deeply plausible. It is a profoundly cunning advertisement for a world whose enclosed spaces—and infinite domains within the skull—we had better be prepared to join."

—*THE WASHINGTON POST BOOK WORLD*

"Gibson's vision is disturbing, his speculation brilliant and his prose immaculate, cementing his reputation as the premier visionary working in SF today."

—*PUBLISHERS WEEKLY* (starred review)

"Gibson envisions a future in which the lines between the virtual and the actual are terminally blurred. How 'real' are today's celebrities? . . . What will happen when the Web allows anyone—anyone at all—to be a star? With characteristic brilliance, the writer who invented the word *cyberspace* looks for answers."

—*ROLLING STONE*

continued...

"Full of color, texture, and depth from beginning to end . . . His technology is both dazzling and disturbing. Gibson's style is vivid, graceful, and dense. At the same time, *Idoru* moves faster than the Roadrunner on crack. A wonderful story. Don't pass it up—even if you don't own a computer."

—Poppy Z. Brite, *VILLAGE VOICE*

"Gibson, like Hemingway, possesses the ability to paint a living, breathing portrait of the world around his characters. His intelligence and imagination take readers into worlds they have never dreamed of, but Gibson makes it seem more real than a dream."

—*HARTFORD COURANT*

"Prose simultaneously as hard and laconic as Elmore Leonard's and as galactically poetic as J. G. Ballard's. Gibson finds new and compelling ways to couch the SF questions first asked by Philip K. Dick: what is reality? And who is human? [*Idoru* is] a speed-bumped tour of a sexy, scary future that seems just around the next temporal corner. Gibson's work is powered by an unparalleled instinct for the metaphors through which technology reveals our own unconscious desires."

—*NEW STATESMAN & SOCIETY*

Also by William Gibson

NEUROMANCER
COUNT ZERO
BURNING CHROME
JOHNNY MNEMONIC: THE SCREENPLAY
MONA LISA OVERDRIVE
VIRTUAL LIGHT

WILLIAM GIBSON

BERKLEY BOOKS, NEW YORK

IDORU

A Berkley Book / published by arrangement with the author

PRINTING HISTORY
G.P. Putnam's Sons edition / September 1996
Berkley edition / September 1997

Cover illustration by Honi Werner (with details from a photograph by Ralph Mercer/Gamma Liaison).

For information address: The Berkley Publishing Group, a member of Penguin Putnam Inc., 200 Madison Avenue, New York, New York 10016.

The Putnam Berkley World Wide Web site address is http://www.berkley.com

ISBN: 0-425-15864-0

BERKLEY®
Berkley Books are published by The Berkley Publishing Group, 200 Madison Avenue, New York, New York 10016, a member of Penguin Putnam Inc.
BERKLEY and the "B" design are trademarks belonging to Berkley Publishing Corporation.

PRINTED IN THE UNITED STATES OF AMERICA

10 9 8 7 6 5 4 3 2 1

for
CLAIRE

Thanks

Sogho Ishii, the Japanese director, introduced me to Kowloon Walled City via the photographs of Ryuji Miyamoto. It was Ishii-san's idea that we should make a science fiction movie there. We never did, but the Walled City continued to haunt me, though I knew no more about it than I could gather from Miyamoto's stunning images, which eventually provided most of the texture for the Bridge in my novel *Virtual Light.*

Architect Ken Vineberg drew my attention to an article about the Walled City in *Architectural Review*, where I first learned of *City of Darkness*, the splendid record assembled by Greg Girard and Ian Lambrot (Watermark, London, 1993). From London, John Jarrold very kindly arranged for me to receive a copy.

Anything I know of the toecutting business, I owe to the criminal memoirs of Mark Brandon "Chopper" Read (*Chopper from the Inside*, Sly Ink, Australia, 1991). Mr. Read is a great deal scarier than Blackwell, and has even fewer ears.

Karl Taro Greenfeld's *Speed Tribes* (HarperCollins, New York, 1994) richly fed my dreams of Laney's jet lag.

Stephen P. ("Plausibility") Brown rode shotgun on the work in progress for many months, commenting daily, sometimes more often, and always with a fine forbearance, as I faxed him a bewildering flurry of disconnected fragments he was somehow expected to interpret as "progress." His constant encouragement and seemingly endless patience were absolutely essential to this book's completion.

My publishers, on both sides of the Atlantic, also demonstrated great patience, and I thank them.

Death Cube K

After Slitscan, Laney heard about another job from Rydell, the night security man at the Chateau. Rydell was a big quiet Tennessean with a sad shy grin, cheap sunglasses, and a walkie-talkie screwed permanently into one ear.

"Paragon-Asia Dataflow," Rydell said, around four in the morning, the two of them seated in a pair of huge old armchairs. Concrete beams overhead had been hand-painted to vaguely resemble blond oak. The chairs, like the rest of the furniture in the Chateau's lobby, were oversized to the extent that whoever sat in them seemed built to a smaller scale.

"Really?" Laney asked, keeping up the pretense that someone like Rydell would know where he could still find work.

"Tokyo, Japan," Rydell said, and sucked iced latte through a plastic straw. "Guy I met in San Francisco last year. Yamazaki. He's working for 'em. Says they need a serious netrunner."

Netrunner. Laney, who liked to think of himself as a researcher, suppressed a sigh. "Contract job?"

"Guess so. Didn't say."

"I don't think I'd want to live in Tokyo."

Rydell used his straw to stir the foam and ice remaining at the bottom of his tall plastic cup, as though he were hoping to find a secret prize. "He didn't say you'd have to." He looked up. "You ever been to Tokyo?"

"No."

"Must be an interesting place, after that quake and all." The walkie-talkie ticked and whispered. "I gotta go on out and check the gate by the bungalows now. Feel like coming?"

"No," Laney said. "Thanks."

Rydell stood, automatically straightening the creases in his khaki uniform trousers. He wore a black nylon web-belt hung with various holstered devices, all of them black, a short-sleeved white shirt, and a peculiarly immobile black tie. "I'll leave the number in your box," he said.

Laney watched the security man cross the terra cotta and the various rugs, to vanish past the darkly polished panels of the registration desk. He'd had something going on cable once, Laney had gathered. Nice guy. Loser.

Laney sat there until dawn came edging in through the tall, arched windows, and Taiwanese stainless could be heard to rattle, but gently, from the darkened cave of the breakfast room. Immigrant voices, in some High Steppe dialect the Great Khans might well have understood. Echoes woke from the tiled floor, from the high beams surviving from an age that must once have seen the advent of Laney's kind or predecessors, their ecology of celebrity and the terrible and inviolable order of that food chain.

•

Rydell left a folded sheet of Chateau notepaper in Laney's box. A Tokyo number. Laney found it there the next afternoon, along with an updated estimate of his final bill from the lawyers.

He took them both up to the room he could no longer even pretend to afford.

A week later he was in Tokyo, his face reflected in an elevator's gold-veined mirror for this three-floor ascent of the aggressively nondescript O My Golly Building. To be admitted to Death Cube K, apparently a Franz Kafka theme bar.

Stepping from the elevator into a long space announced in acid-etched metal as The Metamorphosis. Where salarimen in white shirts had removed their suit jackets and loosened their dark ties, and sat at a bar of artfully corroded steel, drinking, the high backs of their chairs molded from some brown and chitinous resin. Insectoid mandibles curved above the drinkers' heads like scythes.

He moved forward into brown light, a low murmur of conversation. He understood no Japanese. The walls, unevenly transparent, repeated a motif of wing cases and bulbous abdomens, spikey brown limbs folded in at regular intervals. He increased his pace, aiming for a curving stairway molded to resemble glossy brown carapaces.

The eyes of Russian prostitutes followed him from tables opposite the bar, flat and doll-like in this roach-light. The Natashas were everywhere, working girls shipped in from Vladivostok by the Kombinat. Routine plastic surgery lent them a hard assembly-line beauty. Slavic Barbies. A simpler operation implanted a tracking device for the benefit of their handlers.

The stairway opened into The Penal Colony, a disco, deserted at this hour, pulses of silent red lightning marking Laney's steps across the dance floor. A machine of some kind was suspended from the ceiling. Each of its articulated arms, suggestive of antique dental equipment, was tipped with sharp steel. Pens, he thought, vaguely remembering Kafka's story. Sentence of guilt, graven in the flesh of the condemned man's back. Wincing at a memory of upturned eyes unseeing. Pushed it down. Moved on.

A second stairway, narrow, more steep, and he entered The Trial, low-ceilinged and dark. Walls the color of anthracite. Small flames shivered behind blue glass. He hesitated, nightblind and jet-lagged.

"Colin Laney, is it?"

Australian. Enormous. Who stood behind a little table, shoulders sloping bearlike. Something strange about the shape of his shaven head. And another, much smaller figure, seated there. Japanese, in a long-sleeved plaid shirt buttoned up to its oversized collar. Blinking up at Laney through circular lenses.

"Have a seat, Mr. Laney," the big man said.

And Laney saw that this man's left ear was missing, sheared away, leaving only a convoluted stump.

When Laney had worked for Slitscan, his supervisor was named Kathy Torrance. Palest of pale blonds. A pallor bordering on translucence, certain angles of light suggesting not blood but some fluid the shade of summer straw. On her left thigh the absolute indigo imprint of something twisted and multibarbed, an expensively savage pictoglyph. Visible each Friday, when she made it her habit to wear shorts to work.

She complained, always, that the nature of celebrity was much the worse for wear. Strip-mined, Laney gathered, by generations of her colleagues.

She propped her feet on the ledge of a hotdesk. She wore meticulous little reproductions of lineman's boots, buckled across the instep and stoutly laced to the ankle. He looked at her legs, their taut sweep from wooly sock tops to the sandpapered fringe of cut-off jeans. The tattoo looked like something from another planet, a sign or message burned in from the depths of space, left there for mankind to interpret.

He asked her what she meant. She peeled a mint-flavored toothpick from its wrapper. Eyes he suspected were gray regarded him through mint-tinted contacts.

"Nobody's really famous anymore, Laney. Have you noticed that?"

"No."

"I mean *really* famous. There's not much fame left, not in the old sense. Not enough to go around."

"The old sense?"

"We're the media, Laney. We *make* these assholes celebrities. It's a push-me, pull-you routine. They come to us to be created." Vibram cleats kicked concisely off the hotdesk. She tucked her boots in, heels against denim haunches, white knees hiding her mouth. Balanced there on the pedestal of the hotdesk's articulated Swedish chair.

"Well," Laney said, going back to his screen, "that's still fame, isn't it?"

"But is it real?"

He looked back at her.

"We learned to print money off this stuff," she said. "Coin of our realm. Now we've printed too much; even the audience knows. It shows in the ratings."

Laney nodded, wishing she'd leave him to his work.

"Except," she said, parting her knees so he could

see her say it, "when we decide to destroy one."

Behind her, past the anodyzed chainlink of the Cage, beyond a framing rectangle of glass that filtered out every tint of pollution, the sky over Burbank was perfectly blank, like a sky-blue paint chip submitted by the contractor of the universe.

The man's left ear was edged with pink tissue, smooth as wax. Laney wondered why there had been no attempt at reconstruction.

"So I'll remember," the man said, reading Laney's eyes.

"Remember what?"

"Not to forget. Sit down."

Laney sat on something only vaguely chairlike, an attenuated construction of black alloy rods and laminated Hexcel. The table was round and approximately the size of a steering wheel. A votive flame licked the air, behind blue glass. The Japanese man with the plaid shirt and metal-framed glasses blinked furiously. Laney watched the large man settle himself, another slender chair-thing lost alarmingly beneath a sumo-sized bulk that appeared to be composed entirely of muscle.

"Done with the jet lag, are we?"

"I took pills." Remembering the SST's silence, its lack of apparent motion.

"Pills," the man said. "Hotel adequate?"

"Yes," Laney said. "Ready for the interview."

"Well then," vigorously rubbing his face with heavily scarred hands. He lowered his hands and stared at Laney, as if seeing him for the first time. Laney, avoiding the gaze of those eyes, took in the man's outfit, some sort of nanopore exercise gear intended to fit loosely on a smaller but still very large man. Of no particular color in the darkness of The Trial. Open from collar to breastbone. Straining against abnormal mass. Exposed flesh tracked and crossed by an atlas of scars, baffling in their variety of shape and texture. "Well, then?"

Laney looked up from the scars. "I'm here for a job interview."

"Are you?"

"Are you the interviewer?"

" 'Interviewer'?" The ambiguous grimace revealing an obvious dental prosthesis.

Laney turned to the Japanese in the round glasses. "Colin Laney."

"Shinya Yamazaki," the man said, extending his hand. They shook. "We spoke on the telephone."

"You're conducting the interview?"

A flurry of blinks. "I'm sorry, no," the man said. And then, "I am a student of existential sociology."

"I don't get it," Laney said. The two opposite said nothing. Shinya Yamazaki looked embarrassed. The one-eared man glowered.

"You're Australian," Laney said to the one-eared man.

"Tazzie," the man corrected. "Sided with the South in the Troubles."

"Let's start over," Laney suggested. " 'Paragon-Asia Dataflow.' You them?"

"Persistent bugger."

"Goes with the territory," Laney said. "Professionally, I mean."

"Fair enough." The man raised his eyebrows, one of which was bisected by a twisted pink cable of scar tissue. "Rez, then. What do you think of *him?*"

"You mean the rock star?" Laney asked, after struggling with a basic problem of context.

A nod. The man regarded Laney with utmost gravity.

"From Lo/Rez? The band?" Half Irish, half Chinese. A broken nose, never repaired. Long green eyes. "What do I *think* of him?"

In Kathy Torrance's system of things, the singer had been reserved a special disdain. She had viewed him as a living fossil, an annoying survival from an earlier, less evolved era. He was at once massively and meaninglessly famous, she maintained, just as he was both massively and meaninglessly wealthy. Kathy thought of celebrity as a subtle fluid, a universal element, like the phlogiston of the ancients, something spread evenly at creation through all the universe, but prone now to accrete, under specific conditions, around certain individuals and their careers. Rez, in Kathy's view, had simply lasted far too long. Monstrously long. He was affecting the unity of her theory. He was defying the proper order of the food chain. Perhaps there was nothing big enough to eat him, not even Slitscan. And while Lo/Rez, the band, still extruded product on an annoyingly regular basis, in a variety of media, their singer stubbornly refused to destroy himself, murder someone, become active in politics, admit to an interesting substance-abuse problem or an arcane sexual addiction—indeed to do anything at all worthy of an opening segment on Slitscan. He glimmered, dully perhaps, but steadily, just beyond Kathy Torrance's reach. Which was, Laney had always assumed, the real reason for her hating him so.

"Well," Laney said, after some thought, and feeling a peculiar compulsion to attempt a truthful answer, "I remember buying their first album. When it came out."

"Title?" The one-eared man grew graver still.

" 'Lo Rez Skyline,' " Laney said, grateful for whatever minute synaptic event had allowed the recall. "But I couldn't tell you how many they've put out since."

"Twenty-six, not counting compilations," said Mr. Yamazaki, straightening his glasses.

Laney felt the pills he'd taken, the ones that were supposed to cushion the jet lag, drop out from under him like some kind of rotten pharmacological scaffolding. The walls of The Trial seemed to grow closer.

"If you aren't going to tell me what this is about,"

he said to the one-eared man, "I'm going back to the hotel. I'm tired."

"Keith Alan Blackwell," extending his hand. Laney allowed his own to be taken and briefly shaken. The man's palm felt like a piece of athletic equipment. " 'Keithy.' We'll have a few drinks and a little chat."

"First you tell me whether or not you're from Paragon-Asia," Laney suggested.

"Firm in question's a couple of lines of code in a machine in a backroom in Lygon Street," Blackwell said. "A dummy, but you could say it's *our* dummy, if that makes you feel better."

"I'm not sure it does," Laney said. "You fly me over to interview for a job, now you're telling me the company I'm supposed to be interviewing for doesn't exist."

"It *exists,*" said Keith Alan Blackwell. "It's on the machine in Lygon Street."

A waitress arrived. She wore a shapeless gray cotton boilersuit and cosmetic bruises.

"Big draft. Kirin. Cold one. What's yours, Laney?"

"Iced coffee."

"Coke Lite, please," said the one who'd introduced himself as Yamazaki.

"Fine," said the earless Blackwell, glumly, as the waitress vanished into the gloom.

"I'd appreciate it if you could explain to me what we're doing here," Laney said. He saw that Yamazaki was scribbling frantically on the screen of a small notebook, the lightpen flashing faintly in the dark. "Are you taking this down?" Laney asked.

"Sorry, no. Making note of waitress' costume."

"Why?" Laney asked.

"Sorry," said Yamazaki, saving what he'd written and turning off the notebook. He tucked the pen carefully into a recess on the side. "I am a student of such things. It is my habit to record ephemera of popular culture. Her costume raises the question: does it merely reflect the theme of this club, or does it represent some deeper response to trauma of earthquake and subsequent reconstruction?"

Lo Rez Skyline

They met in a jungle clearing.

Kelsey had done the vegetation: big bright Rousseau leaves, cartoon orchids flecked with her idea of tropical colors (which reminded Chia of that mall chain that sold ''organic'' cosmetic products in shades utterly unknown to nature). Zona, the only one telepresent who'd ever seen anything like a real jungle, had done the audio, providing birdcalls, invisible but realistically dopplering bugs, and the odd vegetational rustle artfully suggesting not snakes but some shy furry thing, soft-pawed and curious.

The light, such as there was, filtered down through high, green canopies, entirely too Disneyesque for Chia—though there was no real need for ''light'' in a place that consisted of nothing else.

Zona, her blue Aztec death's-head burning bodiless, ghosts of her blue hands flickering like strobe-lit doves: "Clearly, this dickless whore, the disembodied, has contrived to ensnare his soul." Stylized lightning zig-zags rose around the crown of the neon skull in deliberate emphasis.

Chia wondered what she'd really said. Was "dickless whore" an artifact of instantaneous on-line translation, or was that really something you could or would say in Mexican?

"Waiting hard con-firm from Tokyo chapter," Kelsey reminded them. Kelsey's father was a Houston tax lawyer, something of his particular species of biz-speak tending to enter his daughter around meeting time; also a certain ability to *wait* that Chia found irritating, particularly as manifested by a saucer-eyed nymph-figure out of some old *anime*. Which Chia was double damn sure Kelsey would *not* look like real-time, were they ever to meet that way. (Chia herself was presenting currently as an only slightly tweaked, she felt, version of how the mirror told her she actually looked. Less nose, maybe. Lips a little fuller. But that was it. Almost.)

"Exactly," Zona said, miniature stone calendars whirling angrily in her eye-holes. "We *wait.* While *he* moves ever closer to his fate. We wait. If my girls and I were to wait like this, the Rats would sweep us from the avenues." Zona was, she claimed, the leader of a knife-packing *chilanga* girl gang. Not the meanest in Mexico City, maybe, but serious enough about turf and tribute. Chia wasn't sure she believed it, but it made for some interesting attitude in meetings.

''Really?'' Kelsey drew her nymph-self up with elvin dignity, batting *manga*-doe lashes in disbelief. ''In *that* case, Zona Rosa, why don't you just get yourself over to *Tokyo* and find out what's really going *on?* I mean, did Rez *say* that, that he was going to marry her, or what? And while you're at it, find out whether she *exists* or not, okay?''

The calendars stopped on a dime.

The blue hands vanished.

The skull seemed to recede some infinite distance yet remain perfectly in focus, clear in every textural detail.

Old trick, Chia thought. Stalling.

''You know that I cannot do that,'' Zona said. ''I have responsibilities here. Maria Conchita, the Rat warlord, has stated that—''

''As if *we* care, right?'' Kelsey launched herself straight up, her nymphness a pale blur against the rising tangle of green, until she hovered just below the canopy, a beam of sunlight flattering one impossible cheekbone. ''Zona Rosa's full of shit!'' she bellowed, not at all nymphlike.

''Don't fight,'' Chia said. ''This is *important.* Please.''

Kelsey descended, instantly. ''Then *you* go,'' she said.

''Me?''

''You,'' Kelsey said.

"I can't," Chia said. "To Tokyo? How could I?"

"In an airplane."

"We don't have your kind of money, Kelsey."

"You've got a passport. We know you do. Your mother had to get one for you when she was doing the custody thing. And we know that you are, to put it delicately, 'between schools,' yes?"

"Yes—"

"Then what's the prob?"

"Your father's a big tax lawyer!"

"I know," Kelsey said. "And he flies back and forth, all over the world, making money. But you know what else he earns, Chia?"

"What?"

"Frequent-flyer points. *Big-ass* frequent-flyer points. On Air Magellan."

"Interesting," said the Aztec skull.

"Tokyo," said the mean nymph.

Shit, Chia thought.

The wall opposite Chia's bed was decorated with a six-by-six laser blowup of the cover of *Lo Rez Skyline,* their first album. Not the one you got if you bought it today, but the original, the group shot they'd done for that crucial first release on the indie Dog Soup label. She'd pulled the file off the club's site the week she'd joined, found a place near the Market that could print it out that big. It was still her favorite, and not just, as her mother too frequently suggested, because they all still looked so young. Her mother didn't like that the members of Lo/Rez were nearly as old as she was. Why wasn't Chia into music by people her own age?

—Please, mother, who?

—That Chrome Koran, say.

—Gag, mother.

Chia suspected that her mother's perception of time differed from her own in radical and mysterious ways. Not just in the way that a month, to Chia's mother, was not a very long time, but in the way that her mother's "now" was such a narrow and literal thing. News-governed, Chia believed. Cable-fed. A present honed to whatever very instant of a helicopter traffic report.

Chia's "now" was digital, effortlessly elastic, instant recall supported by global systems she'd never have to bother comprehending.

Lo Rez Skyline had been released, if you could call it that, a week (well, six days) before Chia had been born. She estimated that no hard copies would have reached Seattle in time for her nativity, but she liked to believe there had been listeners here even then, PacRim visionaries netting new sounds from indies as obscure, even, as East Teipei's Dog Soup. Surely the opening chords of "Positron Premonition" had shoved molecules of actual Seattle air, somewhere, in somebody's basement room, at the fateful moment of her birth. She knew that, somehow, just as she knew that "Stuck Pixel," barely even a song, just Lo noodling around on some pawnshop guitar, must have been playing *somewhere* when her mother, who'd spoken very little English at that point, chose Chia's name from something cycling past on the Shopping Channel, the phonetic caress of those syllables striking her there in Postnatal Recovery as some optimally gentle combination of sounds Italian and English; her baby, red-haired even then, subsequently christened Chia Pet McKenzie (somewhat, Chia later gathered, to the amazement of her absent Canadian father).

These thoughts arriving in the pre-alarm dark, just before the infrared winkie on her alarm clock stuttered silently to the halogen gallery-spot, telling it to illuminate Lo/Rez in all their Dog Soup glory. Rez with his shirt open (but entirely ironically) and Lo with his grin and a prototype mustache that hadn't quite grown in.

Hi, guys. Fumbling for her remote. Zapping infrared into the shadows. Zap: Espressomatic. Zap: cubic space heater.

Beneath her pillow the unfamiliar shape of her passport, like a vintage game cartridge, hard navy blue plastic, textured like leatherette, with its stamped gold seal and eagle. The Air Magellan tickets in their limp beige plastic folder from the travel agent in the mall.

Going now.

She took a deep breath. Her mother's house seemed to take one as well, but more tentatively, its wooden bones creaking in the winter morning cold.

• • •

The cab arriving as scheduled, but magically nonetheless, and no, it didn't honk, exactly as requested. Kelsey having explained how these things were done. Just as Kelsey, briskly interviewing Chia on the circumstances of her life, had devised the cover for her impending absence: ten days in the San Juans with Hester Chen, whose well-heeled luddite mother so thoroughly feared electromagnetic radiation that she lived phoneless, in a sod-roofed castle of driftwood, no electricity allowed whatever. "Tell her you're doing a media fast, before your new school thing comes together," Kelsey had said. "She'll like that." And Chia's mother, who felt that Chia spent entirely too much time gloved and goggled, did.

Chia was actually fond of the gentle Hester, who seemed to get what Lo/Rez were about, though somehow without being quite as fundamentally moved as could have been expected, and Chia had in fact already tried the pleasures of Mrs. Chen's island retreat. But Hester's mother had made them both wear special baseball caps, sewn from some EMR-proof fabric, so that their young brains might not be bathed quite so constantly in the invisible soup of bad media.

Chia had complained to Hester that the caps made them both look like meshbacks.

—Don't be racist, Chia.

—I'm not.

—Classist, then.

—It's a matter of *aesthetics.*

And now in the overheated cab, her one bag beside her on the seat, she felt guilt at this deception, her mother sleeping there behind those darkened windows matted with frost, under the weight of her thirty-five years and the flowered duvet Chia had bought at Nordstrom's. When Chia had been small, her mother had worn her hair in a long braid, its tip skewered with turquoise and abalone and carved bits of bone, like the magical tail of some mythical animal, swaying there for Chia to grab. And the house looked sad, too, as if it regretted her leaving, white paint peeling from the underlying gray of ninety-year-old cedar clapboards. Chia shivered. What if she never came back?

"Where to?" the driver said, a black man in a puffy nylon jacket and a flat plaid cap.

"SeaTac," Chia said, and pushed her shoulders back into the seat.

Pulling out past the old Lexus the neighbors kept up on concrete blocks in the driveway.

Airports were spooky places, early in the morning. There was a hollowness that could settle on you there, something sad and empty. Corridors and people moving away down them. Standing in line behind people she'd never seen before and would never see again. Her bag over her shoulder and her passport and ticket in her hand. She wanted another cup of coffee. There was one back in her room, in the Espressomatic. Which she should've emptied and cleaned, because now it would go moldy while she was away.

"Yes?" The man behind the counter wore a striped shirt, a tie with the Air Magellan logo repeated down it diagonally, and a green jade labret stud. Chia wondered what his lower lip looked like when he took it out. She never would, she decided, if she had one of those. She handed him her ticket. He sighed and removed them from the folder, letting her know that she should've done that herself.

She watched him run a scanner over her ticket.

"Air Magellan one-oh-five to Narita, economy return."

"That's right," Chia said, trying to be helpful. He didn't seem to appreciate that.

"Travel document."

Chia handed him her passport. He looked at it as though he'd never seen one before, sighed, and plugged it into a slot in the top of his counter. The slot had beat-up aluminum lips, and someone had covered these with transparent tape, peeling now and dirty. The man was looking at a monitor Chia couldn't see. Maybe he was going to tell her she couldn't go. She thought about the coffee in her Espressomatic. It would still be warm.

"Twenty-three D," he said, as a boarding-pass spooled from a different slot. He pulled her passport out and handed it to her, along with her ticket and the boarding pass. ''Gate fifty-two, blue concourse. Checking anything?''

''No.''

''Passengers who've cleared security may be subject to noninvasive DNA sampling,'' he said, the words all run together because he was only saying it because it was the law that he had to.

She put her passport and ticket away in the special pocket inside her parka. She kept the boarding pass in her hand. She went looking for the blue concourse. She had to go downstairs to find it, and take one of those trains that was like an elevator that ran sideways. Half an hour later she was through security, looking at the seals they'd put on the zippers of her carry-on. They looked like rings of rubbery red candy. She hadn't expected them to do that; she'd thought she could find a pay-station in the departure lounge, link up, and give the club an update. They never sealed her carry-on when she went to Vancouver to stay with her uncle, but that wasn't really international, not since the Agreement.

She was riding a rubber sidewalk toward Gate 52 when she saw the blue light flashing, up ahead. Soldiers there, and a little barricade. The soldiers were lining people up as they came off the sidewalk. They wore fatigues and didn't seem to be much older than the guys at her last school.

''Shit,'' she heard the woman in front of her say, a big-haired blond with obvious extensions woven in. Big red lips, multilevel mascara, padded shoulders out to here, tiny little skirt, white cowboy boots. Like that country singer her mother liked, Ashleigh Modine Carter. Kind of a meshback thing, but with money.

Chia stepped off the end of the rubber sidewalk and took her place in line behind the woman who looked like Ashleigh Modine Carter.

The soldiers were taking hair samples and slotting people's passports. Chia assumed that was to prove you really were who you said you were, because your DNA was there in your passport, converted into a kind of bar code.

The sampler was a little silver wand that vacuumed the tips of a couple of strands in and clipped them off. They'd wind up with the world's biggest collection of split ends, Chia thought. Now it was the blond's turn. There were two boy-soldiers there, one to work the sampler and one to rattle off the line about how you'd already agreed to this by coming this far, and please produce your passport.

Chia watched as the woman handed over her passport, becoming somehow instantly and up-front sexy, like a lightbulb coming on, with a big smile for the soldier that made him blink and swallow and nearly drop the passport. Grinning, he stuck the passport into a little console attached to the barricade. The other soldier raised his wand. Chia saw the woman reach up and choose one of her hair-extensions, offering the end of this for sampling. The whole thing taking maybe eight seconds, including the return of her passport, and the first soldier was still smiling now that it was Chia's turn.

The woman moved on, having just committed what Chia felt fairly certain would be a federal offense. Should she tell the soldier?

But she didn't, and then they were handing back her passport and Chia was on her way to Gate 53. Where she looked for the woman but didn't see her.

She watched the ads cycle by on the walls, until they were called to board by rows.

Seat 23E remained empty as Chia waited for takeoff, sucking on a peppermint the flight attendant had given her. The only empty seat on the plane, she figured. If nobody arrived to take it, she thought, she'd be able to fold the armrest away and curl up there. She tried putting out a negative mental field, a vibe that would keep anyone from getting on at the last minute and sitting there. Zona Rosa was into that, part of her whole girl-gang martial arts thing. Chia didn't see how you could seriously believe it would work.

And it didn't, because here came that blond down the aisle, and wasn't that an eye-click of recognition Chia saw there?

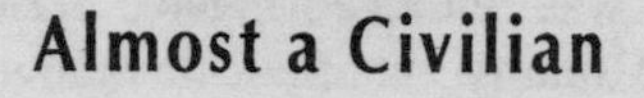

Almost a Civilian

It had been a weeknight, a Wednesday, when Laney had last seen Kathy Torrance, and her tattoo had not been visible. She'd stood there in the Cage, screaming as he cleaned out his locker. She was wearing an Armani blazer cut from gun-metal fustian, its matching skirt concealing the sign from outer space. A single strand of pearls was visible at the open throat of her white, man-tailored blouse. Her dress uniform. Called on the carpet for her subordinate's defection.

He knew that she was screaming because her mouth was open, but the syllables of her rage couldn't penetrate the seamless hissing surf of the white-noise generator provided by his lawyers. He'd been advised to wear the generator at all times, during this last visit to the Slitscan offices. He'd been instructed to make no statements. Certainly he would hear none.

And later he would sometimes wonder exactly how she might have framed her fury. Some restatement of her theory of celebrity and the nature of its price, of Slitscan's place in that, of Laney's inability to function there? Or would she have focused on his treason? But he hadn't heard; he'd only put these things he didn't really want into a corrugated plastic carton that still smelled faintly of Mexican oranges. The notebook, screen cracked now, useless, that he'd carried through college. Insulated mug with the Nissan County logo peeling away. Notes he'd made on paper, counter to office policy. A coffee-stained fax from a woman he'd slept with in Ixtapa, someone whose initials couldn't be deciphered now and whose name he'd forgotten. Pointless pieces of the self, destined for a cannister in the building's parking lot. But he'd leave nothing here, and Kathy kept on screaming.

Now, in Death Cube K, he imagined that she'd told him that he'd never work in that town again, and indeed it seemed he might not. Disloyalty to one's employers being a particularly difficult notch on anyone's ticket, and perhaps particularly so, in that town, when the act itself had sprung from what Laney recalled had once been called scruples.

The word itself striking him now as singularly ridiculous.

"You smiled." Blackwell staring at him from across the tiny table.

"Seratonin depletion."

"Food," said Blackwell.

"I'm not really hungry."

"Need to carbo-load," Blackwell said, standing. He took up a remarkable amount of space.

Laney and Yamazaki got to their feet and followed Blackwell down out of Death Cube K, to descend the O My Golly Building itself. Out of roach-light, into the chrome and neon gulch of Roppongi Dori. A reek of putrid fish and fruit even in this chill damp night, though muted somewhat by the baking-sugar sweetness of Chinese gasohol from the vehicles whirring past on the expressway. But there was comfort in the steady voice of traffic, and Laney found it better to be upright, moving.

If he kept moving, perhaps he could puzzle out the meaning of Keith Alan Blackwell and Shinya Yamazaki.

Blackwell leading the way across a pedestrian overpass. Laney's hand brushed an irregularity on the alloy rail. He saw that it was an accidental fold or pucker in a bright little sticker; a bare-breasted girl smiling up at him from a palm-sized silvery hologram. As his angle of vision changed, she seemed to gesture at the telephone number above her head. The railing, end to end, was dressed with these small ads, though there were precise gaps where a few had been peeled away for later perusal.

Blackwell's bulk parted the sidewalk crowd on the far side like a freighter through a bobbing stream of pleasure craft. "Carbohydrates," he said, over a mountainous shoulder. He steered them down an alley, a narrow maw of colored light, past an all-night veterinary clinic in whose window a pair of white-gowned surgeons were performing an operation on what Laney hoped was a cat. A relaxed little tableau of pedestrians paused here, observing from the pavement.

Blackwell eased himself edgewise into a bright cave, where steam rose from cookers behind a counter of reconstituted granite.

Laney and Yamazaki followed him in, the counterman already ladling out fragrant messes of broth-slick beige to the Australian's order.

Laney watched Blackwell raise the bowl to his mouth and apparently inhale the bulk of his noodles, severing them from the remainder with a neat snap of his bright plastic teeth. Muscles in the man's thick neck worked mightily as he swallowed.

Laney stared.

Blackwell wiped his mouth with the back of one vast and pinkly jigsawed hand. He belched. "Give us one of those baby tubes of Dry. . . ." He downed the entire beer in a single swallow, absently crushing the sturdy steel can as though it were a paper cup. "Similar," he said, rattling his bowl for the counterman.

Laney, suddenly ravenous in spite or because of this gluttonous display, gave his attention to his own bowl, where dyed pink slices of mystery meat, thin as paper, basked atop a sargasso of noodles.

Laney ate in silence, as did Yamazaki, Blackwell

downing another three beers to no apparent effect. As Laney drank off the remaining broth, and put his bowl down on the counter, he noticed an ad behind the counter for something called Apple Shires Authentic Fine Fruit Beverage. Misreading it initially as Alison Shires, once the object of his scruples.

"Taste the wet warm life in Apple Shires," the ad advised.

Alison Shires, glimpsed first as animated headshots, five months into his time at Slitscan, had been a rather ordinarily attractive girl murmuring her stats to imagined casting directors, agents, someone, anyone.

Kathy Torrance had watched his face, as he watched the screen. " 'Babed out' yet, Laney? Allergic reaction to *cute?* First symptoms are a sort of underlying irritation, a resentment, a vague but persistent feeling that you're being gotten at, taken advantage of . . ."

"She isn't even as 'cute' as the last two."

"Exactly. She's almost normal-looking. Almost a civilian. Tag her."

Laney looked up. "What for?"

"Tag her. He could get off pretending she's a waitress or something."

"You think she's the one?"

"You've got another three hundred in there easy, Laney. Picking probables is a start."

"At random?"

"We call it 'instinct.' Tag her."

Laney cursor-clicked, the pale blue arrow resting by chance in the shadowed orbit of the girl's lowered eye. Marking her for closer examination as the possible sometime partner of a very publicly married actor, famous in a way that Kathy Torrance understood and approved of. One who must obey the dictates of the food chain. Not too big for Slitscan to swallow. But he or his handlers had so far been very cautious. Or very lucky.

But no more. A rumor had reached Kathy, via one of those "back channels" she depended on, and now the food chain must have its way.

"Wake up," Blackwell said. "You're falling asleep in your bowl. Time you tell us how you lost your last job, if we're going to offer you another."

"Coffee," Laney said.

Laney was not, he was careful to point out, a voyeur. He had a peculiar knack with data-collection architectures, and a medically documented concentration-deficit that he could toggle, under certain conditions, into a state of pathological hyperfocus. This made him, he continued over lattes in a Roppongi branch of Amos 'n' Andes, an extremely good researcher. (He made no mention of the Federal Orphanage in Gainesville, nor of any attempts that might have been made there to cure his concentration-deficit. The 5-SB trials or any of that.)

The relevant data, in terms of his current employability, was that he was an intuitive fisher of patterns of information: of the sort of signature a particular individual inadvertently created in the net as he or she went about the mundane yet endlessly multiplex business of life in a digital society. Laney's concentration-deficit, too slight to register on some scales, made him a natural channel-zapper, shifting from program to program, from database to database, from platform to platform, in a way that was, well, intuitive.

And that was the catch, really, when it came to finding employment: Laney was the equivalent of a dowser, a cybernetic water-witch. He couldn't explain how he did what he did. He just didn't know.

He'd come to Slitscan from DatAmerica, where he'd been a research assistant on a project code named TIDAL. It said something about the corporate culture of DatAmerica that Laney had never been able to discover whether or not TIDAL was an acronym, or (even remotely) what TIDAL was about. He'd spent his time skimming vast floes of undifferentiated data, looking for "nodal points" he'd been trained to recognize by a team of French scientists who were all keen tennis players, and none of whom had had any interest in explaining these nodal points to Laney, who came to feel that he served as a kind of native guide. Whatever the Frenchmen were after, he was there to scare it up for them. And it beat Gainesville, no contest. Until TIDAL, whatever it was, had been cancelled, and there didn't seem to be anything else for Laney to do at DatAmerica. The Frenchmen were gone, and when Laney tried to talk to other researchers about what they'd been doing, they looked at him as though they thought he was crazy.

When he'd gone to interview for Slitscan, the interviewer had been Kathy Torrance. He'd had no way of knowing that she was a department head, or that she would soon be his boss. He told her the truth about himself. Most of it, anyway.

She was the palest woman Laney had ever seen. Pale to the point of translucence. (Later he'd learned this had a lot to do with cosmetics, and in particular a British line that boasted of peculiar light-bending properties.)

"Do you always wear Malaysian imitations of Brooks Brothers blue oxford button-downs, Mr. Laney?"

Laney had looked down at his shirt, or tried to. "Malaysia?"

"The stitch-count's dead on, but they still haven't mastered the thread-tension."

"Oh."

"Never mind. A little prototypic nerd chic could actually lend a certain frisson, around here. You could lose the tie, though. Definitely lose the tie. And keep a collection of felt-tipped pens in your pocket. Unchewed, please. Plus one of those fat flat highliners, in a really nasty fluorescent shade."

"Are you joking?"

"Probably, Mr. Laney. May I call you Colin?"

"Yes."

She never did call him "Colin," then or ever. "You'll find that humor is essential at Slitscan, Laney. A necessary survival tool. You'll find the type that's most viable here is fairly oblique."

"How do you mean, Ms. Torrance?"

"Kathy. I mean difficult to quote effectively in a memo. Or a court of law."

Yamazaki was a good listener. He'd blink, swallow, nod, fiddle with the top button of his plaid shirt, whatever, all of it managing to somehow convey that he was getting it, the drift of Laney's story.

Keith Alan Blackwell was something else. He sat there inert as a bale of beef, utterly motionless except when he'd raise his left hand and squeeze and twiddle the lobe-stump that was all that remained of his left ear. He did this without hesitation or embarrassment, and Laney formed the impression that it was affording him some kind of relief. The scar tissue reddened slightly under Blackwell's ministrations.

Laney sat on an upholstered bench, his back to the wall. Yamazaki and Blackwell faced him across the narrow table. Behind them, over the uniformly black-haired heads of late-night Roppongi coffee-drinkers, the holographic features of the chain's namesake floated in front of a lurid sunset vista of snow-capped Andean peaks. The lips of the 'toon-Amos were like inflated red rubber sausages, a racial parody that would've earned the place a firebombing anywhere in the L.A. basin. He was holding up a steaming coffee cup, white and smoothly iconic, in a big, white-gloved, three-fingered ur-Disney hand.

Yamazaki coughed, delicately. "You are telling us, please, about your experiences at Slitscan?"

Kathy Torrance began by offering Laney a chance to net-surf, Slitscan style.

She checked a pair of computers out of the Cage, shooed four employees from an SBU, invited Laney in, and closed the door. Chairs, a round table, a large softboard on the wall. He watched as she jacked the computers into dataports and called up identical images of a longhaired dirty-blond guy in his mid-twenties. Goatee and a gold earring. The face meant nothing to Laney. It might have been a face he'd passed on the street an hour before, the face of a minor player in daytime soap, or the face of someone whose freezer had recently been discovered to be packed with his victims' fingers.

"Clinton Hillman," Kathy Torrance said. "Hairdresser, sushi chef, music journalist, extra in mid-budget hardcore. This headshot's tweaked, of course." She tapped keys, detweaking it. Clint Hillman's eyes and chin, on her screen, grew several clicks smaller. "Probably did it himself. With a professional job, there'd be nothing to work back from."

"He acts in porno?" Laney felt obscurely sorry for Hillman, who looked lost and vulnerable without his chin.

"It isn't the size of his chin they're interested in," Kathy said. "It's mainly motion-capture, in porno. Extreme close. They're all body-doubles. Map on better faces in post. But somebody's still gotta get down in the trenches and bump uglies, right?"

Laney shot her a sideways look. "If you say so."

She handed Laney an industrial-strength pair of rubberized Thomson eyephones. "Do him."

"Do?"

"Him. Go for those nodal points you've been telling me about. The headshot's a gateway to everything we've got on him. Whole gigs of sheer boredom. Data like a sea of tapioca, Laney. An endless vanilla plane. He's boring as the day is long, and the day *is* long. Do it. Make my day. Do it and you've got yourself a job."

Laney looked at the tweaked Hillman on his screen. "You haven't told me what I'm looking for."

"Anything that might be of interest to Slitscan. Which is to say, Laney, anything that might be of interest to Slitscan's audience. Which is best visualized as a vicious, lazy, profoundly ignorant, perpetually hungry organism craving the warm god-flesh of the anointed. Personally I like to imagine something the size of a baby hippo, the color of a week-old boiled potato, that lives by itself, in the dark, in a double-wide on the outskirts of Topeka. It's covered with eyes and it sweats constantly. The sweat runs into those eyes and makes them sting. It has no mouth, Laney, no genitals, and can only express its mute extremes of murderous rage and infantile desire by changing the channels on a universal remote. Or by voting in presidential elections."

"SBU?"

Yamazaki had his notebook out, lightpen poised. Laney found that he didn't mind. It made the man look so much more comfortable. "Strategic Business Unit," he said. "A small conference room. Slitscan's post office."

"Post office?"

"California plan. People don't have their own desks. Check a computer and a phone out of the Cage when you come in. Hotdesk it if you need more peripherals. The SBUs are for meetings, but it's hard to get one when you need it. Virtual meetings are a big thing there, better for sensitive topics. You get a locker to keep your personal stuff in. You don't want them to see any printouts. And they hate Post-its."

"Why?"

"Because you might've written something down from the in-house net, and it might get out. That notebook of yours would never have been allowed out of the Cage. If there was no paper, they had a record of every call, every image called up, every keystroke."

Blackwell nodded now, his stubbled dome catching the red of Amos's inner-tube lips. "Security."

"And you were successful, Mr. Laney?" Yamazaki asked. "You found the . . . nodal points?"

4

Venice Decompressed

''Shut up now,'' the woman in 23E said, and Chia hadn't said anything at all. ''Sister's going to tell you a story.''

Chia looked up from the seatback screen, where she'd been working her way through the eleventh level of a lobotomized airline version of Skull Wars. The blond was looking straight ahead, not at Chia. Her screen was down so that she could use the back of it for a tray, and she'd finished another glass of the iced tomato juice she kept paying the flight attendant to bring her. They came, for some reason, with squared-off pieces of celery stuck up in them, like a straw or stir-stick, but the blond didn't seem to want these. She'd stacked five of them in a square on the tray, the way a kid might build the walls of a little house, or a corral for toy animals.

Chia looked down at her thumbs on the disposable Air Magellan touchpad. Back up at the mascaraed eyes. Looking at her now.

"There's a place where it's always light," the woman said. "Bright, everywhere. No place dark. Bright like a mist, like something falling, always, every second. All the colors of it. Towers you can't see the top of, and the light falling. Down below, they pile up bars. Bars and strip clubs and discos. Stacked up like shoe boxes, one on top of the other. And no matter how far you worm your way in, no matter how many stairs you climb, how many elevators you ride, no matter how small a room you finally get to, the light still finds you. It's a light that blows in under the door, like powder. Fine, so fine. Blows in under your eyelids, if you find a way to get to sleep. But you don't *want* to sleep there. Not in Shinjuku. Do you?"

Chia was suddenly aware of the sheer physical mass of the plane, of the terrible unlikeliness of its passage through space, of its airframe vibrating through frozen night somewhere above the sea, off the coast of Alaska now—impossible but true. "No," Chia heard herself say, as Skull Wars, noting her inattention, dumped her back a level.

"No," the woman agreed, "you *don't.* I know. But they make you. They make you. At the center of the world.'' And then she put her head back, closed her eyes, and began to snore.

Chia exited Skull Wars and tucked the touchpad into the seatback pocket. She felt like screaming. What had *that* been about?

The attendant came by, scooped up the corral of celery sticks in a napkin, took the woman's glass, wiped the tray, and snapped it up into position in the seatback.

''My bag?'' Chia said. ''In the bin?'' She pointed.

He opened the hatch above her, pulled out her bag, and lowered it into her lap.

''How do you undo these?'' She touched the loops of tough red jelly that held the zip-tabs together.

He took a small black tool from a black holster on his belt. It looked like something she'd seen a vet use to trim a dog's nails. He held his other hand cupped, to catch the little balls the loops became when he snipped them with the tool.

''Okay to run this?'' She pulled a zip and showed him her Sandbenders, stuffed in between four pairs of rolled-up tights.

''You can't port back here; only in business or first,'' he said. ''But you can access what you've got. Cable to the seatback display, if you want.''

''Thanks,'' she said. ''Got gogs.'' He moved on.

The blond's snore faltered in mid-buzz as they jolted over a pocket of turbulence. Chia dug her glasses and tip-sets from their nests of clean underwear, putting them beside her, between her hip and the armrest. She pulled the Sandbenders out, zipped the bag shut, and used her free hand and both feet to wedge the bag under the seat in front of her. She wanted out of here so bad.

With the Sandbenders across her thighs, she thumbed a battery check. Eight hours on miser mode, if she was lucky. But right now she didn't care. She uncoiled the lead from around the bridge of her glasses and jacked it. The tip-sets were tangled, like they always were. Take your time, she told herself. A torn sensor-band and she'd be here all night with an Ashleigh Modine Carter clone. Little silver thimbles, flexy framework fingers; easy did it. . . . Plug for each one. Jack and *jack* . . .

The blond said something in her sleep. If sleep was what you called it.

Chia picked up her glasses, slid them on, and hit big red.

—My ass *out* of here.

And it was.

There on the edge of her bed, looking at the Lo Rez Skyline poster. Until Lo noticed. He stroked his half-grown mustache and grinned at her.

"Hey, Chia."

"Hey." Experience kept it subvocal, for privacy's sake.

"What's up, girl?"

"I'm on an airplane. I'm on my way to Japan."

"Japan? Kicky. You do our Budokan disk?"

"I don't feel like talking, Lo." Not to a software agent, anyway, sweet as he might be.

"Easy." He shot her that catlike grin, his eyes wrinkling at the corners, and became a still image. Chia looked around, feeling disappointed. Things weren't quite the right size, somehow, or maybe she should've used those fractal packets that messed it all up a little, put dust in the corners and smudges around the light switch. Zona Rosa swore by them. When she was home, Chia liked it that the construct was cleaner than her room ever was. Now it made her homesick; made her miss the real thing.

She gestured for the living room, phasing past what would've been the door to her mother's bedroom. She'd barely wireframed it, here, and there was no there there, no interiority. The living room had its sketchy angles as well, and furniture she'd imported from a Playmobil system that predated her Sandbenders. Wonkily bit-mapped fish swam monotonously around in a glass coffee table she'd built when she was nine. The trees through the front window were older still: perfectly cylindrical Crayola-brown trunks, each supporting an acid-green cotton ball of undifferentiated foliage. If she looked at these long enough, the Mumphalumphagus would appear outside, wanting to play, so she didn't.

She positioned herself on the Playmobil couch and looked at the programs scattered across the top of the coffee table. The Sandbenders system software looked like an old-fashioned canvas water bag, a sort of canteen (she'd had to consult *What Things Are,* her icon dictionary, to figure that out). It was worn and spectacularly organic, with tiny beads of water bulging through the tight weave of fabric. If you got in super close you saw things reflected in the individual droplets: circuitry that was like beadwork or the skin on a lizard's throat, a long empty beach under a gray sky, mountains in the rain, creek water over different-colored stones. She loved Sandbenders; they were the best. THE SANDBENDERS, OREGON, was screened faintly across the sweating canvas, as though it had almost faded away under a desert sun. SYSTEM 5.9. (She had all the upgrades, to 6.3. People said 6.4 was buggy.)

Beside the water bag lay her schoolwork, represented by a three-ring binder suffering the indignities of artificial bit-rot, its wire-frame cover festered with digital mung. She'd have to reformat that before she started her new school, she reminded herself. Too juvenile.

Her Lo/Rez collection, albums, compilations and bootlegs, were displayed as the original cased disks. These were stacked up, as casually as possible, beside the archival material she'd managed to assemble since being accepted into the Seattle chapter. This looked, thanks to a fortuitous file-swap with a member in Sweden, like a lithographed tin lunch box, Rez and Lo peering stunned and fuzzy-eyed from its flat, rectangular lid. The Swedish fan had scanned the artwork from the five printed surfaces of the original, then mapped it over wireframe. The original was probably Nepalese, definitely unlicensed, and Chia appreciated the reverse cachet. Zona Rosa coveted a copy, but so far all she'd offered were a set of cheesy tv spots for the fifth Mexico Dome concert. They weren't nearly cheesy *enough,* and Chia wasn't prepared to swap. There was a shadowy Brazilian tour documentary supposed to have been made by a public-access subsidiary of Globo. Chia wanted *that,* and Mexico was the same direction as Brazil.

She ran a finger down the stacked disks, her hand wireframed, the finger tipped with quivering mercury, and thought about the Rumor. There had been rumors before, there were rumors now, there would always be rumors. There had been the rumor about Lo and that Danish model, that they were going to get married, and that had probably been true, even though they never did. And there were always rumors about Rez and different people. But that was *people.* The Danish model was people, as much as Chia thought she was a snotbag. The Rumor was something else.

What, exactly, she was on her way to Tokyo to find out.

She selected *Lo Rez Skyline.*

The virtual Venice her father had sent for her thirteenth birthday looked like an old dusty book with leather covers, the smooth brown leather scuffed in places into a fine suede, the digital equivalent of washing denim in a machine full of golf balls. It lay beside the featureless, textureless gray file that was her copy of the divorce decree and the custody agreement.

She pulled the Venice toward her, opened it. The fish flickered out of phase, her system launching a subroutine.

Venice decompressed.

The Piazza in midwinter monochrome, its facades texture-mapped in marble, porphyry, polished granite, jasper, alabaster (the rich mineral names scrolling at will in the menu of peripheral vision). This city of winged lions and golden horses. This default hour of gray and perpetual dawn.

She could be alone here, or visit with the Music Master.

Her father, phoning from Singapore to wish her a happy birthday, had told her that Hitler, during his first and only visit, had slipped away to range the streets alone, in these same small hours, mad perhaps, and trotting like a dog.

Chia, who had only a vague idea who Hitler might have been, and that mainly from references in songs, understood the urge. The stones of the Piazza flowed beneath her like silk, as she raised a silvered finger and sped into the maze of bridges, water, arches, walls.

She had no idea what this place was meant to mean, the how or why of it, but it fit so perfectly into itself and the space it occupied, water and stone slotting faultlessly into the mysterious whole.

The gnarliest piece of software ever, and here came the opening chords of "Positron Premonition."

5

Nodal Points

Clinton Emory Hillman, twenty-five: hairdresser, sushi chef, music journalist, porno extra, reliable purveyor of proscribed fetal tissue cultures to three of the more endomorphic members of the decidedly mesh-backed Dukes of Nuke 'Em, whose ''Gulf War Baby'' was eighteen with a bullet on the *Billboard* chart, in heavy rotation on I (heart) America, and had already been the subject of diplomatic protests from several Islamic states.

Kathy Torrance looked as though she might be prepared to be pleased. ''And the fetal tissue, Laney?''

''Well,'' Laney said, putting the 'phones down beside the computer, ''I think that might be the good part.''

''Why?''

''It has to be Iraqi. They make a point of insisting on that. They won't shoot up any other kind.''

''You're hired.''

''I am?''

''You must have correlated the calls to Ventura with the parking charges from the garage in the Beverly Center. Although that running gag about 'Gulf War babies' would've been hard to miss.''

''Wait a minute,'' Laney said. ''You knew.''

''It's the top segment on Wednesday's show.'' She closed the computer without bothering to turn off Clint Hillman's detweaked chin. ''But now I've had a chance to watch you work, Laney. You're a natural. I could almost believe there might actually be something to that nodal point bullshit. Some of your moves made no logical sense whatever, but I've just watched you hone in, cold, on something it took three experienced researchers a month to excavate. You did it in just under half an hour.''

''Some of that was illegal,'' Laney said. ''You're tied into parts of DatAmerican that you aren't supposed to be.''

''Do you know what a nondisclosure agreement is, Laney?''

Yamazaki looked up from his notebook. ''Very good,'' he said, probably to Blackwell. ''This is very good.''

Blackwell shifted his weight, the chair's polycarbon frame creaking faintly in protest. "But he didn't last there, did he?"

"A little over six months," Laney said.

Six months could be a very long time, at Slitscan.

He used most of his first month's salary to lease a micro-bachelor in a retrofitted parking structure on Broadway Avenue, Santa Monica. He bought shirts he thought were more like the ones people wore at Slitscan, and kept his Malaysian button-downs to sleep in. He bought an expensive pair of sunglasses and made sure he never displayed as much as a single felt-pen in his shirt pocket.

Life at Slitscan had a certain focused quality. Laney's colleagues limited themselves to a particular bandwidth of emotion. A certain kind of humor, as Kathy had said, was highly valued, but there was remarkably little laughter. The expected response was eye contact, a nod, the edge of a smile. Lives were destroyed here, and sometimes re-created, careers crushed or made anew in guises surreal and unexpected. Because Slitscan's business was the ritual letting of blood, and the blood it let was an alchemical fluid: celebrity in its rawest, purest form.

Laney's ability to locate key data in apparently random wastes of incidental information earned him the envy and grudging admiration of more experienced researchers. He became Kathy's favorite, and was almost pleased when he discovered that a rumor had spread that they were having an affair.

They weren't—except for that one time at her place in Sherman Oaks, and that hadn't been a good idea. Nothing either of them wanted to repeat.

But Laney was still narrowing down, getting focused, pushing the envelope of whatever it was that manifested as this talent, his touch. And Kathy liked that. With his eyephones on and Slitscan's dedicated landline feeding him the bleak reaches of DatAmerica, he felt increasingly at home. He went where Kathy suggested he go. He found the nodal points.

Sometimes, falling asleep in Santa Monica, he wondered vaguely if there might be a larger system, a field of greater perspective. Perhaps the whole of DatAmerica possessed its own nodal points, infofaults that might be followed down to some other kind of truth, another mode of knowing, deep within gray shoals of information. But only if there were someone there to pose the right question. He had no idea at all what that question might be, if indeed there were one, but he somehow doubted it would ever be posed from an SBU at Slitscan.

Slitscan was descended from "reality" programming and the network tabloids of the late twentieth century, but it resembled them no more than some large, swift, bipedal carnivore resembled its sluggish, shallow-dwelling ancestors. Slitscan was the mature form, supporting fully global franchises. Slitscan's revenues had paid for entire satellites and built the building he worked in in Burbank.

Slitscan was a show so popular that it had evolved into something akin to the old idea of a network. It was flanked and buffered by spinoffs and peripherals, each designed to shunt the viewer back to the crucial core, the familiar and reliably bloody altar that one of Laney's Mexican co-workers called Smoking Mirror.

It was impossible to work at Slitscan without a sense of participating in history, or else in what Kathy Torrance would argue had *replaced* history. Slitscan itself, Laney suspected, might be one of those larger nodal points he sometimes found himself trying to imagine, an informational peculiarity opening into some unthinkably deeper structure.

In his quest for lesser nodal points, the sort that Kathy sent him into DatAmerica to locate, Laney had already affected the courses of municipal elections, the market in patent gene futures, abortion laws in the State of New Jersey, and the spin on an ecstatic pro-euthanasia movement (or suicide cult, depending) called Cease Upon The Midnight, not to mention the lives and careers of several dozen celebrities of various kinds.

Not always for the worst, either, in terms of what the show's subjects might have wished for themselves. Kathy's segment on the Dukes of Nuke 'Em, exposing the band's exclusive predilection for Iraqi fetal tissue, had sent their subsequent release instant platinum (and had resulted in show-trials and public hangings in Baghdad, but he supposed life was hard there to begin with).

Laney had never been a Slitscan viewer, himself, and he suspected that this had counted in his favor when he'd applied as a researcher. He had no strong opinion of the show either way. He accepted it, to the extent that he'd thought of it at all, as a fact of life. Slitscan was how a certain kind of news was done. Slitscan was where he worked.

Slitscan allowed him to do the one thing he possessed a genuine talent for, so he'd managed to avoid thinking in terms of cause and effect. Even now, attempting to explain himself to the attentive Mr. Yamazaki, he found it difficult to feel any clear linkage of responsibility. The rich and the famous, Kathy had once said, were seldom that way by accident. It was possible to be one or the other, but very seldom, accidentally, to be both.

Celebrities who were neither were something else again, and Kathy viewed these as crosses she must bear: a mass-murderer, for instance, or his most recent victim's parents. No star quality (though she always held out hope for the murderers, feeling that at least the potential was there).

It was the other kind that Kathy wanted, directing the attentions of Laney and as many as thirty other researchers to the more private aspects of the lives of those who were deliberately and at least moderately famous.

Alison Shires wasn't famous at all, but the man Laney had confirmed she was having an affair with was famous enough.

And then something began to come clear to Laney.

Alison Shires *knew,* somehow, that he was there, watching. As though she felt him gazing down, into the pool of data that reflected her life, its surface made of all the bits that were the daily record of her life as it registered on the digital fabric of the world.

Laney watched a nodal point begin to form over the reflection of Alison Shires.

She was going to kill herself.

6

DESH

Chia had programmed her Music Master to have an affinity for bridges. He appeared in her virtual Venice whenever she crossed one at moderate speed: a slender young man with pale blue eyes and a penchant for long, flowing coats.

He'd been the subject of a look-and-feel action, in his beta release, when lawyers representing a venerable British singer had protested that the Music Master's designers had scanned in images of their client as a much younger man. This had been settled out of court, and all later versions, including Chia's, were much more carefully generic. (Kelsey had told her that it had mainly had to do with changing one of his eyes, but why only the one?)

She'd fed him into Venice on her second visit, to

keep her company and provide musical variety, and keying his appearances to moments when she crossed bridges had seemed like a good idea. There were lots of bridges in Venice, some of them no more than a little arc of stone steps spanning the narrowest of waterways. There was the Bridge of Sighs, which Chia avoided because she found it sad and creepy, and the Bridge of Fists, which she liked mainly for its name, and so many others. And there was the Rialto, big and humped and fantastically old, where her father said men had invented banking, or a particular kind of banking. (Her father worked for a bank, which was why he had to live in Singapore.)

She'd slowed her rush through the city now, and was cruising at a walking pace up the stepped incline of the Rialto, the Music Master striding elegantly beside her, his putty-colored trenchcoat flapping in the breeze.

"DESH," he said, triggered by her glance, "the Diatonic Elaboration of Static Harmony. Also known as the Major Chord with Descending Bassline. Bach's 'Air on a G String,' 1730. Procol Harum's 'A Whiter Shade of Pale,' 1967." If she made eye contact now, she'd hear his samples, directionless and at just the right volume. Then more about DESH, and more samples. She had him here for company, though, and not for a lecture. But lectures were all there was to him, aside from his iconics, which were about being blond and fine-boned and wearing clothes more beautifully than any human ever could. He knew everything there was to know about music, and nothing else at all.

She didn't know how long she'd been in Venice, this visit. It was still that minute-before-dawn that she liked best, because she kept it that way.

"Do you know anything about Japanese music?" she asked.

"What sort, exactly?"

"What people listen to."

"Popular music?"

"I guess so."

He paused, turning, hands in his trouser pockets and the trenchcoat swinging to reveal its lining.

"We could begin with a music called *enka,*" he said, "although I doubt you'd like it." Software agents did that, learned what you liked. "The roots of contemporary Japanese pop came later, with the wholesale creation of something called 'group sounds.' That was a copy-cat phenomenon, flagrantly commercial. Extremely watered-down Western pop influences. Very bland and monotonous."

"But do they really have singers who don't exist?"

"The idol-singers," he said, starting up the hump-backed incline of the bridge. "The *idoru.* Some of them are enormously popular."

"Do people kill themselves over them?"

"I don't know. They could do, I suppose."

"Do people marry them?"

"Not that I know of."

"How about Rei Toei?" Wondering if that was how you pronounced it.

"I'm afraid I don't know her," he said, with the slight wince that came when you asked him about music that had come out since his own release. This always made Chia feel sorry for him, which she knew was ridiculous.

"Never mind," she said, and closed her eyes.

She removed her glasses.

After Venice, the plane felt even more low-ceilinged and narrow, a claustrophobic tube packed with seats and people.

The blond was awake, watching her, looking a lot less like Ashleigh Modine Carter now that she'd removed most of her makeup. Her face only inches away.

Then she smiled. It was a slow smile, modular, as though there were stages to it, each one governed by a separate shyness or hesitation.

"I like your computer," she said. "It looks like it was made by Indians or something."

Chia looked down at her Sandbenders. Turned off the red switch. "Coral," she said. "These are turquoise. The ones that look like ivory are the inside of a kind of nut. Renewable."

"The rest is silver?"

"Aluminum," Chia said. "They melt old cans they dig up on the beach, cast it in sand molds. These panels are micarta. That's linen with this resin in it."

"I didn't know Indians could make computers," the woman said, reaching out to touch the curved edge of the Sandbenders. Her voice was hesitant, light, like a child's. The nail on the finger that rested on her Sandbenders was bright red, the lacquer chipped through and ragged. A tremble, then the hand withdrew.

"I drank too much. And with tequila in them, too. 'Vitamin T,' Eddie calls it. I wasn't *bad,* was I?"

Chia shook her head.

"I can't always remember, if I'm bad."

"Do you know how much longer it is to Tokyo?" Chia asked, all she could think of to say.

"Nine hours easy," the blond said, and sighed. "Subsonics just *suck,* don't they? Eddie had me booked on a super, in full business, but then he said something went wrong with the ticket. Eddie gets all the tickets from this place in Osaka. We went on Air France once, first class, and your seat turns into a bed and they tuck you in with a little quilt. And they have an open bar right there and they just leave the bottles out, and champagne and just the best food." The memory didn't seem to cheer her up. "And they give you perfume and makeup in its own case, from Hermès. Real leather, too. Why are you going to Tokyo?"

"Oh," Chia said. "Oh. Well. My friend. To see my friend."

"It's so strange. You know? Since the quake."

"But they've built it all back now. Haven't they?"

"Sure, but they did it all so fast, mostly with that nanotech, that just grows? Eddie got in there before the dust had settled. Told me you could *see* those towers growing, at night. Rooms up top like a honeycomb, and walls just sealing themselves over, one after another. Said it was like watching a candle melt, but in reverse. That's too scary. Doesn't make a sound. Machines too small to see. They can get into your body, you know?''

Chia sensed an underlying edge of panic there. ''Eddie?'' she asked, hoping to change the subject.

''Eddie's like a businessman. He went to Japan to make money after the earthquake. He says the infa, infa, the *structure* was wide open, then. He says it took the spine out of it, sort of, so you could come in and root around, quick, before it healed over and hardened up again. And it healed over *around* Eddie, like he's an implant or something, so now he's part of the infa, the infa—''

''Infrastructure.''

''The structure. Yeah. So now he's plugged in, to all that juice. He's a landlord, and he owns these clubs, and has deals in music and vids and things.''

Chia leaned over, dragging her bag from beneath the seat in front, putting away the Sandbenders. ''Do you live there, in Tokyo?''

''Part of the time.''

''Do you like it?''

''It's . . . I . . . well . . . *Weird,* right? It's not like anyplace. This huge thing happened there, then they fixed it with what was maybe even a huger thing, a bigger change, and everybody goes around pretending it never happened, that nothing *happened.* But you know what?''

''What?''

''Look at a map. A map from before? A lot of it's *not even where it used to be.* Nowhere near. Well, a few things are, the Palace, that expressway, and that big city hall thing in Shinjuku, but a lot of the rest of it's like they just made it up. They pushed all the quake-junk into the water, like landfill, and now they're building that up, too. New islands.''

''You know,'' Chia said, ''I'm really sleepy. I think I'll try to go to sleep now.''

''My name's Maryalice. Like it's one word.''

''Mine's Chia.''

Chia closed her eyes and tried to put her seat back a little more, but that was as far as it could go.

''Pretty name,'' Maryalice said.

Chia thought she could hear the Music Master's DESH behind the sound of the engines, not so much a sound now as a part of her. That whiter shade of something, but she could never quite make it out.

7

The Wet, Warm Life in Alison Shires

''She'll try to kill herself,'' Laney said.

''Why?'' Kathy Torrance sipped espresso. A Monday afternoon in the Cage.

''Because she knows. She can feel me watching.''

''That's impossible, Laney.''

''She knows.''

''You aren't 'watching' her. You're examining the data she generates, like the data all our lives generate. She can't know that.''

''She does.''

The white cup clicking down into its saucer. ''Then how can you know that she does? You're looking at her phone records, what she chooses to watch and when, the music she accesses. How could you possibly know that she's aware of your attention?''

The nodal point, he wanted to say. But didn't.

"I think you're working too hard, Laney. Five days off."

"No, I'd rather—"

"I can't afford to let you burn yourself out. I know the signs, Laney. Recreational leave, full pay, five days."

She added a travel bonus. Laney was sent to Slit-scan's in-house agency and booked into a hollowed-out hilltop above Ixtapa, a hotel with vast stone spheres ranged across the polished concrete of its glass-walled lobby. Beyond the glass, iguanas regarded the registration staff with an ancient calm, green scales bright against dusty brown branches.

Laney met a woman who said she edited lamps for a design house in San Francisco. Tuesday evening. He'd been in Mexico three hours. Drinks in the lobby bar.

He asked her what that meant, to edit lamps. Laney had recently noticed that the only people who had titles that clearly described their jobs had jobs he wouldn't have wanted. If people asked him what he did, he said he was a quantitative analyst. He didn't try to explain the nodal points, or Kathy Torrance's theories about celebrity.

The woman replied that her company produced short-run furniture and accessories, lamps in particular. The actual manufacturing took place at any number of different locations, mainly in Northern California. Cottage industry. One maker might contract to do two hundred granite bases, another to lacquer and distress two hundred steel tubes in a very specific shade of blue. She brought out a notebook and showed him animated sketches. All of the things had a thin, spiky look that made him think of African insects he'd seen on the Nature Channel.

Did she design them? No. They were designed in Russia, in Moscow. She was the editor. She selected the suppliers of components. She oversaw manufacture, transport to San Francisco, assembly in what once had been a cannery. If the design documents specified something that couldn't be provided, she either found a new supplier or negotiated a compromise in material or workmanship.

Laney asked who they sold to. People who wanted things other people didn't have, she said. Or that other people didn't like? That too, she said. Did she enjoy it? Yes. Because she generally liked the things the Russians designed, and she tended to like the people who manufactured the components. Best of all, she told him, she liked the feeling of bringing something new into the world, of watching the sketches from Moscow finally become objects on the floor of the former cannery.

It's there, one day, she said, and you can look at it, and touch it, and know whether or not it's good.

Laney considered this. She seemed very calm. Shadows lengthened with almost visible speed across the floor of glossy concrete.

He put his hand over hers.

And touch it, and know whether or not it's good.

Just before dawn, the editor of lamps asleep in his bed, he watched the curve of the bay from the suite's balcony, the moon a milky thing, translucent, nearly gone.

In the night, in the Federal District, somewhere east of here, there had been rocket attacks and rumors of chemical agents, the latest act in one of those obscure and ongoing struggles that made up the background of his world.

Birds were waking in the trees around him, a sound he knew from Gainesville, from the orphanage and other mornings there.

Kathy Torrance announced herself satisfied with Laney's recuperation. He looked rested, she said.

He took to the seas of DatAmerica without comment, suspecting that another leave might prove permanent. She was watching him the way an experienced artisan might watch a valued tool that had shown the first signs of metal-fatigue.

The nodal point was different now, though he had no language to describe the change. He sifted the countless fragments that had clustered around Alison Shires in his absence, feeling for the source of his earlier conviction. He called up the music she'd accessed while he'd been in Mexico, playing each song in the order of her selection. He found her choices had grown more life-affirming; she'd moved to a new provider, Upful Groupvine, whose relentlessly positive product was the musical equivalent of the Good News Channel.

Cross-indexing her charges against the records of her credit-provider and its client retailers, he produced a list of everything she'd purchased in the past week. Six-pack, blades, Tokkai carton opener. Did she own a Tokkai carton opener? But then he remembered Kathy's advice, that this was the part of research most prone to produce serious transference, the point at which the researcher's intimacy with the subject could lead to loss of perspective. "It's often easiest for us to identify at the retail level, Laney. We're a shopping species. Find yourself buying a different brand of frozen peas because the subject does, watch out."

The floor of Laney's apartment was terraced against the original slope of the parking garage. He slept at the deep end, on an inflatable guest bed he'd ordered from the Shopping Channel. There were no windows. Regulations required a light-pump, and reconstituted sunlight sometimes fell from a panel in the ceiling, but he was seldom there during daylight hours.

He sat on the slippery edge of the inflatable, picturing Alison Shires in her Fountain Avenue apartment. Larger than this, he knew, but not by much.

Windows. Her rent was paid, Slitscan had finally determined, by her married actor. Via a fairly intricate series of blinds, but paid nonetheless. ''His reptile fund,'' Kathy called it.

He could hold Alison Shires' history in his mind like a single object, like the perfectly detailed scale model of something ordinary but miraculous, made luminous by the intensity of his focus. He'd never met her, or spoken to her, but he'd come to know her, he supposed, in more ways than anyone ever had or would. Husbands didn't know their wives this way, or wives their husbands. Stalkers might aspire to know the objects of their obsession this way, but never could.

Until the night he woke after midnight, head throbbing. Too hot, something wrong with the conditioning again. Florida. The blue shirt he slept in clinging to his back and shoulders. What would she be doing now?

Was she staring up, awake, at faint bars of reflected light on the ceiling, listening to Upful Groupvine?

Kathy suspected he might be cracking up. He looked at his hands. They could be anybody's. He looked at them as though he'd never seen them before.

He remembered the 5-SB in the orphanage. The taste of it coming while it was still being injected. Rotting metal. The placebo brought no taste at all.

He got up. The Kitchen Korner, sensing him, woke. The fridge door slid aside. A single ancient leaf of lettuce sagged blackly through the plastic rods of one white shelf. A half-empty bottle of Evian on another. He held his cupped hands above the lettuce, willing himself to feel something radiating from its decay, some subtle life force, orgones, particles of an energy unknown to science.

Alison Shires was going to kill herself. He knew he'd seen it. Seen it somehow in the incidental data she generated in her mild-mannered passage through the world of things.

"Hey there," the fridge said. "You've left me open."

Laney said nothing.

"Well, do you *want* the door open, partner? You know it interferes with the automatic *de*-frost . . ."

"Be quiet." His hands felt better. Cooler.

He stood there until his hands were quite cold, then withdrew them and pressed the tips of his fingers against his temples, the fridge taking this opportunity to close itself without further comment.

Twenty minutes later he was on the Metro, headed for Hollywood, a jacket over his sleep-creased Malaysian oxford shirt. Isolated figures on station platforms, whipped sideways by perspective in the wind of the train's passing.

"We're not talking conscious decision, here?" Blackwell kneaded what was left of his right ear.

"No," Laney said, "I don't know what I thought I was doing."

"You were trying to save her. The girl."

"It felt like something snapped. A rubber band. It felt like gravity."

"That's what it feels like," Blackwell said, "when you decide."

Somewhere down the hill from the Sunset Metro exit he passed a man watering his lawn, a rectangle perhaps twice the size of a pooltable, illuminated by the medicinal glow of a nearby streetlight. Laney saw the water beading on the perfectly even blades of bright green plastic. The plastic lawn was fenced back from the street with welded steel, upright prison bars supporting bright untarnished coils of razor-wire. The man's house was scarcely larger than his glittering lawn; a survival from a day when this slope to the hills had been covered with bungalows and arbors. There were others like it, tucked between the balconied, carefully varied faces of condos and apartment complexes, tiny properties dating from before the area's incorporation into the city. There was a hint of oranges in the air, but he couldn't see them.

The waterer looked up, and Laney saw that he was blind, eyes hidden by the black lozenges of video units coupled directly to the optic nerve. You never knew what they were watching.

Laney went on, letting whatever drew him set his

course through these sleeping streets and the occasional scent of a blooming tree. Distant brakes sounded on Santa Monica.

Fifteen minutes later he was in front of her building on Fountain Avenue. Looking up. Fifth floor. 502.

The nodal point.

''You don't want to talk about it?''

Laney looked up from his empty cup, meeting Blackwell's eyes across the table.

''I've never really told this to anyone,'' he said, and it was true.

''Let's walk,'' Blackwell said, and stood, his bulk seeming to lift effortlessly, as though he were a helium parade float. Laney wondered what time it might be, here or in L.A. Yamazaki was taking care of the bill.

He left Amos 'n' Andes with them, out into a falling mist that wasn't quite rain, the sidewalk a bobbing stream of black umbrellas. Yamazaki produced a black object no larger than a business card, slightly thicker, and flexed it sharply between his thumbs. A black umbrella flowered. Yamazaki handed it to him. The curve of the black handle felt dry and hollow and very slightly warm.

''How do you fold it?''

''You don't,'' Yamazaki said. ''It goes away.'' He opened another for himself. Hairless Blackwell, in his micropore, was evidently immune to rain. ''Please continue with your account, Mr. Laney.''

Through a gap between two distant towers, Laney glimpsed the side of another, taller building. He saw vast faces there, vaguely familiar, contorted in inexplicable drama.

The nondisclosure agreement Laney had signed was intended to cover any incidences of Slitscan using its connections with DatAmerica in ways that might be construed as violations of the law. Such incidences, in Laney's experience, were frequent to the point of being constant, at least at certain advanced levels of research. Since DatAmerica had been Laney's previous employer, he hadn't found any of this particularly startling. DatAmerica was less a power than a territory; in many ways it was a law unto itself.

Laney's protracted survey of Alison Shires had already involved any number of criminal violations, one of which had provided him with the codes required to open the door into her building's foyer, activate the elevator, unlock the door of her fifth-floor apartment, and cancel the private security alarm that would automatically warrant an armed response if she did these things without keying in two extra digits. This last was intended as insurance against endemic home invasion, a crime in which residents were accosted in parking garages and induced to surrender their codes.

Alison Shires' code consisted of her month, date, and year of birth, something any security service strongly advised against. Her back-up code was 23, her age the year before, when she'd moved in and become a subscriber.

Laney softly reciting these as he stood before her building, its eight-story facade feinting toward someone's idea of Tudor Revival. Everything looking so sharply and comprehensively detailed, in these first moments of an L.A. dawn.

23.

"So," Blackwell supposed, "you just walked in. Punched up her codes and bang, there you were." The three of them waiting to cross at an intersection.

—Bang.

No sound at all in the mirrored foyer. A sense of vacuum. A dozen Laneys reflected there as he crossed an expanse of new carpet. Into an elevator smelling of something floral, where he used part of the code again. It took him straight to five. The door slid open. More new carpet. Beneath a fresh coat of cream enamel the corridor's walls displayed the faint irregularities of old-fashioned plaster.

502.

"What do you think you're doing?" Laney asked

aloud, though whether to himself or to Alison Shires he did not nor would he ever know.

The brass round of an antique security fish-eye regarded him from the door, partially occluded by a cataract of pale paint.

The key-pad was set flush with the door's steel frame, not quite level with the fish-eye. He watched his finger finding its way through the sequence.

23.

But Alison Shires, naked, opened the door before the code could key, Upful Groupvine soaring joyfully behind her as Laney grabbed her blood-slick wrists. And saw there in her eyes what he took then and forever as a look of simple recognition, not even of blame.

"This isn't working," she said, as though she were indicating a minor appliance, and Laney heard himself whimper, a sound he hadn't made since childhood. He needed to see those wrists, but couldn't, holding her. He was walking her backward, toward a wicker armchair he wasn't even aware he'd seen.

"Sit," he said, as if to a stubborn child, and she did. He let go of her wrists. Ran for where he guessed the bathroom had to be. Towels there and some kind of tape.

And discovered himself kneeling beside her where she sat, red fingers curled in toward red palms, as if in meditation. He rolled a dark green hand towel around her left wrist and whipped the tape around it, some rubbery beige product meant to mask specific areas during the application of aerosol cosmetics. He knew that from her product-purchase data.

Were her fingers turning blue, beneath their coat of red? He looked up. Into that same recognition. One cheekbone brushed with blood.

"Don't," he said.

"It's slowing."

Laney wrapping her right forearm now, the tape-roll dangling from his teeth.

"I missed the artery."

"Don't move," Laney said, and sprang up, tripping over his own feet, crashing face-first into what he recognized, just before it broke his nose, as the work of the editor of lamps. The carpet seemed to whip up and smack him playfully in the face.

"Alison—"

Her ankle stepping past him, kitchenward.

"Alison, sit *down!*"

"Sorry," he thought he heard her say, and then the shot.

Blackwell's shoulders heaved as he sighed, making a sound that Laney heard above the traffic. Yamazaki's glasses were filled with jittering pastels, the walls here all neon, a glare to shame Vegas, every surface lit and jumping.

Blackwell was staring at Laney. "This way," he said, finally, and rounded a corner, into relative darkness and an edge of urine. Laney followed, Yamazaki behind him. At the far end of the narrow passage, they emerged into fairyland.

No neon here at all. Ambient glow from the towers overhead. Austere rectangles of white frosted glass, the size of large greeting cards, were daubed with black ideograms, each sign marking a tiny structure like some antique bathing cabin on a forgotten beach. Crowded shoulder to shoulder down one side of the cobbled lane, their miniature facades suggested a shuttered sideshow in some secret urban carnival. Age-silvered cedar, oiled paper, matting; nothing to pin the place in time but the fact that the signs were electric.

Laney stared. A street built by leprechauns.

''Golden Street,'' said Keith Alan Blackwell.

8

Narita

Chia deplaned behind Maryalice, who'd had a couple of those vitamin drinks and then tied up one of the toilets for twenty minutes while she teased her extensions and put on lipstick and mascara. Chia couldn't say much for the result, which looked less like Ashleigh Modine Carter than something Ashleigh Modine Carter had slept on.

When Chia stood up, she felt like she had to tell her body to do every single thing she needed it to. Legs: move.

She'd gotten a few more hours sleep, somewhere back there. She'd packed her Sandbenders back in her bag, and now she was putting one foot in front of the other, as Maryalice, in front of her, shuffle-swayed along the narrow aisle in her white cowboy boots.

It seemed to take forever to get out of the plane, but then they were breathing airport air in a corridor, under big logos that Chia had known all her life, all those Japanese companies, and everything crowded and moving in one direction. "You check anything?" Maryalice asked, beside her.

"No," Chia said.

Maryalice let Chia go ahead of her through Passport Control, where Chia gave the Japanese policeman her passport and the Cashflow smartcard Zona Rosa had forced Kelsey to come up with because this was all Kelsey's idea anyway. In theory, the amount in the card represented the bulk of the Seattle chapter's treasury, but Chia suspected Kelsey would wind up footing the bill for the whole thing, and probably wouldn't even care.

The policeman pulled her passport out of the counter-slot and handed it back to her. He hadn't bothered to check the smartcard. "Two week maximum stay," he said, and nodded her on.

Frosted glass slid open for her. It was crowded here, way more than SeaTac. So many planes must've come in at once, to have all these people waiting for their luggage. She edged aside to let a little robot stacked with suitcases pass. It had dirty pink rubber tires and big cartoon eyes that rolled morosely as it made its way through the crowd.

"Now, that was easy," said Maryalice, behind her. Chia turned in time to see her take a long deep breath, hold it, and let it out. Maryalice's eyes looked pinched, like she was having a headache.

"Do you know which way I should go to get the train?" Chia asked. She had maps in her Sandbenders, but she didn't want to have to get it out now.

"This way," Maryalice said.

Maryalice worked her way between people, Chia following with her bag under her arm. Emerging in front of a carousel where bags were sliding down a ramp, bumping, swinging past and away.

"Here's one," Maryalice said, snagging a black one and sounding so forcefully cheerful that it made Chia look at her. "And . . . *two*." Another one like it, except this one had a sticker on the side from Nissan County, the third largest gated attraction in the Californias. "Would you mind carrying this for me, honey? My back goes out on long plane rides." Passing Chia the bag with the sticker. It wasn't too heavy, like maybe it was only half-full of clothes. But it was too large for her; she had to lean over in the opposite direction to keep it off the ground.

"Thanks," Maryalice said. "Here," and she handed Chia a crumpled square of sticky-backed paper with a bar code on it. "That's the check. Now we just want to go this way . . ."

It was even harder getting through the crowd, lugging Maryalice's bag. Chia had to concentrate on not stepping on people's feet, and not bumping them too hard with the bag, and the next thing she knew, she'd lost Maryalice. She looked around, expecting to see hair-extensions bobbing above the crowd, who were mostly shorter than Maryalice, but Maryalice was nowhere in sight.

ALL ARRIVING PASSENGERS MUST EXIT THROUGH CUSTOMS.

Chia watched the sign twist itself up into Japanese letters, then pop back out as English.

Well, that was the way to go. She got in line behind a man in a red leather jacket that said ''Concept Collision'' across the back in gray chenille letters. Chia stared at that, imagining concepts colliding, which she guessed was a concept in itself, but then she thought it was probably just the name of a company that fixed cars, or one of those slogans the Japanese made up in English, the ones that almost seemed to mean something but didn't. This trans-Pacific jet lag thing was serious.

''Next.''

They were feeding Concept Collision's suitcase through a machine the size of a double bed, but taller. There was an official of some kind in a video-helmet, evidently reading feed off the scanners, and another policeman, to take your passport, slot it in the machine, then put your bags through. Chia let him take Maryalice's suitcase and flip it up, onto the conveyor. Chia handed him her carry-on. ''There's a computer in there. This scan okay for that?'' He didn't seem to hear her. She watched her carry-on follow Maryalice's bag into the machine.

The man in the helmet, eyes hidden, was bobbing

his head from side to side as he accessed gaze-activated menus.

"Baggage check," the policeman said, and Chia remembered she had it in her hand. It struck her as strange, handing it over, that Maryalice had thought to give her that. The policeman ran a hand-scanner over it.

"You packed these bags yourself?" asked the man in the helmet. He couldn't see her directly, but she assumed he could see the clips stored in her passport, and he could probably see her on live feed as well. Airports were full of cameras.

"Yes," Chia said, deciding it was easier than trying to explain that it was Maryalice's bag, not hers. She tried to read the expression on the helmeted man's lips, but it was hard to say if he even had one.

"You packed this?"

"Yes . . ." Chia said, not sounding nearly as certain this time.

The helmet bobbed.

"Next," he said.

Chia went to the other end of the machine and collected her bag and the black suitcase.

Through another sliding wall of frosted glass: she was in a larger hall, beneath a higher ceiling, bigger ads overhead but no thinning of the crowd. Maybe this wasn't so much a matter of crowds as it was of Tokyo, maybe of Japan in general: more people, closer together.

More of those robot baggage carts. She wondered

what it cost to rent one. You could lie down on top of your luggage, maybe, tell it where you wanted to go, and then just go to sleep. Except she wasn't sure she felt sleepy, exactly. She transferred Maryalice's bag from her left to her right hand, wondering what to do with it if she didn't find Maryalice inside the next, say, five minutes. She'd had enough of airports and the space between them, and she wasn't even sure where she was supposed to sleep tonight. Or if it *was* night, even.

She was looking up, hoping to find some kind of time display, when a hand closed around her right wrist. She looked down at the hand, saw gold rings and a watch to match, fat links of a gold bracelet, the rings connected to the watch with little gold chains.

"That's my suitcase."

Chia's eyes followed the hand's wrist to a length of bright white cuff, then up the arm of a black jacket. To pale eyes in a long face, each cheek seamed vertically, as if with a modelling instrument. For a second she took him for her Music Master, loose somehow in this airport. But her Music Master would never wear a watch like that, and this one's hair, a darker blond, was swept back, long and wet-looking, from his high forehead. He didn't look happy.

"Maryalice's suitcase," Chia said.

"She gave it to you? In Seattle?"

"She asked me to carry it."

"From Seattle?"

"No," Chia said. "Back there. She sat beside me on the plane."

"Where is she?"

"I don't know," Chia said.

He wore a black, long-coated suit, buttoned high. Like something from an old movie, but new and expensive-looking. He seemed to notice that he was still holding her wrist; now he let it go.

"I'll carry it for you," he said. "We'll find her."

Chia didn't know what to do. "Maryalice wanted *me* to carry it."

"You did. Now I'll carry it." He took it from her.

"Are you Maryalice's boyfriend? Eddie?"

The corner of his mouth twitched.

"You could say that," he said.

Eddie's car was a Daihatsu Graceland with the steering wheel on the wrong side. Chia knew that because Rez had ridden in the back of one in a video, except that that one had had a bath in it, black marble, big gold faucets shaped like tropical fish. People had posted that that was an ironic take on money, on the really ugly things you could do with it if you had too much. Chia had told her mother about that. Her mother said there wasn't much point in worrying what you might do if you had too much, because most people never even had enough. She said it was better to try to figure out what "enough" actually meant.

But Eddie had one, a Graceland, all black and

chrome. From the outside it looked sort of like a cross between an RV and one of those long, wedge-shaped Hummer limousines. Chia couldn't imagine there'd be much of a Japanese market; the cars here all looked like little candy-colored lozenges. The Graceland was meshback pure and simple, designed to sell to the kind of American who made a point of trying not to buy imports. Which, when it came to cars, definitely narrowed your options. (Hester Chen's mother had one of those really ugly Canadian trucks that cost a fortune but were guaranteed to last for eighty-five years; that was supposed to be better for the ecology.)

Inside, the Graceland was all burgundy velour, puffed up in diamonds, with little chrome nubs where the points of the diamonds met. It was about the tackiest thing Chia had ever seen, and she guessed Maryalice thought so too, because Maryalice, seated next to her, was explaining that it was an "image" thing, that Eddie had this very hot, very popular country-music club called Whiskey Clone, so he'd gotten the Graceland to go with that, and he'd also started dressing the way they did in Nashville. Maryalice thought that look suited him, she said.

Chia nodded. Eddie was driving, talking in Japanese on a speakerphone. They'd found Maryalice at a tiny little bar, just off the arrivals area. It was the third one they'd looked in. Chia got the feeling that Eddie wasn't very happy to see Maryalice, but Maryalice hadn't seemed to care.

It was Maryalice's idea that they give Chia a ride into Tokyo. She said the train was too crowded and it cost a lot anyway. She said she wanted to do Chia a favor, because Chia had carried her bag for her. (Chia had noticed that Eddie had put one bag in the Graceland's trunk, but kept the one with the Nissan County sticker up front, next to him, beside the driver's seat.)

Chia wasn't really listening to Maryalice now; it was some time at night and the jet lag was too weird and they were on this big bridge that seemed to be made out of neon, with however many lanes of traffic around them, the little cars like strings of bright beads, all of them shiny and new. There were screens that kept blurring past, tall and narrow, with Japanese writing jumping around on some of them, and people on others, faces, smiling as they sold something.

And then a woman's face: Rei Toei, the idoru Rez wanted to marry. And gone.

Out of Control

"Rice Daniels, Mr. Laney. Out of control." Pressing a card of some kind to the opposite side of the scratched plastic that walled the room called Visitors away from those who gave it its name. Laney had tried to read it, but the attempt at focusing had driven an atrocious spike of pain between his eyes. He'd looked at Rice Daniels instead, through tears of pain: close-cropped dark hair, close-fitting sunglasses with small oval lenses, the black frames gripping the man's head like some kind of surgical clamp.

Nothing at all about Rice Daniels appeared to be out of control.

"The series," he said. " 'Out of Control.' As in: aren't the media? Out of Control: the cutting edge of counter-investigative journalism."

Laney had gingerly tried touching the tape across the bridge of his nose: a mistake. "Counter-investigative?"

"You're a quant, Mr. Laney." A quantitative analyst. He wasn't, really, but that was technically his job description. "For Slitscan."

Laney didn't respond.

"The girl was the focus of intensive surveillance. Slitscan was all over her. You know why. We believe a case can be made here for Slitscan's culpability in the death of Alison Shires."

Laney looked down at his running shoes, their laces removed by the Deputies. "She killed herself," he said.

"But we know why."

"No," Laney said, meeting the black ovals again, "I don't. Not exactly." The nodal point. Protocols of some other realm entirely.

"You're going to need help, Laney. You might be looking at a manslaughter charge. Abetting a suicide. They'll want to know why you were up there."

"I'll tell them why."

"Our producers managed to get me in here first, Laney. It wasn't easy. There's a spin-control team from Slitscan out there now, waiting to talk with you. If you let them, they'll turn it all around. They'll get you off, because they have to, in order to cover the show. They can do it, with enough money and the right lawyers. But ask yourself this: do you want to *let* them do it?"

Daniels still had his business card thumbed up against the plastic. Trying to focus on it again, Laney saw that someone had scratched something in from the other side, in small, uneven mirror-letters, so that he could read it left to right:

I NO U DIDIT

"I've never heard of Out of Control."

"Our hour-long pilot is in production as we speak, Mr. Laney." A measured pause. "We're all very excited."

"Why?"

"Out of Control isn't just a series. We think of it as an entirely new paradigm. A new way to do television. Your story—Alison Shires' story—is *precisely* what we intend to get out there. Our producers are people who want to *give something back* to the audience. They've done well, they're established, they've proven themselves; now they want to give something back—to restore a degree of honesty, a new opportunity for perspective." The black ovals drew slightly closer to the scratched plastic. "Our producers are the producers of 'Cops in Trouble' and 'A Calm and Deliberate Fashion.' "

"A what?"

"Factual accounts of premeditated violence in the global fashion industry."

• • •

" 'Counter-investigative'?" Yamazaki's pen hovered over the notebook.

"It was a show *about* shows like Slitscan," Laney explained. "Supposed abuses." There were no stools at the bar, which might have been ten feet long. You stood. Aside from the bartender, in some kind of Kabuki drag, they had the place to themselves. By virtue of filling it, basically. It was probably the smallest freestanding commercial structure Laney had ever seen, and it seemed to have been there forever, like a survival from ancient Edo, a city of shadows and minute dark lanes. The walls were shingled with faded postcards, gone a uniform sepia under a glaze of accumulated nicotine and cooking smoke.

"Ah," Yamazaki said at last, "a 'meta-tabloid.' "

The bartender was broiling two sardines on a doll's hotplate. He flipped them with a pair of steel chopsticks, transferred them to a tiny plate, garnished them with some kind of colorless, translucent pickle, and presented them to Laney.

"Thanks," Laney said. The bartender ducked his shaven eyebrows.

In spite of the modest decor, there were dozens of bottles of expensive-looking whiskey arranged behind the bar, each one with a hand-written brown paper sticker: the owner's name in Japanese. Yamazaki had explained that you bought one and they kept it there for you. Blackwell was on his second tumbler of the local vodka-analog, on the rocks. Yamazaki was sticking to Coke Lite. Laney had an untouched shot of surrealistically expensive Kentucky straight bourbon whiskey in front of him, and wondered vaguely what it would do to his jet lag if he were actually to drink it.

"So," Blackwell said, draining the tumbler, ice clinking against his prosthetic, "they get you out so they can have a go at these other bastards."

"That was it, basically," Laney said. "They had their own legal team waiting, to do that, and another team to work on the nondisclosure agreement I'd signed with Slitscan."

"And the second team had the bigger job," Blackwell said, shoving his empty glass toward the bartender, who swept it smoothly out of sight, producing a fresh replacement just as smoothly, as if from nowhere.

"That's true," Laney said. He'd had no idea, really, of what he'd be getting into when he'd found himself agreeing to the general outlines of Rice Daniels' offer. But there was something in him that didn't want to see Slitscan walk away from the sound of that one single shot from Alison Shires' kitchen. (Produced, the cops had pointed out, by a Russian-made device that was hardly more than a cartridge, a tube to contain it, and the simplest possible firing mechanism; these were designed with suicide almost exclusively in mind; there was no way to aim them at anything more than two inches away. Laney had heard of them, but had never seen one before; for some reason, they were called Wednesday Night Specials.)

And Slitscan would walk away, he knew; they'd drop the sequence on Alison's actor, if they felt they had to, and the whole thing would settle to the sea floor, silting over almost instantly with the world's steady accretion of data.

And Alison Shires' life, as he'd known it in all that terrible, banal intimacy, would lie there forever, forgotten and finally unknowable.

But if he went with Out of Control, her life might retrospectively become something else, and he wasn't sure, exactly, sitting there on the hard little chair in Visitors, what that might be.

He thought of coral, of the reefs that grew around sunken aircraft carriers; perhaps she'd become something like that, the buried mystery beneath some exfoliating superstructure of supposition, or even of myth.

It seemed to him, in Visitors, that that might be a slightly less dead way of being dead. And he wished her that.

"Get me out of here," he said to Daniels, who smiled beneath his surgical clamp, whipping the card triumphantly away from the plastic.

"Steady," said Blackwell, laying his huge hand, with its silvery-pink fretwork of scars, over Laney's wrist. "You haven't even had your drink yet."

• • •

Laney had met Rydell when the Out of Control team installed him in a suite at the Chateau, that ancient simulacrum of a still more ancient original, its quaint concrete eccentricities pinched between the twin brutalities of a particularly nasty pair of office buildings dating from the final year of the previous century. These reflected all the Millennial anxiety of the year of their creation, while refracting it through some other, more mysterious, weirdly muted hysteria that seemed somehow more personal and even less attractive.

Laney's suite, much larger than his apartment in Santa Monica, was like an elongated 1920s apartment following the long, shallow concrete balcony that faced Sunset, this in turn overlooking a deeper balcony on the floor below and the tiny circular lawn that was all that remained of the original gardens.

Laney thought it was a strange choice, considering his situation. He would have imagined they'd choose something more corporate, more fortified, more heavily wired, but Rice Daniels had explained that the Chateau had advantages all its own. It was a good choice in terms of image, because it humanized Laney; it looked like a *habitation,* basically, something with walls and doors and windows, in which a guest could be imagined to be living something akin to a life—not at all the case with the geometric solids that were serious business hotels. It also had deeply rooted associations with the Hollywood star system, and with human tragedy as well. Stars had lived here, in the heyday of old Hollywood, and, later, certain stars had died here. Out of Control planned to frame the death of Alison Shires as a tragedy in a venerable Hollywood tradition, but one that had been brought on by Slitscan, a very contemporary entity. Besides, Daniels explained, the Chateau was far more secure than it might at first look. And at this point Laney had been introduced to Berry Rydell, the night security man.

Daniels and Rydell, it seemed to Laney, had known one another prior to Rydell working at the Chateau, though how, exactly, remained unclear. Rydell seemed oddly at home with the workings of the infotainment industry, and at one point, when they'd found themselves alone together, he'd asked Laney who was representing him.

"How do you mean?" Laney had said.

"You've got an agent, don't you?"

Laney said he didn't.

"You better get one," Rydell had said. "Not that it'll necessarily come out the way you'd wanted, but, hey, it's show business, right?"

It was indeed show business, to an extent that very quickly made Laney wonder if he'd made the right decision. There had been sixteen people in his suite, for a four-hour meeting, and he'd only been out of the lock-up for six hours. When they'd finally gone, Laney had staggered the length of the place, mistakenly trying several closet doors in his search for the bedroom. Finding it, he'd crawled onto the bed and fallen asleep in the clothes they'd sent Rydell to the Beverly Center to buy for him.

Which he thought he might well do right here, now, in this Golden Street bar, thereby answering the question of what the bourbon was doing to his jet lag. But now, finishing the remainder of the shot, he felt one of thosc tidal reversals begin, perhaps less to do with the drink than with some in-built chemistry of fatigue and displacement.

"Was Rydell happy?" Yamazaki asked.

It seemed a strange question, to Laney, but then he'd remembered Rydell mentioning someone Japanese, someone he'd known in San Francisco, and that, of course, had been Yamazaki.

"Well," Laney said, "he didn't strikc me as desperately unhappy, but there *was* something sort of down about him. You could say that. I mean, I don't really know him well at all."

"It is too bad," Yamazaki said. "Rydell is a brave man."

"How about you, Laney," Blackwell said, "you think of yourself as a brave man?" The wormlike scar that bisected his eyebrow writhed into a new degree of concentration.

"No," Laney said, "I don't."

"But you went up against Slitscan, didn't you, because of what they did to the girl? You had a job, you had food, you had a place to sleep. You got all that from Slitscan, but they did the girl, so you opted to do 'em back. Is that right?''

''Nothing's ever that simple,'' Laney said.

When Blackwell spoke, Laney was unexpectedly aware of another sort of intelligence, something the man must ordinarily conceal. ''No,'' Blackwell said, almost gently, ''it fucking well isn't, is it?'' One large, pinkly jigsawed hand, like some clumsy animal in its own right, began to root in the taut breast pocket of Blackwell's micropore. Producing a small, gray, metallic object that he placed on the bar.

''Now that's a nail,'' Blackwell said, ''galvanized, one-and-a-half-inch, roofing. I've nailed men's hands to bars like this, with nails like that. And some of them were right bastards.'' There was nothing at all of threat in Blackwell's voice. ''And some of those, you nail their one hand, their other comes up with a razor, or a pair of needle-nose pliers.'' Blackwell's forefinger absently found an angry-looking scar beneath his right eye, as though something had entered there and been deflected along the cheekbone. ''To have a go, right?''

''Pliers?''

''Bastards,'' Blackwell said. ''You have to kill 'em, then. Now that's one kind of 'brave,' Laney. What I mean is, how's that so different from what you tried to do to Slitscan?''

''I just didn't want them to let it drop. To let her . . . settle to the bottom. Be forgotten. I didn't really care how badly Slitscan got hurt, or even if they were damaged or not. I wasn't thinking of revenge, as much as of a way of . . . keeping her alive?''

''There's other men, you nail their hand to a table, they'll sit there and look at you. That's your true hard man, Laney. Do you think you're one of those?''

Laney looked from Blackwell to the empty bourbon glass, back to Blackwell; the bartender moved, as if to refill it, but Laney covered it with his hand. ''If you nail my hand to the bar, Blackwell,'' and here he spread his other hand, flat, palm down, on the dark wood, the drink-ringed varnish, ''I'll scream, okay? I don't know what *any* of this is about. You might be crazy. But what I most definitely am not is anybody's idea of a hero. I'm not now, and I wasn't back there in L.A.''

Blackwell and Yamazaki exchanged glances. Blackwell pursed his lips, gave a tiny nod. ''Good on you then,'' he said. ''I think you just might be right for the job.''

''No job,'' Laney said, but let the bartender pour him a second bourbon. ''I don't want to hear about any job at all, not until I know who's hiring me.''

''I'm chief of security for Lo/Rez,'' Blackwell said, ''and I owe that silly bastard my life. The last five of which I'd've passed in the punitive bowels of the State of fucking Victoria. If it hadn't been for him. Though I'd've topped myself first, no fear.''

''The band? You're security for them?''

''Rydell spoke well of you, Mr. Laney.'' Yamazaki's neck bobbed in the collar of his plaid shirt.

"I don't know Rydell," Laney said. "He was just the night watchman at a hotel I couldn't afford."

"Rydell has a good sense of people, I think," Yamazaki said.

To Blackwell: "Lo/Rez? They're in trouble?"

"Rez," Blackwell said. "He says he's going to marry this Jap twist doesn't fucking *exist!* And he *knows* she doesn't, and says we've *no fucking imagination!* Now hear me," and Blackwell produced, from some unspecific region of his clothing, a mirror-polished rectangle with a round hole through its uppermost, leading corner. Something not much larger than a cashcard, to see it in his big hand. "Someone's *got* to our boy, hear? Got *to* him. Don't know how, don't know who. Though personally myself I'd bet on the fucking Kombinat. Those Russ bastards. But you, my friend, you're going to do your nodal thing for us, on our Rez, and you are going to find fucking *out. Who.*" And the rectangle came down with a concise little thunk, to be left standing, crosswise to the counter's grain, and Laney saw that it was a very small meat cleaver, with round steel rivets through its tidy rosewood handle.

"And when you do," Blackwell said, "we shall sort them well and fucking out."

Whiskey Clone

Eddie's club was way up in something like an office building. Chia didn't think there were music clubs on the upper floors of buildings like that in Seattle, but she wasn't sure. She'd fallen asleep in the Graceland, and only woke up as Eddie was driving into a garage entrance, and then up into something vaguely like a Ferris wheel, or the cylinder of an old-fashioned revolver, except the bullets were cars. She watched out the windows as it swung them up and over, to stop at the top, where Eddie drove forward into a parking garage that might've been anywhere, except the cars were all big and black, though none as big as the Graceland.

"Come on up with us and freshen up, honey," Maryalice said. "You look wrecked."

''I have to port,'' Chia said. ''Find my friend I'm staying with . . .''

''Easy enough,'' Maryalice said, sliding across the velour and opening the door. Eddie got out the driver's side, taking the bag with the Nissan County sticker with him. He still didn't look very happy. Chia took her bag with her and followed Maryalice. They all got into an elevator. Eddie pressed his palm against a hand-shaped outline on the wall and said something in Japanese. The elevator said something back, then the door closed and they were going up. Fast, it felt like, but they just kept going.

Being in the elevator didn't seem to be improving Eddie's mood. He had to stand right up close to Maryalice, and Chia could see a little muscle working, in the hinge of his jaw, as he looked at her. Maryalice just looked right back at him.

''You oughta lighten up,'' Maryalice said. ''It's done.''

The little muscle went into overdrive. ''That was not the deal,'' he said, finally. ''That was not the arrangement.''

Maryalice lifted an eyebrow. ''You used to appreciate a little innovation.''

Eddie glanced from Maryalice to Chia, then, quick, back to Maryalice. ''You call that an innovation?''

''You used to have a sense of humor, too,'' Maryalice said, as the elevator stopped and the door slid open. Eddie glared, then stepped out, Chia and Maryalice following. ''Never mind him,'' Maryalice said. ''Just how he gets, sometimes.''

Chia wasn't sure what she'd expected, but this definitely wasn't it. A messy room jammed with shipping cartons, and a bank of security monitors. The low ceiling was made of those fibery tiles that were hung on little metal rails; about half of them were missing, with wires and cables looping down from dusty-looking shadow. There were a couple of small desk lamps, one of them illuminating a stack of used instant-noodle containers and a black coffee mug filled with white plastic spoons. A Japanese man in a black meshback that said ''Whiskey Clone'' across the front was sitting in a swivel chair in front of the monitors, pouring himself a hot drink out of a big thermos with pink flowers on the side.

''Yo, Calvin,'' Maryalice said, or that was what it sounded like.

''Hey,'' the man said.

''Calvin's from Tacoma,'' Maryalice said, as Chia watched Eddie, still carrying the suitcase, march straight through the room, through a door, and out of sight.

''Boss looks happy,'' the man said, sounding no more Japanese than Maryalice. He took a sip from his thermos cup.

''Yeah,'' Maryalice said. ''He's so glad to see me, he's beside himself.''

''This too will pass.'' Another sip. Looking at Chia from beneath the bill of the meshback. The letters in

"Whiskey Clone" were the kind they'd use in a mall when they wanted you to think a place was traditional.

"This is Chia," Maryalice said. "Met her in SeaTac," and Chia noticed that she hadn't said she'd met her on the plane. Which made her remember that business with the DNA sampling and the hair-extensions.

"Glad to hear it's still there," the man said. "Means there's some way back out of this batshit."

"Now, Calvin," Maryalice said, "you know you love Tokyo."

"Sure. Had a place in Redmond had a bathroom the size of the whole apartment I got here, and it wasn't even a big bathroom. I mean, it had a shower. No tub or anything."

Chia looked at the screens behind him. Lots of people there, but she couldn't tell what they were doing.

"Looks like a good night," Maryalice said, surveying the screens.

"Just fair," he said. "Fair to middling."

"Quit talking like that," Maryalice said. "You'll have me doing it."

Calvin grinned. "But you're a good old girl, aren't you, Maryalice?"

"Please," Chia said, "may I use a dataport?"

"There's one in Eddie's office," Maryalice said. "But he's probably on the phone now. Why don't you go in the washroom there," indicating another door, closed, "and have a wash. You're looking a little blurry. Then Eddie'll be done and you can call your friend.''

The washroom had an old steel sink and a very new, very complicated-looking toilet with at least a dozen buttons on top of the tank. These were labeled in Japanese. The polymer seat squirmed slightly, taking her weight, and she almost jumped up again. It's okay, she reassured herself, just foreign technology. When she was done, she chose one of the controls at random, producing a superfine spray of warm, perfumed water that made her gasp and jump back. She wiped her eyes with the back of her hand, then stood well to the side and tried another button. This one seemed to do the trick: the toilet flushed, with a jet-stream sound that reminded her of being on the plane.

As she washed her hands, and then her face, at the reassuringly ordinary sink, using pale blue liquid soap from a pump-top dispenser shaped like a one-eyed dinosaur, she heard the flushing stop and another sound begin. She looked back and saw a ring of purplish light oscillating, somewhere below the toilet seat. UV, she supposed, sterilizing it.

There was a poster of the Dukes of Nuke 'Em taped on the wall, this hideous 'roidhead metal band. They were sweaty and blank-eyed, grinning, and the drummer was missing his front teeth. The lettering was in Japanese. She wondered why anyone in Japan would be into that, because groups like the Dukes were all about hating anything that wasn't their idea of American. But Kelsey, who'd been to Japan lots, with her father, had said that you couldn't tell what the Japanese would make of anything.

There wasn't anything here to dry your hands on. She got a t-shirt out of her bag and used that, although it didn't work very well. As she was kneeling to stuff the shirt back in, she noticed a corner of something she didn't recognize, but then Calvin cracked the door behind her.

"Excuse me," he said.

"It's okay," Chia said, zipping the bag shut.

"It's not," he said, looking back over his shoulder, then back at her. "You really meet Maryalice at SeaTac?"

"On the plane," Chia said.

"You're not part of it?"

Chia stood up, which made her feel kind of dizzy. "Part of what?"

He looked at her from beneath the brim of the black cap. "Then you really ought to get out of here. I mean right now."

"Why?" Chia asked, although it didn't strike her as a bad idea at all.

"Nothing you want to know anything about." There was a crash, somewhere behind him. He winced. "It's okay. She's just throwing things. They haven't gotten serious yet. Come on," and he grabbed her bag by the shoulder strap and lifted it up. He was moving fast now, and she had to hustle to keep up with him. Out past the closed door of Eddie's office, past the bank of screens (where she thought she saw people line-dancing in cowboy hats, but she was never sure).

Calvin slapped his hand on the sensor-plate on the elevator door. ''Take you to the garage,'' he said, as the sound of breaking glass came from Eddie's office. ''Hang a left, about twenty feet, there's another elevator. Skip the lobby; we got cameras there. Bottom button gets you the subway. Get on a train.'' He passed her her bag.

''Which one?'' Chia asked.

Maryalice screamed. Like something really, really hurt.

''Doesn't matter,'' Calvin said, and quickly said something in Japanese to the elevator. The elevator answered, but he was already gone, the door closing, and then she was descending, her bag seeming to lighten slightly in her arms.

Eddie's Graceland was still there when the door slid open, a hulking wedge beside those other black cars. She found the second elevator Calvin had told her to take, its door scratched and dented. It had reg ular buttons, and it didn't talk, and it took her down to malls bright as day, crowds moving through them, to escalators and platforms and mag-levs and the eternal logos tethered overhead.

She was in Tokyo at last.

11

Collapse of New Buildings

Laney's room was high up in a narrow tower faced with white ceramic tile. It was trapezoidal in cross section and dated from the eighties boomtown, the years of the Bubble. That it had survived the great earthquake was testimony to the skill of its engineers; that it had survived the subsequent reconstruction testified to an arcane tangle of ownership and an ongoing struggle between two of the city's oldest criminal organizations. Yamazaki had explained this in the cab, returning from New Golden Street.

"We were uncertain how you might feel about new buildings," he'd said.

"You mean the nanotech buildings?" Laney had been struggling to keep his eyes open. The driver wore spotless white gloves.

"Yes. Some people find them disturbing."

"I don't know. I'd have to see one."

"You can see them from your hotel, I think."

And he could. He knew their sheer brutality of scale from constructs, but virtuality had failed to convey the peculiarity of their apparent texture, a streamlined organicism. "They are like Giger's paintings of New York," Yamazaki had said, but the reference had been lost on Laney.

Now he sat on the edge of his bed, staring blankly out at these miracles of the new technology, as banal and as sinister as such miracles usually were, and they were only annoying: the world's largest inhabited structures. (The Chernobyl containment structure was larger, but nothing human would ever live there.)

The umbrella Yamazaki had given him was collapsing into itself, shrinking. Going away.

The phone began to ring. He couldn't find it.

"Telephone," he said. "Where is it?"

A nub of ruby light, timed to the rings, began to pulse from a flat rectangle of white cedar arranged on a square black tray on a bedside ledge. He picked it up. Thumbed a tiny square of mother-of-pearl.

"Hey," someone said. "That Laney?"

"Who's calling?"

"Rydell. From the Chateau. Hans let me use the phone." Hans was the night manager. "I get the time right? You having breakfast?"

Laney rubbed his eyes, looked out again at the new buildings. "Sure."

"I called Yamazaki," Rydell said. "Got your number."

"Thanks," Laney said, yawning, "but I—"

"Yamazaki said you got the gig."

"I think so," Laney said. "Thanks. Guess I owe—"

"Slitscan," Rydell said. "All over the Chateau."

"No," Laney said, "that's over."

"You know any Katherine Torrance, Laney? Sherman Oaks address? She's up in the suite you had, with about two vans worth of sensing gear. Hans figures they're trying to get a read on what you were doing up there, any dope or anything."

Laney stared out at the towers. Part of a facade seemed to move, but it had to be his eyes.

"But Hans says there's no way they can sort the residual molecules out in those rooms anyway. Place has too much of a history."

"Kathy Torrance? From Slitscan?"

"Not like they said they were, but they've got all these techs, and techs always talk too much, and Ghengis down in the garage saw the decals on some of the cases, when they were unloading. There's about twenty of 'em, if you don't count the gophers. Got two suites and four singles. Don't tip."

"But what are they *doing?*"

"That sensor stuff. Trying to figure out what you got up to in the suite. And one of the bellmen saw them setting up a camera."

The entire facade of one of the new buildings

seemed to ripple, to crawl slightly. Laney closed his eyes and pinched the bridge of his nose, discovering a faint trace of pain residing there from the break. He opened his eyes. "But I never got *up* to anything."

"Whatever." Rydell sounded slightly hurt. "I just thought you ought to know, is all."

Something was definitely happening to that facade. "I know. Thanks. Sorry."

"I'll let you know if I hear anything," Rydell said. "What's it like over there, anyway?"

Laney was watching a point of reflected light slide across the distant structure, a movement like osmosis or the sequential contraction of some sea creature's palps. "It's strange."

"Bet it's interesting," Rydell said. "Enjoy your breakfast, okay? I'll keep in touch."

"Thanks," Laney said, and Rydell hung up.

Laney put the phone back on the lacquer tray and stretched out on the bed, fully clothed. He closed his eyes, not wanting to see the new buildings. But they were still there, in the darkness and the light behind his lids. And as he watched, they slid apart, deliquesced, and trickled away, down into the mazes of an older city.

He slid down with them.

Mitsuko

Chia used a public dataport in the deepest level of the station. The Sandbenders sent the number they'd given her for Mitsuko Mimura, the Tokyo chapter's "social secretary" (everyone in Tokyo chapter seemed to have a formal title). A girl's sleepy voice in Japanese from the Sandbenders' speakers. The translation followed instantly: "Hello? Yes? May I help you?"

"It's Chia McKenzie, from Seattle."

"You are still in Seattle?"

"I'm here. In Tokyo." She upped the scale on the Sandbenders' map. "In a subway station called Shinjuku."

"Yes. Very good. Are you coming here now?"

"I'd sure like to. I'm really tired."

The voice began to explain the route.

"It's okay," Chia said, "my computer can do it. Just tell me the station I have to get to." She found it on the map, set a marker. "How long will it take to get there?"

"Twenty to thirty minutes, depending on how crowded the trains are. I will meet you there."

"You don't have to do that," Chia said. "Just give me your address."

"Japanese addresses are difficult."

"It's okay," Chia said, "I've got global positioning." The Sandbenders, working the Tokyo telco, was already showing her Mitsuko Mimura's latitude and longitude. In Seattle, that only worked for business numbers.

"No," Mitsuko said, "I must greet you. I am the social secretary."

"Thanks," Chia said. "I'm on my way."

With her bag over her shoulder, left partly unzipped so she could follow the Sandbenders' verbal prompts, Chia rode an escalator up, two levels, bought a ticket with her cashcard, and found her platform. It was really crowded, as crowded as the airport, but when the train came she let the crowd pick her up and squash her into the nearest car; it would've been harder *not* to get on.

As they pulled out, she heard the Sandbenders announce that they were leaving Shinjuku station.

• • •

The sky was like mother-of-pearl when Chia emerged from the station. Gray buildings, pastel neon, a streetscape dotted with vaguely unfamiliar shapes. Dozens of bicycles were parked everywhere, the fragile-looking kind with paper-tube frames spun with carbon fiber. Chia took a step back as an enormous turquoise garbage truck rumbled past, its driver's white-gloved hands visible on the high wheel. As it cleared her field of vision, she saw a Japanese girl wearing a short plaid skirt and black biker jacket. The girl smiled. Chia waved.

Mitsuko's second-floor room was above the rear of her father's restaurant. Chia could hear a steady thumping sound from below, and Mitsuko explained that that was a food-prep robot that chopped and sliced things.

The room was smaller than Chia's bedroom in Seattle, but much cleaner, very neat and organized. So was Mitsuko, who had a razor-edged coppery diagonal bleached into her black bangs, and wore sneakers with double soles. She was thirteen, a year younger than Chia.

Mitsuko had introduced Chia to her father, who wore a white, short-sleeved shirt, a tie, and was supervising three white-gloved men in blue coveralls, who were cleaning his restaurant with great energy and determination. Mitsuko's father had nodded, smiled, said something in Japanese, and gone back to what he was doing. On their way upstairs, Mitsuko, who didn't speak much English, told Chia that she'd told her father that Chia was part of some cultural-exchange program, short-term homestay, something to do with her school.

Mitsuko had the same poster on her wall, the original cover shot from the Dog Soup album.

Mitsuko went downstairs, returning with a pot of tea and a covered, segmented box that contained a California roll and an assortment of less familiar things. Grateful for the familiarity of the California roll, Chia ate everything except the one with the orange sea-urchin goo on top. Mitsuko complimented her on her skill with chopsticks. Chia said she was from Seattle and people there used chopsticks a lot.

Now they were both wearing wireless ear-clip headsets. The translation was generally glitch-free, except when Mitsuko used Japanese slang that was too new, or when she inserted English words that she knew but couldn't pronounce.

Chia wanted to ask her about Rez and the idoru, but they kept getting onto other things. Then Chia fell asleep, sitting up cross-legged on the floor, and Mitsuko must have managed to roll her onto a hard little futon-thing that she'd unfolded from somewhere, because that was where Chia woke up, three hours later.

A rainy silver light was at the room's narrow window.

Mitsuko appeared with another pot of tea, and said

something in Japanese. Chia found her ear-clip and put it on.

"You must have been exhausted," the ear-clip translated. Then Mitsuko said she was taking the day off from school, to be with Chia.

They drank the nearly colorless tea from little nubbly ceramic cups. Mitsuko explained that she lived here with her father, her mother, and a brother, Masahiko. Her mother was away, visiting a relative in Kyoto. Mitsuko said that Kyoto was very beautiful, and that Chia should go there.

"I'm here for my chapter," Chia said. "I can't do tourist things. I have things to find out."

"I understand," Mitsuko said.

"So is it true? Does Rez really want to marry a software agent?"

Mitsuko looked uncomfortable. "I am the social secretary," she said. "You must first discuss this with Hiromi Ogawa."

"Who's she?"

"Hiromi is the president of our chapter."

"Fine," Chia said. "When do I talk to her?"

"We are erecting a site for the discussion. It will be ready soon." Mitsuko still looked uncomfortable.

Chia decided to change the subject. "What's your brother like? How old is he?"

"Masahiko is seventeen," Mitsuko said. "He is a 'pathological-techno-fetishist-with-social-deficit,' " this last all strung together like one word, indicating a concept that taxed the lexicon of the ear-clips. Chia wondered briefly if it would be worth running it through her Sandbenders, whose translation functions updated automatically whenever she ported.

"A what?"

"Otaku," Mitsuko said carefully in Japanese. The translation burped its clumsy word string again.

"Oh," Chia said, "we have those. We even use the same word."

"I think that in America they are not the same," Mitsuko said.

"Well," Chia said, "it's a *boy* thing, right? The otaku guys at my last school were into, like, plastic anime babes, military simulations, and trivia. Bigtime into trivia." She watched Mitsuko listen to the translation.

"Yes," Mitsuko said, "but you say they go to school. Ours do not go to school. They complete their studies on-line, and that is bad, because they cheat easily. Then they are tested, later, and are caught, and fail, but they do not care. It is a social problem."

"Your brother's one?"

"Yes," Mitsuko said. "He lives in Walled City."

"In where?"

"A multi-user domain. It is his obsession. Like a drug. He has a room here. He seldom leaves it. All his waking hours he is in Walled City. His dreams, too, I think."

• • •

Chia tried to get more of a sense of Hiromi Ogawa, before the noon meeting, but with mixed results. She was older, seventeen (as old as Zona Rosa) and had been in the club for at least five years. She was possibly overweight (though this had had to be conveyed in intercultural girl-code, nothing overt) and favored elaborate iconics. But overall Chia kept running up against Mitsuko's sense of her duty to her chapter, and of her own position, and of Hiromi's position.

Chia hated club politics, and she was beginning to suspect they might pose a real problem here.

Mitsuko was getting her computer out. It was one of those soft, transparent Korean units, the kind that looked like a flat bag of clear white jelly with a bunch of colored jujubes inside. Chia unzipped her bag and pulled her Sandbenders out.

"What is that?" Mitsuko asked.

"My computer."

Mitsuko was clearly impressed. "It is by Harley-Davidson?"

"It was made by the Sandbenders," Chia said, finding her goggles and gloves. "They're a commune, down on the Oregon coast. They do these and they do software."

"It is American?"

"Sure."

"I had not known Americans made computers," Mitsuko said.

Chia worked each silver thimble over the tips of her fingers and thumbs, fastened the wrist straps.

"I'm ready for the meeting," she said.

Mitsuko giggled nervously.

13

Character Recognition

Yamazaki phoned just before noon. The day was dim and overcast. Laney had closed the curtains in order to avoid seeing the nanotech buildings in that light.

He was watching an NHK show about champion top-spinners. The star, he gathered, was a little girl with pigtails and a blue dress with an old-fashioned sailor's collar. She was slightly cross-eyed, perhaps from concentration. The tops were made of wood. Some of them were big, and looked heavy.

"Hello, Mr. Laney," Yamazaki said. "You are feeling better now?"

Laney watched a purple-and-yellow top blur into action as the girl gave the carefully wound cord an expert pull. The commentator held a hand mike near the top to pick up the hum it was producing, then said something in Japanese.

"Better than last night," Laney said.

"It is being arranged for you to access the data that surrounds . . . our friend. It is a complicated process, as this data has been protected in many different ways. There was no single strategy. The ways in which his privacy has been protected are complexly incremental."

"Does 'our friend' know about this?"

There was a pause. Laney watched the spinning top. He imagined Yamazaki blinking. "No, he does not."

"I still don't know who I'll really be working for. For him? For Blackwell?"

"Your employer is Paragon-Asia Dataflow, Melbourne. They are employing me as well."

"What about Blackwell?"

"Blackwell is employed by a privately held corporation, through which portions of our friend's income pass. In the course of our friend's career, a structure has been erected to optimize that flow, to minimize losses. That structure now constitutes a corporate entity in its own right."

"Management," Laney said. "His management's scared because it looks like he might do something crazy. Is that it?"

The purple-and-yellow top was starting to exhibit the first of the oscillations that would eventually bring it to a halt. "I am still a stranger to this business-culture, Mr. Laney. I find it difficult to assess these things."

"What did Blackwell mean, last night, about Rez wanting to marry a Japanese girl who isn't real?"

"Idoru," Yamazaki said.

"What?"

" 'Idol-singer.' She is Rei Toei. She is a personality-construct, a congeries of software agents, the creation of information-designers. She is akin to what I believe they call a 'synthespian,' in Hollywood."

Laney closed his eyes, opened them. "Then how can he marry her?"

"I don't know," Yamazaki said. "But he has very forcefully declared this to be his intention."

"Can you tell me what it is they've hired *you* to do?"

"Initially, I think, they hoped I would be able to explain the idoru to them: her appeal to her audience, therefore perhaps her appeal to him. Also, I think that, like Blackwell, they remain unconvinced that this is not the result of a conspiracy of some kind. Now they want me to acquaint you with the cultural background of the situation."

"Who are they?"

"I cannot be more specific now."

The top was starting to wobble. Laney saw something like terror in the girl's eyes. "You don't think there's a conspiracy?"

"I will try to answer your questions this evening. In the meantime, while it is being arranged for you to access the data, please study these . . ."

"Hey," Laney protested, as his top-spinning girl was replaced by an unfamiliar logo: a grinning cartoon bulldog with a spiked collar, up to its muscular neck in a big bowl of soup.

"Two documentary videos on Lo/Rez," Yamazaki said. "These are on the Dog Soup label, originally a small independent based in East Taipei. They released the band's first recordings. Lo/Rez later purchased Dog Soup and used it to release less commercial material by other artists."

Laney stared glumly at the grinning bulldog, missing the girl with pigtails. "Like documentaries about themselves?"

"The documentaries were not made subject to the band's approval. They are not Lo/Rez corporate documents."

"Well, I guess we've got that to be thankful for."

"You are welcome." Yamazaki hung up.

The virtual POV zoomed, rotating in on one of the spikes on the dog's collar: in close-up, it was a shining steel pyramid. Reflected clouds whipped past in time-lapse on the towering triangular face as the Universal Copyright Agreement warning scrolled into view.

Laney watched long enough to see that the video was spliced together from bits and pieces of the band's public relations footage. "Art-warning," he said, and went into the bathroom to decipher the shower controls.

He managed to miss the first six minutes, showering and brushing his teeth. He'd seen things like that before, art videos, but he'd never actually tried to pay attention to one. Putting on the hotel's white terry robe, he told himself he'd better try. Yamazaki seemed capable of quizzing him on it later.

Why did people make things like this? There was no narration, no apparent structure; some of the same fragments kept repeating throughout, at different speeds . . .

In Los Angeles there were whole public-access channels devoted to things like this, and home-made talkshows hosted by naked Encino witches, who sat in front of big paintings of the Goddess they'd done in their garages. Except you could *watch* that. The logic of these cut-ups, he supposed, was that by making one you could somehow push back at the medium. Maybe it was supposed to be something like treading water, a simple repetitive human activity that temporarily provided at least an illusion of parity with the sea. But to Laney, who had spent many of his waking hours down in the deeper realms of data that underlay the worlds of media, it only looked hopeless. And tedious, too, although he supposed that that boredom was somehow meant to be harnessed, here, another way of pushing back.

Why else would anyone have selected and edited all these bits of Lo and Rez, the Chinese guitarist and the half-Irish singer, saying stupid things in dozens of different television spots, most of them probably intended for translation? Greetings seemed to be a theme. "We're happy to be here in Vladivostok. We hear you've got a great new aquarium!" "We congratulate you on your free elections and your successful dengue-abatement campaign!" "We've always loved London!" "New York, you're . . . *pragmatic!*"

Laney explored the remains of his breakfast, finding a half-eaten slice of cold brown toast under a steel plate cover. There was an inch of coffee left in the pot. He didn't want to think about the call from Rydell or what it might mean. He'd thought he was done with Slitscan, done with the lawyers . . .

"Singapore, you're beautiful!" Rez said, Lo chiming in with "Hell-o, Lion City!"

He picked up the remote and hopefully tried the fast-forward. No. Mute? No. Yamazaki was having this stuff piped in for his benefit. He considered unplugging the console, but he was afraid they'd be able to tell.

It was speeding up now, the cuts more frequent, the whole more content-free, a numbing blur. Rez's grin was starting to look sinister, something with an agenda of its own that jumped unchanged from one cut to the next.

Suddenly it all slid away, into handheld shadow, highlights on rococo gilt. There was a clatter of glassware. The image had a peculiar flattened quality that he knew from Slitscan: the smallest lapel-cameras did that, the ones disguised as flecks of lint.

A restaurant? Club? Someone seated opposite the camera, beyond a phalanx of green bottles. The darkness and the bandwidth of the tiny camera making the features impossible to read. Then Rez leaned forward, recognizable in the new depth of focus. He gestured toward the camera with a glass of red wine.

"If we could ever once stop talking about the music, and the industry, and all the politics of that, I think I'd probably tell you that it's easier to desire and pursue the attention of tens of millions of total strangers than it is to accept the love and loyalty of the people closest to us."

Someone, a woman, said something in French. Laney guessed that she was the one wearing the camera.

"Ease up, Rozzer. She doesn't understand half you're saying." Laney sat forward. The voice had been Blackwell's.

"Doesn't she?" Rez receded, out of focus. "Because if she did, I think I'd tell her about the loneliness of being misunderstood. Or is it the loneliness of being afraid to allow ourselves to be understood?"

And the frame froze on the singer's blurred face. A date and time-stamp. Two years earlier. The word "Misunderstood" appeared.

The phone rang.

"Yeah?"

"Blackwell says there is a window of opportunity. The schedule has been moved up. You can access now." It was Yamazaki.

''Good,'' Laney said. ''I don't think I'm getting very far with this first video.''

''Rez's quest for renewed artistic meaning? Don't worry; we will screen it for you again, later.''

''I'm relieved,'' Laney said. ''Is the second one as good?''

''Second documentary is more conventionally structured. In-depth interviews, biographical detail, BBC, three years ago.''

''Wonderful.''

''Blackwell is on his way to the hotel. Goodbye.''

Tokyo Chapter

The site Mitsuko's chapter had erected for the meeting reminded Chia of Japanese prints she'd seen on a school trip to the museum in Seattle; there was a brownish light that seemed to arrive through layers of ancient varnish. There were hills in the distance with twisted trees, their branches like quick black squiggles of ink. She came vectoring in, beside Mitsuko, toward a wooden house with deep overhanging eaves, its shape familiar from anime. It was the sort of house that ninjas crept into in the dark, to wake a sleeping heroine and tell her that all was not as she thought, that her uncle was in league with the evil warlord. She checked how she was presenting in a small peripheral window; put a nudge more depth into her lips.

Nearing the house, she saw that everything had been worked up out of club archives, so that the whole environment was actually made of Lo/Rez material. You noticed it first in the wood-and-paper panels of the walls, where faint image-fragments, larger than life, came and went with the organic randomness of leaf-dappled sun and shadow: Rez's cheekbone and half a pair of black glasses, Lo's hand chording the neck of his guitar. But these changed, were replaced with a mothlike flicker, and there would be more, all the way down into the site's finest resolution, its digital fabric. She wasn't sure if you could do that with enough of the right kind of fractal packets, or if you needed some kind of special computer. Her Sandbenders managed a few effects like that, but mainly in its presentation of Sandbenders software.

Screens slid aside as she and Mitsuko, seated cross-legged, entered the house. Coming to a neat halt side by side, still seated, floating about three inches off the tatami (which Chia avoided focusing on after she'd seen that it was woven from concert-footage; too distracting). It was a nice way to make an entrance. Mitsuko was wearing the kimono and the wide belt-thing, the whole traditional outfit, except there was some low-key animation going on in the weave of the fabric. Chia herself had downloaded this black Silke-Marie Kolb blouson-and-tights set, even though she hated paying for virtual designer stuff that they wouldn't even let you keep or copy. She'd used Kelsey's cashcard number for that, though, which had made her feel better about it.

There were seven girls waiting there, all in kimonos, all floating just off the tatami. Except the one sitting by herself, at the head of the imaginary table, was a robot. Not like any real robot, but a slender, chrome-skinned thing like mercury constrained within the form of a girl. The face was smooth, only partially featured, eyeless, with twin straight rows of small holes where a mouth should have been. That would be Hiromi Ogawa, and Chia immediately decided to believe that she was overweight.

Hiromi's kimono was crawling with animated sepia-tone footage from band interviews.

The introductions took a while, and everyone there definitely had a title, but Chia had stopped paying attention after Hiromi's introduction, except to bow when she thought she was supposed to. She didn't like it that Hiromi would turn up that way for a first meeting. It was rude, she thought, and it had to be deliberate, and the trouble they'd gone to with the space just seemed to make it more deliberate.

"We are honored to welcome you, Chia McKenzie. Our chapter looks forward to affording you every assistance. We are proud to be a part of the ongoing global appreciation of Lo/Rez, their music and their art."

"Thank you," Chia said, and sat there as a silence lengthened. Mitsuko quietly cleared her throat. Uh-oh, Chia thought. Speech time. "Thank you for offering to help,'' Chia said. ''Thanks for your hospitality. If any of you ever comes to Seattle, we'll find a way to put you up. But mainly thanks for your help, because my chapter's been really worried about this story that Rez claims he wants to marry some kind of software agent, and since he's supposed to have said it when he was over here, we thought—'' Chia had had the feeling that she was moving along a little too abruptly, and this was confirmed by another tiny throat-clearing signal from Mitsuko.

''Yes,'' Hiromi Ogawa said, ''you are welcome, and now Tomo Oshima, our chapter's historian, will favor us with a detailed and accurate account of our chapter's story, how we came, from simple but sincere beginnings, to be the most active, the most respectful chapter in Japan today.''

Chia couldn't believe it.

The girl nearest Hiromi, on Chia's right, bowed and began to recite the chapter's history in what Chia immediately understood would be the most excruciatingly boring detail. The two boarding-school roommates, best friends and the most loyal of buddies, who discovered a copy of the Dog Soup album in a bin in Akihabara. How they returned to school with it, played it, were immediate converts. How their schoolmates mocked them, at one point even stealing and hiding the precious recording . . . And on, and on, and Chia already felt like screaming, but there was nothing for it but to sit there. She pulled up a clock and stuck it on the mirrored robot's face, where the eyes should have been. Nobody else could see it, but it made her feel a little better.

Now they were into the first Japanese national Lo/Rez convention, snapshots flashing on the white paper walls, little girls in jeans and t-shirts drinking Coca-Cola in some function room in an Osaka airport hotel, a few obvious parents standing around in the background.

Forty-five minutes later, by the red read-out stuck to Hiromi Ogawa's blank metallic face, Tomo Oshima concluded: "Which brings us to the present, and the historic visit of Chia McKenzie, the representative of our sister chapter in Seattle, in the State of Washington. And now I hope that she will honor us by recounting the history of her own chapter, how it was founded, and the many activities it has undertaken to honor the music of Lo/Rez . . ."

There was a soft burst of applause. Chia didn't join in, uncertain whether it was for her or for Tomo Oshima.

"Sorry," Chia said. "Our historian put all that together for you, but it got corrupted when they ran my computer through that big scanner at the airport."

"We are very sorry to hear that," the silver robot said. "How unfortunate."

"Yeah," Chia said, "but I guess it gives us more time to discuss what brings me here, right?"

"We had hoped—"

"To help us understand this whole Rez thing, right? We know. We're glad you do. Because we're all really worried about this rumor. Because it seems like it started here, and this Rei Toei's a local product, so if anybody can tell us what's going on, it's you."

The silver robot said nothing. It was expressionless as ever, but Chia took the clock away just to be sure.

"That's why I'm here," Chia said. "To find out if it's true he wants to marry her."

She sensed a general uneasiness. The six girls were looking at the texture-mapped tatami, unwilling to meet her eye. She wanted to look at Mitsuko, but it would have been too obvious.

"We are an *official* chapter," Hiromi said. "We have the honor of working closely with actual employees of the band. Their publicists are also concerned with the rumor you mention, and they have requested that we assist them in seeing that it not spread further."

"Spread? It's been on the net for a week!"

"It is rumor only."

"Then they should issue a denial."

"Denial would add weight to the rumor."

"The posting said that Rez had announced that he was in love with Rei Toei, that he was going to marry her. There was a long quote." Chia was definitely starting to get the feeling that something was wrong here. This was not what she'd come all this physical distance for; she might as well have been sitting in her bedroom in Seattle.

"We think that the original posting was a hoax. It would not be the first."

"You think? Doesn't that mean you don't know?"

"Our sources within the organization assure us there is no cause for concern."

"Spin control," Chia said.

"You imply that Lo/Rez employees are lying to us?"

"Look," Chia said, "I'm as into the band as anybody. I came all this way, right? But the people who work for them are just people who work for them. If Rez gets up in a club one night, takes the mike, and announces that he's in love with this idoru and swears he's going to marry her, the PR people are going to say whatever they think they have to say."

"But you have no evidence that any of this occurred. Only an anonymous posting, claiming to be a transcription of a recording made in a club in Shinjuku."

" 'Monkey Boxing.' We looked it up; it's there."

"Really? Perhaps you should go there."

"Why?"

"There is no longer a club called Monkey Boxing."

"There isn't?"

"Clubs in Shinjuku are extremely short-lived. There is no Monkey Boxing." All of Hiromi's smug satisfaction came through in the Sandbenders' translation.

Chia stared at the smooth silver face. Stonewalling bitch. What to do? What would Zona Rosa do if she were in Chia's place? Something symbolically violent, Chia decided. But that wasn't her style.

"Thank you," Chia said. "We just wanted to make sure it wasn't happening. Sorry I hit on you that way, but we had to be certain. If you say it's not happening, we'll accept that. We all care about Rez and the rest of the band, and we know you do too." Chia added a bow of her own, one that seemed to take Hiromi off guard.

Now it was the robot's turn to hesitate. She hadn't expected Chia to just roll over that way. "Our friends in the Lo/Rez organization are very concerned that this pointless hoax not affect the public's perception of Rez. You are aware that there has always been a tendency to portray him as the most creative but least stable member of the band."

This last, at least, was true, though Rez's style of instability was fairly mild, compared with most of his pop-cultural forebears. He had never been arrested, never spent a night in jail. But he was still the one most likely to get into trouble. It had always been part of his charm.

"Sure," Chia said, playing along, relishing the uncertainty she was sure she was causing Hiromi. "And they try to make Lo out as some kind of boring techie, the practical one, but we know that isn't true either." She tagged it with a smile.

"Yes," Hiromi said, "of course. But you are satisfied, then? You will explain to your chapter that this was all the result of some prank, and that all is well with Rez?"

"If you say so," Chia said, "absolutely. And if that settles it, then I've got three more days to kill in Japan."

"To kill?"

"Idiom," Chia said. "Free time. Mitsuko says I ought to see Kyoto."

"Kyoto is very beautiful . . ."

"I'm on my way," Chia said. "Thanks for putting this site together for our meeting. It's really great, and if you'll save it, I'd love to access it later with the rest of my chapter. Maybe we could all get together here when I'm back in Seattle, introduce our chapters."

"Yes . . ." Hiromi definitely didn't know what to make of Chia's attitude.

So worry about it, Chia thought.

"You knew," Chia said. "You knew she'd do that."

Mitsuko was blushing, bright red. Looking at the floor, her jelly-bag computer on her lap. "I am sorry. It was her decision."

"They got to her, right? They told her to get rid of me, hush it up."

"She communicates with the Lo/Rez people privately. It is one of the privileges of her position."

Chia still had her tip-sets on. "I have to talk with my chapter now. Can you give me a few minutes alone?" She felt sorry for Mitsuko, but she was still angry. "I'm not angry with *you,* okay?"

"I will make tea," Mitsuko said.

When Mitsuko had closed the door behind her, Chia checked that the Sandbenders was still ported, put the goggles back on, and selected the Seattle chapter's main site.

She never got there. Zona Rosa was waiting to cut her out.

Akihabara

Low gray cloud pressing down on the sheer gray city. A glimpse of new buildings, through the scaled-down limo's tinted, lace-curtained windows.

They passed an Apple Shires ad, a cobbled lane leading away into some hologram nursery land, where smiling juice bottles danced and sang. Laney's jet lag was back, in some milder but more baroque format. Something compounded of a pervasive sense of guilt and a feeling of physical distance from his own body, as though the sensory signals arrived stale, after too long a passage, through some other country that he himself was never privy to.

"I thought we'd done with all of that when we got rid of those Siberian neuropaths," Blackwell said. He was dressed entirely in black, which had the effect of somewhat reducing his bulk. He wore a soft, smock-like garment sewn from very black denim, multiple pockets around its wide hem. Laney thought it looked vaguely Japanese, in some medieval way. Something a carpenter might wear. "Bent as a dog's hind legs. Picked them up touring the Kombinat states."

"Neuropaths?"

"Filling Rez's head with their garbage. He's vulnerable to influences, touring. Combination of stress and boredom. Cities start to look the same. One hotel room after another. It's a syndrome, is what it is."

"Where are we going?"

"Akihabara."

"Where?"

"Where we're going." Blackwell consulted an enormous, elaborately dialed, steel-braceleted chronometer that looked as though it had been designed to do double duty as brass knuckles. "Took a month before they'd let me have a go, do what was needed. Then we got him over to a clinic in Paris and they told us what those bastards had been feeding him had made a pig's breakfast of his endocrine system. Put him right, in the end, but it needn't have happened, none of it."

"But you got rid of them?" Laney had no idea what Blackwell was talking about, but it seemed best to keep up the illusion of conversation.

"Told them I was thinking about putting them face-first through a little Honda tree-shredder I'd purchased, just on the off chance," Blackwell said. "Not necessary. Showed them it, though. In the end, they were sent along with no more than a moderate touch-up.''

Laney looked at the back of the driver's head. The right-hand drive worried him. He felt like there was nobody in the driver's seat. ''How long did you say you'd worked for the band?''

''Five years.''

Laney thought of the video, Blackwell's voice in the darkened club. Two years ago. ''Where are we going?''

''Be there, soon enough.''

They entered an area of narrower streets, of featureless, vaguely shabby buildings covered with unlit, inactivated advertising. Huge representations of media platforms Laney didn't recognize. Some of the buildings revealed what he assumed was quake damage. Head-sized gobs of a brownish, glasslike substance protruded from cracks that ran diagonally across one facade, like a cheap toy repaired badly by a clumsy giant. The limo pulled to the curb.

'' 'Electric Town,' '' Blackwell said. ''I'll page you,'' he said to the driver, who nodded in a way that struck Laney as being not particularly Japanese. Blackwell opened the door and got out with that same unlikely grace Laney had noted before, the car bucking noticeably with the departure of his weight. Laney, sliding across the gray velour seat, felt tired and wooden.

''Somehow I was expecting a more upscale destination,'' he said to Blackwell. It was true.

''Stop expecting,'' Blackwell said.

The building with the cracks and the brown, saplike knobs opened into a white-and-pastel sea of kitchen appliances. The ceiling was low, laced with temporary-looking pipes and conduits. Laney followed Blackwell down a central aisle. A few figures stood along other aisles to either side, but he had no way of knowing whether these were salespeople or potential customers.

An old-fashioned escalator was grinding away, at the end of the central aisle, the rectilinear steel teeth at the edges of each ascending step worn sharp and bright. Blackwell kept walking. Levitated ahead of Laney, climbing, his feet barely seeming to move. Laney mounted hard behind him.

They rose up to a second level, this one displaying a less consistent range of goods: wallscreens, immersion consoles, automated recliners with massage-modules bulging from their cushions like the heads of giant mechanical grubs.

Along an aisle walled with corrugated plastic cartons, Blackwell with his scarred hands tucked deep in the pockets of his ninja smock. Into a maze of bright blue plastic tarps, slung from pipes overhead. Unfamiliar tools. A worker's dented thermos standing on a red toolkit that spanned a pair of aluminum sawhorses. Blackwell holding a final tarp aside. Laney ducked, entering.

''We've been holding it open for the past hour,

Blackwell,'' someone said. ''Not an easy thing.''

Blackwell let the tarp fall into place behind him. ''Had to collect him from the hotel.''

The space, walled off with the blue tarps on three sides, was twice the size of Laney's hotel room but considerably more crowded. A lot of hardware was assembled there: a collection of black consoles were cabled together in a white swamp of Styrofoam packing-forms, torn corrugated plastic, and crumpled sheets of bubble-pack. Two men and a woman, waiting. It was the woman who had spoken. As Laney shuffled forward, ankle-deep through the packing materials, the stuff creaked and popped, slippery under the soles of his shoes.

Blackwell kicked at it. ''You might have tidied up.''

''We aren't set-dressers,'' the woman said. She sounded to Laney as though she was from Northern California. She had short brown hair cut in bangs, and something about her reminded him of the quants who worked at Slitscan. Like the other two, men, one Japanese and one red-haired, she wore jeans and a generic nylon bomber jacket.

''Hell of a job on short notice,'' the redhead said.

''*No* notice,'' the other corrected, and he was definitely from California. His hair was pulled straight back, fastened high in a little samurai ponytail.

''What you're paid for,'' Blackwell said.

''We're paid to tour,'' the redhead said.

''If you want to tour again, you'd better hope that

these work.'' Blackwell looked at the cabled consoles.

Laney saw a folding plastic table set up against the rear wall. It was bright pink. There was a gray computer there, a pair of eyephones. Unfamiliar cables ran to the nearest console: flat ribbons candy-striped in different colors. The wall behind was plastered with an overlay of old advertising; a woman's eye was directly behind the pink table, a yard wide, her laser-printed pupil the size of Laney's head.

Laney moved toward the table, through the Styrofoam, sliding his feet, a motion not unlike cross-country skiing.

''Let's do it,'' he said. ''Let's see what you've got.''

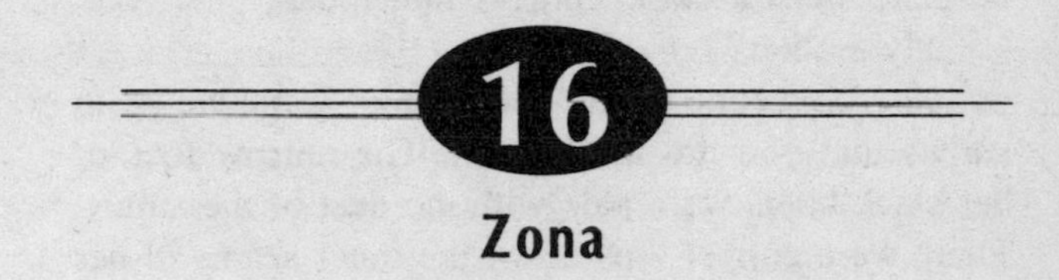

Zona

Zona Rosa kept a secret place, a country carved from what once had been a corporate website.

It was a valley lined with ruined swimming pools, overgrown with cactus and red Christmas flowers. Lizards posed like hieroglyphs on mosaics of shattered tile.

No houses stood in that valley, though sections of broken wall gave shade, or rusting rectangles of corrugated metal set aslant on weathered wooden uprights. Sometimes there were ashes of a cooking fire.

She kept it early evening there.

"Zona?"

"Someone is trying to find you." Zona in her ragged leather jacket over a white t-shirt. In that place she presented as a quick collage, fragments torn from films, magazines, Mexican newspapers: dark eyes, Aztec cheekbones, a dusting of acne scars, her black hair tangled like smoke. She kept the resolution down, never let herself come entirely into focus.

"My mother?"

"No. Someone with resources. Someone who knows that you are in Tokyo." The narrow toes of her black boots were pale with the dust of the valley. There were copper zips down the outer seams of her faded black jeans, waist to ankle. "Why are you dressed that way?"

Chia remembered that she was still presenting in the Silke-Marie Kolb outfit. "There was a meeting. Very formal. *Major* butt-pain. I got this with Kelsey's cashcard."

"Where were you ported, when you paid for it?"

"Where I'm ported now. Mitsuko's place."

Zona frowned. "What other purchases have you made?"

"None."

"Nothing?"

"A subway ticket."

Zona snapped her fingers and a lizard scurried from beneath a rock. It ran up her leg and into her waiting hand. As she stroked it with the fingers of the other hand, the patterns of its coloration changed. She tapped its head and the lizard ran down her leg, vanishing behind a crumpled sheet of rusted roofing. "Kelsey is frightened, frightened enough to come to me."

"Frightened of what?"

"Someone contacted her about your ticket. They were trying to reach her father, because the points used to purchase it were his. But he is traveling. They spoke with Kelsey instead. I think they threatened her."

"With what?"

"I don't know. But she gave them your name and the number of the cashcard."

Chia thought about Maryalice and Eddie.

Zona Rosa took a knife from her jacket pocket and squatted on a shelf of pinkish rock. Golden dragons swirled in the shallow depths of the knife's pink plastic handles. She thumbed a button of plated tin and the dragon-etched blade snapped out, its spine saw-toothed and merciless. "She has no balls, your Kelsey."

"She's not *my* Kelsey, Zona."

Zona picked up a length of green-barked branch and began to shave thin curls from it with the edge of the switchblade. "She would not last an hour, in my world." On a previous visit, she'd told Kelsey stories of the war with the Rats, pitched battles fought through the garbage-strewn playgrounds and collapsing parking garages of vast housing projects. How had that war begun? Over what? Zona never said.

"Neither would I."

"So who is looking for you?"

"My mother would be, if she knew I was here . . ."

"That was not your mother, the one who put the fear into Kelsey."

"If someone knew my seat number on the flight over, they could get a ticket number and trace it back, right?"

"If they had certain resources, yes. It would be illegal."

"From there, they could go to Kelsey—"

"From there they are in the frequent-flyer files of Air Magellan, which implies very serious resources."

"There was a woman, on the plane . . . She had the seat beside me. Then I had to carry her suitcase, and she and her boyfriend gave me a ride into Tokyo . . ."

"You carried her suitcase?"

"Yes."

"Tell me this story. All of it. When did you first see this woman?"

"In the airport, SeaTac. They were doing noninvasive DNA samples and I saw her do this weird thing . . ." Chia began the story of Maryalice and the rest of it, while Zona Rosa sat and peeled and sharpened her stick, frowning.

"Fuck your mother," Zona Rosa said, when Chia had finished her story. The translation rendered her tone as either amazement or disgust, Chia couldn't tell.

"*What?*" Chia's confusion was absolute.

Zona looked at her along the length of the peeled stick. "An idiom. *Idioma.* Very rich and complicated.

It has nothing to do with your mother.'' She lowered the stick and did something to her knife, folding the blade away with a triple click. The lizard she'd adjusted earlier came scurrying low across a narrow ledge of rock, clinging so close as to appear two-dimensional. Zona picked it up and stroked it into yet another color-configuration.

''What are you doing?''

''Harder encryption,'' Zona said, and put the lizard on the lapel of her jacket, where it clung like a brooch, its eyes tiny spheres of onyx. ''Someone is looking for you. Probably they've already found you. We must try to insure that our conversation is secure.''

''Can you do that, with him?'' The lizard's head moved.

''Maybe. He's new. But those are better.'' She pointed up with the stick. Chia squinted into the evening sky, dark cloud tinted with streaks of sunset pink. She thought she saw a sweep of wings, so high. Two things flying. Big. Not planes. But then they were gone. ''Illegal, in your country. Colombian. From the data-havens.'' Zona put the pointed end of her stick on the ground and began to twirl it one way, then the other, between her palms. Chia had seen a rabbit make fire that way, once, in an ancient cartoon. ''You are an idiot.''

''Why?''

''You carried a bag through customs? A stranger's bag?''

“Yes . . .”

“Idiot!”

“I am not.”

“She is a smuggler. You are hopelessly naive.”

But you went along with sending me here, Chia thought, and suddenly felt like crying. “But why are they looking for me?”

Zona shrugged. “In the District, a cautious smuggler would not let a mule go free . . .”

Something silvery and cold executed a tight little flip somewhere behind and below Chia’s navel, and with it came the unwelcome recollection of the washroom at Whiskey Clone, and the corner of something she hadn’t recognized. In her bag. Stuffed down between her t-shirts. When she’d used one to dry her hands.

“What’s wrong?”

“I better go. Mitsuko went to make tea . . .” Talking too quickly, biting off the words.

“Go? Are you insane? We must—”

“Sorry. ’Bye.” Pulling off the goggles and scrabbling at the wrist-fasteners.

Her bag there, where she’d left it.

The Walls of Fame

''We had no time to do this right,'' the woman said, handing Laney the eyephones. He was sitting on a child-sized pink plastic bench that matched the table. ''If there *is* a way to do it right.''

''There are areas we could not arrange access to,'' said the Japanese-American with the ponytail. ''Blackwell said you've had experience with celebrities.''

''Actors,'' Laney said. ''Musicians, politicians . . .''

''You'll probably find this different. Bigger. By a couple of degrees of magnitude.''

''What can't you access?'' Laney asked, settling the 'phones over his eyes.

''We don't know,'' he heard the woman say.

"You'll get a sense of the scale of things, going in. The blanks might be accountancy, tax-law stuff, contracts . . . We're just tech support. He has other people someone pays to make sure parts of it stay as private as possible."

"Then why not bring *them* in?" Laney asked.

He felt Blackwell's hand come down on his shoulder like a bag of sand. "I'll discuss that with you later. Now get in there and have a look. What we pay you for, isn't it?"

In the week following Alison Shires' death, Laney had used Out of Control's DatAmerica account to re-access the site of her personal data. The nodal point was gone, and a certain subtle reduction had taken place. Not a shrinkage so much as a tidying, a folding in.

But the biggest difference was simply that she was no longer generating data. There was no credit activity. Even her Upful Groupvine account had been canceled. As her estate was executed, and various business affairs terminated, her data began to take on a neat rectilinearity. Laney thought of the dead bundled squarely in their graveclothes, of coffins and cairns, of the long straight avenues of cemeteries in the days when the dead had been afforded their own real estate.

The nodal point had formed where she had lived, while she had lived, in the messy, constantly proliferating interface with the ordinary yet endlessly multiplex world. Now there was no longer an interface.

He'd looked, but only briefly, and very cautiously, to see whether her actor might be undertaking tidying activities of his own. Nothing obvious there, but he imagined Out of Control would have set a more careful watch on that.

Her data was very still. Only a faint, methodical movement at its core: something to do with the ongoing legal mechanism of the execution of her estate.

A catalog of each piece of furniture in the bedroom of a guesthouse in Ireland. A subcatalog of the products provided in the seventeenth-century walnut commode at bedside there: toothbrush, toothpaste, analgesic tablets, tampons, razor, shaving gel. Someone would check these periodically, restock to the inventory. (The last guest had taken the gel but not the razor.) In the first catalog, there was a powerful pair of Austrian binoculars, tripod-mounted, which also functioned as a digital camera.

Laney accessed its memory, discovering that the recording function had been used exactly once, on the day the manufacturer's warranty had been activated. The warranty was now two months void, the single recorded image a view from a white-curtained balcony, looking toward what Laney took to be the Irish Sea. There was an unlikely palm tree, a length of chainlink fence, a railbed with a twin dull gleam of track, a deep expanse of grayish-brown beach, and then the gray and silver sea. Closer to the sea, partially cut off by the image's border, there appeared to be a low, broad fort of stone, like a truncated tower. Its stones were the color of the beach.

Laney tried to quit the bedroom, the guesthouse, and found himself surrounded by archaeologically precise records of the restoration of five vast ceramic stoves in an apartment in Stockholm. These were like giant chess pieces, towers of brick faced with elaborately glazed, lavishly molded ceramic. They rose to the fourteen-foot ceilings, and several people could easily have stood upright in one. There was a record of the numbering, disassembly, cleaning, restoration, and reassembly of each brick in each stove. There was no way to access the rest of the apartment, but the proportions of the stoves led Laney to assume that it was very large. He clicked to the end of the stove-record and noted the final price of the work; at current rates it was more than several times his former annual salary at Slitscan.

He clicked back, through points of recession, trying for a wider view, a sense of form, but there were only walls, bulking masses of meticulously arranged information, and he remembered Alison Shires and his apprehension of her data-death.

''The lights are on,'' Laney said, removing the eyephones, ''but there's nobody home.'' He checked the computer's clock: he'd spent a little over twenty minutes in there.

Blackwell regarded him dourly, settled on an injection-molded crate like a black-draped Buddha, the scars in his eyebrows knitted into new configurations of concern. The three technicians looked carefully blank, hands in the pockets of their matching jackets.

"How's that, then?" Blackwell asked.

"I'm not sure," Laney said. "He doesn't seem to *do* anything."

"He doesn't bloody do anything *but* do things," Blackwell declared, "as you'd know if you were orchestrating his bloody security!"

"Okay," Laney said, "then where'd he have breakfast?"

Blackwell looked uncomfortable. "In his suite."

"His suite where?"

"Imperial Hotel." Blackwell glared at the technicians.

"Which empire, exactly?"

"Here. Bloody Tokyo."

"Here? He's in Tokyo?"

"You lot," Blackwell said, "outside." The brown-haired woman shrugged, inside her nylon jacket, and went kicking through the Styrofoam, head down, the other two following in her wake. When the tarp dropped behind them, Blackwell rose from his crate. "Don't think you can try me on for size . . ."

"I'm telling you that I don't think this is going to work. Your man isn't *in* there."

"That's his bloody *life*."

"How did he pay for his breakfast?"

"Signed to the suite."

"Is the suite in his name?"

"Of course not."

"Say he needs to buy something, during the course of the day?"

"Someone *buys* it for him, don't they?"

"And pays with?"

"A card."

"But not in his name."

"Right."

"So if anyone were looking at the transaction data, there'd be no way to connect it directly to him, would there?"

"No."

"Because you're doing your job, right?"

"Yes."

"Then he's invisible. To me. I can't see him. He isn't there. I can't do what you want to pay me to do. It's impossible."

"But what about all the rest of it?"

Laney put the eyephones down on the keyboard. "That isn't a person. That's a corporation."

"But you've got it *all!* His bloody houses! His flats! Where the gardeners put the bloody flowers in the rock wall! All of it!"

"But I don't know who he is. I can't make him out against the rest of it. He's not leaving the traces that make the patterns I need."

Blackwell sucked in his upper lip and kept it there. Laney heard the dislodged prosthesis click against his teeth.

"I have to get some idea of who he really is," Laney said.

The lip re-emerged, damp and gleaming. "Christ," Blackwell said, "*that's* a poser."

"I have to meet him."

Blackwell wiped his mouth with the back of his hand. "His music, then?" He raised his eyebrows hopefully. "Or there's video—"

"I've *got* video, thanks. It really might help if I could meet him."

Blackwell touched his ear-stump. "You meet him, you think you'll be able to get his nodes, nodal, do that thing Yama's on about?"

"I don't know," Laney said. "I can try."

"Bloody hell," Blackwell said. He plowed through the Styrofoam, swept the tarp aside with his arm, barked for the waiting technicians, then turned back to Laney. "Sometimes I'd as soon be back with my mates in Jika Jika. Get things sorted, in there, they'd bloody *stay* that way." The woman with the brown bangs thrust her head in, past the edge of the tarp. "Collect this business in the van," Blackwell told her. "Have it ready to use when we need it."

"We don't have a van, Keithy," the woman said.

"Buy one," Blackwell said.

The Otaku

Something rectangular, yielding to the first touch but hard inside, as she tugged it free. Wrapped in a blue and yellow plastic bag from the SeaTac duty-free, crookedly sealed with wrinkled lengths of slick brown tape. Heavy. Compact.

“Hello.”

Chia very nearly falling backward, where she crouched above her open bag, at the voice and the sight of this boy, who in that first instant she takes to be an older girl, side-parted hair falling past her shoulders.

“I am Masahiko.” No translator. He wore a dark, oversized tunic, vaguely military, buttoned to its high, banded collar, loose around his neck. Old gray sweatpants bagging at the knees. Grubby-looking white paper slippers.

"Mitsuko made tea," indicating the tray, the stoneware pot, two cups. "But you were ported."

"Is she here?" Chia pushed the thing back down into her bag.

"She went out," Masahiko said. "May I look at your computer?"

"Computer?" Chia stood, confused.

"It is Sandbenders, yes?"

She poured some of the tea, which was still steaming. "Sure. You want tea?"

"No," Masahiko said. "I drink coffee only." He squatted on the tatami, beside the low table, and ran an admiring fingertip along the edge of the Sandbenders' cast aluminum. "Beautiful. I have seen a small disk player by the same maker. It is a cult, yes?"

"A commune. Tribal people. In Oregon."

The boy's black hair was long and glossy and smoothly brushed, but Chia saw there was a bit of noodle caught in it, the thin, kinky kind that came in instant ramen bowls.

"I'm sorry I was ported when Mitsuko came back. She'll think I was rude."

"You are from Seattle." Not a question.

"You're her brother?"

"Yes. Why are you here?" His eyes large and dark, his face long and pale.

"Your sister and I are both into Lo/Rez."

"You have come because he wants to marry Rei Toei?"

Hot tea dribbled down Chia's chin. "She told you that?"

"Yes," Masahiko said. "In Walled City, some people worked on her design." He was lost in his study of her Sandbenders, turning it over in his hands. His fingers were long and pale, the nails badly chewed.

"Where's that?"

"Netside," he said, flipping the weight of his hair back, over one shoulder.

"What do they say about her?"

"Original concept. Almost radical." He stroked the keys. "This is very beautiful . . ."

"You learned English here?"

"In Walled City."

Chia tried another sip of tea, then put the cup down. "You have any coffee?"

"In my room," he said.

Masahiko's room, at the bottom of a short flight of concrete stairs, to the rear of the restaurant's kitchen, had probably been a storage closet. It was a boy-nightmare, the sort of environment Chia knew from the brothers of friends, its floor and ledgelike bed long vanished beneath unwashed clothes, ramen-wrappers, Japanese magazines with wrinkled covers. A tower of empty foam ramen bowls in one corner, their hologram labels winking from beyond a single cone of halogen. A desk or table forming a second, higher ledge, cut from some recycled material that looked as though it had been laminated from shredded juice cartons. His computer there, a featureless black cube. A shallower shelf of the juice-carton board supported a pale blue microwave, unopened ramen bowls, and half a dozen tiny steel cans of coffee.

One of these, freshly microwaved, was hot in Chia's hand. The coffee was strong, sugary, thickly creamed. She sat beside him on the lumpy bed ledge, a padded jacket wadded up behind her for a cushion.

It smelled faintly of boy, of ramen, and of coffee. Though he seemed very clean, now that she was this close, and she had a vague idea that Japanese people generally were. Didn't they love to bathe? The thought made her want a shower.

"I like this very much." Reaching to touch the Sandbenders again, which he'd brought from upstairs and placed on the work surface, in front of his black cube, sweeping aside a litter of plastic spoons, pens, nameless bits of metal and plastic.

"How do you see to work yours?" Gesturing toward his computer with the miniature can of coffee.

He said something in Japanese. Worms and dots of pastel neon lit the faces of the cube, crawling and pulsing, then died.

The walls, from floor to ceiling, were thickly covered with successive layers of posters, handbills, graphics files. The wall directly in front of her, above and behind the black computer, was hung with a large scarf, a square of some silky material screened with a map or diagram in red and black and yellow. Hundreds of irregular blocks or rooms, units of some kind, pressing in around a central vacancy, an uneven vertical rectangle, black.

"Walled City," he said, following her eye. He leaned forward, fingertip finding a particular spot. "This is mine. Eighth level."

Chia pointed to the center of the diagram. "What's this?"

"Black hole. In the original, something like an airshaft." He looked at her. "Tokyo has a black hole, too. You have seen this?"

"No," she said.

"The Palace. No lights. From a tall building, at night, the Imperial Palace is a black hole. Watching, once, I saw a torch flare."

"What happened to it in the earthquake?"

He raised his eyebrows. "This of course would not be shown. All now is as before. We are assured of this." He smiled, but only with the corners of his mouth.

"Where did Mitsuko go?"

He shrugged.

"Did she say when she'd be back?"

"No."

Chia thought of Hiromi Ogawa, and then of someone phoning for Kelsey's father. Hiromi? But then there was whatever it was, upstairs in her bag in Mitsuko's room. She remembered Maryalice yelling from behind the door to Eddie's office. Zona had to be right. "You know a club called Whiskey Clone?"

"No." He stroked the buffed aluminum edges of her Sandbenders.

"How about Monkey Boxing?"

He looked at her, shook his head.

"You probably don't get out much, do you?"

He held her gaze. "In Walled City."

"I want to go to this club, Monkey Boxing. Except maybe it isn't called that anymore. It's in a place called Shinjuku. I was in the station there, before."

"Clubs are not open, now."

"That's okay. I just want you to show me where it is. Then I'll be able to find my own way back."

"No. I must return to Walled City. I have responsibilities. Find the address of this place and I will explain to your computer where to go."

The Sandbenders could find its own way there, but Chia had decided she didn't want to go alone. Better to go with a boy than Mitsuko, and Mitsuko's allegiance to her chapter could be a problem anyway. Mainly, though, she just wanted to get out of here. Zona's news had spooked her. Somebody knew she was here. And what to do about the thing in her bag?

"You like this, right?" Pointing at her Sandbenders.

"Yes," he said.

"The software's even better. I've got an emulator in there that'll install a virtual Sandbenders in your computer. Take me to Monkey Boxing and it's yours.''

.

''Have you always lived here?'' Chia asked, as they walked to the station. ''In this neighborhood, I mean?''

Masahiko shrugged. Chia thought the street made him uncomfortable. Maybe just being outside. He'd traded his gray sweats for equally baggy black cotton pants, cinched at the ankle with elastic-sided black nylon gaiters above black leather workshoes. He still wore his black tunic, but with the addition of a short-billed black leather cap that she thought might have once been part of a school uniform. If the tunic was too big for him, the cap was too small. He wore it perched forward at an angle, the bill riding low. ''I live in Walled City,'' he said.

''Mitsuko told me. That's like a multi-user domain.''

''Walled City is unlike anything.''

''Give me the address when I give you the emulator. I'll check it out.'' The sidewalk arched over a concrete channel running with grayish water. It reminded her of her Venice. She wondered if there had been a stream there once.

''It has no address,'' he said.

''That's impossible,'' Chia said.

He said nothing.

She thought about what she'd found when she'd

opened the SeaTac duty-free bag. Something flat and rectangular, dark gray. Maybe made from one of those weird plastics that had metal in them. One end had rows of little holes, the other had complicated shapes, metal, and a different kind of plastic. There didn't seem to be any way to open it, no visible seams. No markings. Didn't rattle when she shook it. Maybe *What Things Are,* the icon dictionary, would recognize it, but she hadn't had time. Masahiko had been downstairs changing when she'd slit the blue and yellow plastic with Mitsuko's serially numbered, commemorative Lo/Rez Swiss Army knife. She'd glanced around the room for a hiding place. Everything too neat and tidy.

Finally she'd put it back in her bag, hearing him coming up the stairs from the kitchen. Which was where it was now, along with her Sandbenders, under her arm, as they entered the station. Which was probably not smart but she just didn't know.

She used Kelsey's cashcard to buy them both tickets.

19

Arleigh

There was a fax from Rydell waiting for Laney when Blackwell dropped him at the hotel. It had been printed on expensive-looking gray letterhead that contrasted drastically with the body of the fax itself, which had been sent from a Lucky Dragon twenty-four-hour convenience store on Sunset. The smiling Lucky Dragon, blowing smoke from its nostrils, was centered just below the hotel's silver-embossed logo, something Laney thought of as the Droopy Evil Elf Hat. Whatever it was supposed to be, the hotel's decorators were very fond of it. It formed a repeating motif in the lobby, and Laney was glad that it didn't seem to have reached the guest rooms yet.

Rydell had hand-printed his fax with a medium-width fiber-pen in scrupulously neat block capitals. Laney read it in the elevator.

It was addressed to C. LANEY, GUEST:

I THINK THEY KNOW WHERE YOU ARE. SHE AND THE DAY MANAGER HAD COFFEE IN THE LOBBY AND HE KEPT LOOKING AT ME. HE COULD'VE CHECKED THE PHONE LOG EASY. WISH I HADN'T CALLED YOU THERE. SORRY. ANYWAY, THEN SHE AND THE OTHERS CHECKED OUT FAST, LEFT THE TECHS TO PACK UP. A TECH TOLD GHENGIS IN THE GARAGE THAT SOME OF THEM WERE ON THEIR WAY TO JAPAN AND HE WAS GLAD HE WASN'T. WATCH OUT, OKAY? RYDELL

''Okay,'' Laney said, and remembered how he'd walked to the Lucky Dragon one night, against Rydell's advice, because he couldn't sleep. There were scary-looking bionic hookers posted every block or so, but otherwise it hadn't felt too dangerous. Someone had painted a memorial mural to J. D. Shapely on one side of the Lucky Dragon, and the management had had the good sense to leave it there, culturally integrating their store into the actual twenty-four-hour life of the Strip. You could buy a burrito there, a lottery ticket, batteries, tests for various diseases. You could do voice-mail, e-mail, send faxes. It had occurred to Laney that this was probably the only store for miles that sold anything that anyone ever really *needed;* the others all sold things that he couldn't even imagine wanting.

He re-read the fax, walking down the corridor, and used the cardkey to open his door.

There was a shallow wicker basket on the bed, spread with white tissue and unfamiliar objects. On closer inspection, these proved to be his socks and underwear, freshly laundered and arranged in little paper holders embossed with the Elf Hat. He opened the narrow, mirrored closet door, activating a built-in light, and discovered his shirts arranged on hangers, including the blue button-downs Kathy Torrance had made fun of. They looked brand new. He touched one of the lightly starched cuffs. "Stitch count," he said. He looked down at Rydell's folded fax. He imagined Kathy Torrance headed straight for him, on an SST from Los Angeles. He discovered that he couldn't imagine her sleeping. He'd never seen her asleep and somehow it didn't seem like something she'd willingly do. In the weird vibrationless quiet of supersonic flight, she'd be staring at the gray blank of the window, or at the screen of her computer.

Thinking of him.

The screen behind him came on with a soft chime and he jumped, four inches, straight up. He turned and saw the BBC logo. Yamazaki's second video.

He was a third of the way through it when the door chimed. Rez was strolling along a narrow trail in the jungle somewhere, wearing sun-bleached khakis and rope-soled sandals. He was singing something as he went, a wordless little melody, over and over, trying different tones and stresses. His bare chest shone with sweat, and when the open shirt swung aside you'd catch a corner of his I Ching tattoo. He had a length of bamboo, and swung it as he walked, swatting at dangling vines. Laney had a sneaking suspicion that the wordless melody had subsequently turned into some global billion-seller, but he couldn't place it yet. The door chimed again.

He got up, crossed to the door, thumbed the speaker button. "Yes?"

"Hello?" A woman's voice.

He touched the card-sized screen set into the doorframe and saw a dark-haired woman. Bangs. The tech from the appliance warehouse. He unlocked the door and opened it.

"Yamazaki thinks we should talk," she said.

Laney saw that she was wearing a black suit with a narrow skirt, dark stockings.

"Aren't you supposed to be shopping for a van?" He stepped back to let her in.

"Got one," closing the door behind her. "When the Lo/Rez machine decides to throw money at a problem, money will be thrown. Usually in the wrong direction." She looked at the screen, where Rez was still swinging along, swatting flies from his neck and chest, lost in composition. "Homework?"

"Yamazaki."

''Arleigh McCrae,'' she said, taking a card from a small black purse and handing it to him. Her name there, then four telephone numbers and two addresses, neither of them physical. ''Do you have a card, Mr. Laney?''

''Colin. No. I don't.''

''They can make them up for you at the desk. Everyone has a card here.''

He put the card in his shirt pocket. ''Blackwell didn't give me one. Neither did Yamazaki.''

''Outside the Lo/Rez organization, I mean. It's like not having socks.''

''I have socks,'' Laney said, indicating the basket on the bed. ''Do you feel like watching a BBC documentary on Lo/Rez?''

''No.''

''I don't think I can turn it off. He'll know.''

''Try lowering the volume. Manually.'' She demonstrated.

''A technician,'' Laney said.

''With a van. And umpti-million yen worth of equipment that didn't seem to do much for you.'' She sat down in one of the room's two small armchairs, crossing her legs.

Laney took the other chair. ''Not your fault. You got me in there just fine. But it's not the kind of data I can work with.''

''Yamazaki told me what you're supposed to be able to do,'' she said. ''I didn't believe him.''

Laney looked at her. ''I can't help you there.''

There were three smiling suns, like black woodblock prints, down the inside of her left calf.

"They're woven into the stockings. Catalan."

Laney looked up. "I hope you're not going to ask me to explain what it is people think they pay me to do," he said, "because I can't. I don't know."

"Don't worry," she said. "I just work here. But what I'm being paid to do, right now, is determine what it is we could give you that would allow you to do whatever it is that you're alleged to be able to do."

Laney looked at the screen. Concert footage now, and Rez was dancing, a microphone in his hand. "You've seen this video, right? Is he serious about that 'Sino-Celtic' thing he was talking about in that interview?"

"You haven't met him yet, have you?"

"No."

"It's not the easiest thing, deciding what Rez is serious about."

"But how can there be 'Sino-Celtic mysticism' when the Chinese and the Celts don't have any shared history?"

"Because Rez himself is half Chinese and half Irish. And if there's one thing he's serious about . . ."

"Yes?"

"It's Rez."

Laney stared glumly at the screen as the singer was replaced by a close-up of Lo's playing, his hands on the black-bodied guitar. Earlier, a venerable British guitarist in wonderful tweeds had opined as how they hadn't really expected the next Hendrix to emerge from Taiwanese Canto-pop, but then again they hadn't actually been expecting the first one, had they?

"Yamazaki told me the story. What happened to you," Arleigh McCrae said. "Up to a certain point."

Laney closed his eyes.

"The show never aired, Laney. Out of Control dropped it. What happened?"

He'd taken to having breakfast beside the Chateau's small oval pool, past the homely clapboard bungalows that Rydell said were a later addition. It was the one time of the day that felt like his own, or did until Rice Daniels arrived, which was usually toward the bottom of a three-cup pot of coffee, just prior to his eggs and bacon.

Daniels would cross the terra cotta to Laney's table with what could only be described as a spring in his step. Laney privately wished to ascribe this to drug-use, of which he'd seen no evidence whatever, and indeed Daniels's most potent public indulgence seemed to be multiple cups of decaf espresso taken with curls of lemon peel. He favored loosely woven beige suits and collarless shirts.

This particular morning, however, Daniels had not been alone, and Laney had detected a lack of temper in the accustomed spring; a certain jangled brittleness there, and the painful-looking glasses seeming to grip his head even more tightly than usual. Beside him came a gray-haired man in a dark brown suit of Western cut, hawk-faced and wind-burnt, the blade of his impressive nose protruding from a huge black pair of sunglasses. He wore black alligator roping-boots and carried a dusty-looking briefcase of age-darkened tan cowhide, its handle mended with what Laney supposed had to be baling wire.

"Laney," Rice Daniels had said, arriving at the table, "this is Aaron Pursley."

"Don't get up, son," Pursley said, though Laney hadn't thought to. "Fella's just bringing you your breakfast." One of the Mongolian waiters was crossing with a tray, from the direction of the bungalows. Pursley put his battle-scarred briefcase down and took one of the white-painted metal chairs. The waiter served Laney's eggs. Laney signed for them, adding a 15-percent tip. Pursley was flipping through the contents of his case. He wore half a dozen heavy silver rings on the fingers of either hand, some of them studded with turquoise. Laney couldn't remember when he'd last seen anyone carry around that much paper.

"You're the lawyer," Laney said. "On television."

"In the flesh as well, son." Pursley was on "Cops in Trouble," and before that he'd been famous for defending celebrity clients. Daniels hadn't taken a seat, and stood behind Pursley now with a hunched, uncharacteristic posture, hands in his trouser pockets. "Here we are," Pursley said. He drew out a sheaf of blue paper. "Don't let your eggs get cold."

"Have a seat," Laney said to Daniels. Daniels winced behind his glasses.

"Now," Pursley said, "you were in a Federal Orphanage, in Gainesville, it says here, from age twelve to age seventeen."

Laney looked at his eggs. "That's right."

"During that time, you participated in a number of drug trials? You were an experimental subject?"

"Yes," Laney said, his eggs looking somehow farther away, or like a picture in a magazine.

"This was voluntary on your part?"

"There were rewards."

"Voluntary," Pursley said. "You get on any of that 5-SB?"

"They didn't tell us what they were giving us," Laney said. "Sometimes we'd get a placebo instead."

"You don't mistake 5-SB for any placebo, son, but I think you know that."

Which was true, but Laney just sat there.

"Well?" Pursley removed his big heavy glasses. His eyes were cold and blue and set into an intricate topography of wrinkles.

"I probably had it," Laney said.

Pursley slapped the blue papers on his thigh. "Well, there you are. You almost certainly did. Now, do you know how that substance eventually affected many of the test subjects?"

Daniels unclamped his glasses and began to knead the bridge of his nose. His eyes were closed.

"Stuff tends to turn males into fixated homicidal stalkers," Pursley said, putting his glasses back on and stuffing the papers into his case. "Comes on years later, sometimes. Go after media faces, politicians. . . . That's why it's now one of *the* most illegal substances, any damn country you care to look. Drug that makes folks want to stalk and kill politicians, well, boy, it'll *get* to be." He grinned dryly.

"I'm not one," Laney said. "I'm not like that."

Daniels opened his eyes. "It doesn't matter," he said. "What matters is that Slitscan can counter all our material by raising the possibility, the merest shadow, however remote, that you are."

"You see, son," Pursley said, "they'd just make out you got into your line of work because you were predisposed to that, spying on famous people. You didn't tell them about any of it, did you?"

"No," Laney said, "I didn't."

"There you go," said Pursley. "They'll say they hired you because you were good at it, but you just got too damn *good* at it."

"But she wasn't famous," Laney said.

"But *he* is," Rice Daniels said, "and they'll say you were after *him*. They'll say the whole thing was your idea. They'll wring their hands about responsibility. They'll talk about their new screening procedures for quantitative analysts. And nobody, Laney, nobody *at all* will be watching *us*."

"That's about the size of it," Pursley said, standing. He picked up the briefcase. "That real bacon there, like off a hog?"

"They say it is," Laney said.

"Damn," Pursley said, "these Hollywood hotels are fast-lane." He stuck out his hand. Laney shook it. "Nice meeting you, son."

Daniels didn't even bother to say goodbye. And two days later, going over the printout of his charges, Laney would notice that it all began, the billing in his own name, with a large pot of coffee, scrambled eggs and bacon, and a 15-percent tip.

Arleigh McCrae was staring at him.

"Do they know that?" she asked. "Does Blackwell?"

"No," Laney said, "not that part, anyway." He could see Rydell's fax, folded on the bedside stand. They didn't know about that, either.

"What happened then? What did you do?"

"I found out I was paying for at least some of the lawyers they'd gotten for me. I didn't know what *to* do. I sat out there by the pool a lot. It was sort of pleasant, actually. I wasn't thinking about anything in particular. Know what I mean?"

"Maybe," she said.

"Then I heard about this job from one of the security people at the hotel."

She slowly shook her head.

"What?" he said.

"Never mind," she said. "You make about as much sense as the rest of it. Probably you'll fit right in."

"Into what?"

She looked at her watch, black-faced stainless on a plain black nylon band. "Dinner's at eight, but Rez will be late. Come out for a walk and a drink. I'll try to tell you what I know about it."

"If you want to," Laney said.

"They're paying me to do it," she said, getting up. "And it probably beats wrestling large pieces of high-end electronics up and down escalators."

Monkey Boxing

Between stations there was a gray shudder beyond the windows of the silent train. Not as of surfaces rushing past, but as if particulate matter were being vibrated there at some crucial rate, just prior to the emergence of a new order of being.

Chia and Masahiko had found two seats, between a trio of plaid-skirted schoolgirls and a businessman who was reading a fat Japanese comic. There was a woman on the cover with her breasts bound up like balls of twine, but conically, the nipples protruding like the popping eyes of a cartoon victim. Chia noticed that the artist had devoted much more time to drawing the twine, exactly how it was wrapped and knotted, than to drawing the breasts themselves. The woman had sweat running down her face and was trying to back away from someone or something cut off by the edge of the cover.

Masahiko undid the top two buttons of his tunic and withdrew a six-inch square of something black and rigid, no thicker than a pane of glass. He brushed it purposefully with the fingers of his right hand, beaded lines of colored light appearing at his touch. Though these were fainter here, washed out by the train's directionless fluorescents, Chia recognized the square as the control-face of the computer she'd seen in his room.

He studied the display, stroked it again, and frowned at the result. "Someone pays attention to my address," he said, "and to Mitsuko's . . ."

"The restaurant?"

"Our user addresses."

"What kind of attention?"

"I do not know. We are not linked."

—Except by me.

"Tell me about Sandbenders," Masahiko said, putting the control-face away and buttoning his tunic.

"It started with a woman who was an interface designer," Chia said, glad to change the subject. "Her husband was a jeweller, and he'd died of that nerve-attenuation thing, before they saw how to fix it. But he'd been a big green, too, and he hated the way consumer electronics were made, a couple of little chips and boards inside these plastic shells. The shells were just point-of-purchase eye-candy, he said, made to wind up in the landfill if nobody recycled it, and usually nobody did. So, before he got sick, he used to tear up her hardware, the designer's, and put the real parts into cases he'd make in his shop. Say he'd make a solid bronze case for a minidisk unit, ebony inlays, carve the control surfaces out of fossil ivory, turquoise, rock crystal. It weighed more, sure, but it turned out a lot of people liked that, like they had their music or their memory, whatever, in something that felt like it was *there.* . . . And people liked touching all that stuff: metal, a smooth stone. . . . And once you had the case, when the manufacturer brought out a new model, well, if the electronics were any better, you just pulled the old ones out and put the new ones in your case. So you still had the same object, just with better functions."

Masahiko's eyes were closed, and he seemed to be nodding slightly, though perhaps only with the motion of the train.

"And it turned out some people liked *that,* too, liked it a lot. He started getting commissions to make these things. One of the first was for a keyboard, and the keys were cut from the keys of an old piano, with the numbers and letters in silver. But then he got sick . . ."

Masahiko's eyes opened, and she saw that not only had he been listening, but that he was impatient for more.

"So after he was dead, the software designer started thinking about all that, and how she wanted to do something that took what he'd been doing into something else. So she cashed out her stock in all the companies she'd worked for, and she bought some land on the coast, in Oregon—''

And the train pulled into Shinjuku, and everyone stood up, heading for the doors, the businessman closing his breast-bondage comic and tucking it beneath his arm.

Chia was leaning back to look at the strangest building she'd ever seen. It was shaped like the old-fashioned idea of a robot, a simplified human figure, its legs and upraised arms made of transparent plastic over a framework of metal. Its torso appeared to be of brick, in red, yellow and blue, arranged in simple patterns. Escalators, stairways, and looping slides twisted through the hollow limbs, and puffs of white smoke emerged at regular intervals from the rectangular mouth of the thing's enormous face. Beyond it the sky all gray and pressing down.

''Tetsujin Building,'' Masahiko said. ''Monkey Boxing was not there.''

''What is it?''

''Osaka Tin Toy Institute,'' he said. ''Monkey Boxing this way.'' He was consulting the swarming squiggles on his control-face. He pointed along the street, past a fast-food franchise called California Reich, its trademark a stylized stainless-steel palm tree against one of those twisted-cross things like the meshbacks had drawn on their hands in her class on

European history. Which had pissed the teacher off totally, but Chia couldn't remember them drawing any palm trees. Then two of them had gotten into a fight over which way you were supposed to draw the twisted parts on the cross, pointing left or pointing right, and one of them had zapped the other with a stungun, the kind they were always making out of those disposable flash-cameras, and the teacher had to call the police.

"Ninth floor, Wet Leaves Fortune Building," he said. He set off down the crowded pavement. Chia followed, wondering how long jet lag lasted, and how you were supposed to separate it from just being tired.

Maybe what she was feeling now was what her civics program at her last school had called culture shock. She felt like everything, every little detail of Tokyo, was just different enough to create a kind of pressure, something that built up against her eyes, as though they'd grown tired of having to notice all the differences: a little sidewalk tree that was dressed up in a sort of woven basketwork jacket, the neon-avocado color of a payphone, a serious-looking girl with round glasses and a gray sweatshirt that said "Free Vagina." She'd been keeping her eyes extra-wide to take all these things in, like they'd be processed eventually, but now her eyes were tired and the differences were starting to back up. At the same time, she felt that if she squinted, maybe, just the right way, she could make all this turn back into Seattle, some downtown part she'd walked through with her mother. Homesick. The strap of her bag digging into her shoulder each time her left foot came down.

Masahiko turned a corner. There didn't seem to be alleys in Tokyo, not in the sense that there were smaller streets behind the big streets, the places where they put out the garbage, and there weren't any stores. There were smaller streets, and smaller ones behind those, but you couldn't guess what you'd find there: a shoe-repair place, an expensive-looking hair salon, a chocolate-maker, a magazine stand where she noticed a copy of that same creepy comic with the woman all wrapped up like that.

Another corner and they were back on what she took to be a main street. Cars here, anyway. She watched one turn into a street-level opening and vanish. Her scalp prickled. What if that were the way up to Eddie's club, that Whiskey Clone? That was right around here, wasn't it? How big was this Shinjuku place, anyway? What if the Graceland pulled up beside her? What if Eddie and Maryalice were out looking for her?

They were passing the opening the car had disappeared into. She looked in and saw that it was a kind of gas station. "Where is it?" she asked.

"Wet Leaves Fortune," he said, pointing up.

Tall and narrow, square signs jutting out at the corners of each floor. It looked like almost all the others, but she thought Eddie's had been bigger. "How do we get up there?"

He led her into a kind of lobby, a ground-floor

arcade lined with tiny stall-like shops. Too many lights, mirrors, things for sale, all blurring together. Into a cramped elevator that smelled of stale smoke. He said something in Japanese and the door closed. The elevator sang them a little song to tinkling music. Masahiko looked irritated.

At the ninth floor the door opened on a dust-covered man with a black headband sagging over his eyes. He looked at Chia. "If you're the one from the magazine," he said, "you're three days early." He pulled the headband off and wiped his face with it. Chia wasn't sure if he was Japanese or not, or what age he might be. His eyes were brown, spectacularly bloodshot under deep brows, and his black hair, pulled straight back and secured by the band, was streaked with gray.

Behind him there was a constant banging and confusion, men yelling in Japanese. Someone pushing a high-sided orange plastic cart crammed with folded, plaster-flecked cables, shards of plastic painted with gold gilt and Chinese red. Part of a suspended ceiling let go with a twanging of wires, crashed to the floor. More cries.

"I'm looking for Monkey Boxing," Chia said.

"Darling," the man said, "you're a bit late." He wore a black paper coverall, its sleeves torn off at the elbows, revealing arms tracked with blobby blue lines and circles, some kind of faux-primitive decoration. He wiped his eyes and squinted at her. "You aren't from the magazine in London?"

"No," Chia said.

"No," he agreed. "You seem a bit young even for them."

"This is Monkey Boxing?"

Another section of ceiling came down. The dusty man squinted at her. "Where did you say you were from?"

"Seattle."

"You heard about Monkey Boxing in Seattle?"

"Yes . . ."

He smiled wanly. "That's fun: heard about it in Seattle. . . . You're on the club scene yourself, dear?"

"I'm Chia McKenzie—"

"Jun. I'm called Jun, dear. Owner, designer, DJ. But you're too late. Sorry. All that's left of Monkey Boxing's going out in these gomi-carts. Landfill now. Like every other broken dream. Had a lovely run while it lasted, better part of three months. You heard about our Shaolin Temple theme? That whole warrior-monk thing?" He sighed extravagantly. "It was *heaven.* Every instant of it. The Okinawan bartenders shaved their heads, after the first three nights, and started to wear the orange robes. I surpassed myself, in the booth. It was a *vision,* you understand? But that's the nature of the floating world, isn't it? We *are* in the water trade, after all, and one tries to be philosophical. But who is your friend here? I like his hair . . ."

"Masahiko Mimura," Chia said.

"I *like* that black-clad boho butch bedsit thing,"

the man said. "Mishima and Dietrich on the same halfshell, if it's done right."

Masahiko frowned.

"If Monkey Boxing is gone," Chia said, "what will you do now?"

Jun retied his headband. He looked less pleased. "Another club, but I won't be designing. They'll say I've sold out. Suppose I have. I'll still be managing the space, very nice salary and an apartment along with it, but the conccpt . . ." He shrugged.

"Were you here the night Rez told them he wanted to marry the idoru?"

His brow creased, behind the headband. "I had to sign *agreements,*" he said. "You *aren't* from the magazine?"

"No."

"If he hadn't come in that night, I suppose we might still be up and running. And really he wasn't the sort of thing we'd tried to be about. We'd had Maria Paz, just after she'd split up with her boyfriend, the public relations monster, and the press were thick as flies. She's huge here, did you know that? And we'd had Blue Ahmed from Chrome Koran and the press scarcely noticed. Rez and his friends, though, press was *not* a problem. Sent in this big minder who looked as though he'd been using his face as a chopping block. Came up to me and said Rez had heard about the place and was about to drop in with a few friends, and could we arrange a table with a bit of privacy. . . . Well, really, I had to think: Rez *who?*

Then it clicked, of course, and I said fine, absolutely, and we put three tables together in the back, and even borrowed a purple cordon from the gumi boys in the hostess place upstairs."

"And he came? Rez?"

"Absolutely. An hour later, there he is. Smiling, shaking hands, signing things if you asked him to, though there wasn't too burning a demand, actually. Four women with him, two other men if you didn't count the minder. Very nice black suit. Yohji. Bit the worse for wear. Rez, I mean. Been out to dinner, it looked like. Had a few drinks with it. Certain amount of laughter, if you follow me." He turned and said something to one of the workmen, who wore shoes like two-toed black leather socks.

Chia, who had no idea what Monkey Boxing had actually been about, imagined Rez at a table with some other people, behind a purple rope, and in the foreground a crowd of Japanese people doing whatever Japanese people did at a club like that. Dancing?

"Then our boy gets up, he's going to the toilet. The big minder makes as if he's getting up to go too, but our boy waves him back. Big laugh from the table, big minder not too happy. Two of the women start to get up, like *they*'re going with him; he'll have none of it, waves 'em back, *more* laughter. Not that anyone else was paying him that much attention. I was going into the booth in five minutes, with a set of *extremely* raw North African; had to judge the crowd, get on it with them, know just when to drop it in. But there he went, right through them, and only one or two even noticed, and they didn't stop dancing."

What kind of club was it, where nobody would stop dancing for Rez?

"So I was thinking about my set, the order of it, and suddenly he's right in front of me. Big grin. Eyes funny, though I wouldn't swear it was anything he'd done in the toilet—if you know what I mean."

Chia nodded her head. What *did* he mean?

"And would I mind, he said, hand on my shoulder, if he just spoke briefly to the crowd? Said he'd been thinking about something for a long time, and now he'd made up his mind and he wanted to tell people. And the big minder just *materialized* there, wanting to know was there any problem? None at all, Rez says, giving my shoulder a squeeze, but he was just going to have a word with the crowd."

Chia looked at Jun's shoulders, wondering which one had been squeezed by Rez's actual hand. "So he did," Jun said.

"But what did he *say?*" Chia asked.

"A load of bollocks, dear. Evolution and technology and passion; man's need to find beauty in the emerging order; his own burning need to get his end in with some software dolly wank toy. Balls. Utter." He pushed his headband up with his thumb, but it fell back. "And *because* he did that, opened his mouth up in my club, Lo slash bloody Rez *bought* my club.

Bought me as well, and I've signed *agreements* that I won't talk to *any* of you about *any* of that. And now if you and your charming friend will excuse me, darling, I have work to do."

Standover Man

There was a man on stilts at the intersection nearest the hotel. He wore a hooded white paper suit, a gas mask, and a pair of rectangular sign-boards. Messages scrolled down the boards in Japanese as he shifted his weight to maintain balance. Streams of pedestrian traffic flowed around and past him.

"What's that?" Laney asked, indicating the man on stilts.

"A sect," Arleigh McCrae said. " 'New Logic.' They say the world will end when the combined weight of all the human nervous tissue on the planet reaches a specific figure."

A very long multi-digit number went scrolling down.

"Is that it?" Laney asked.

"No," she said, "that's their latest estimate of the current total weight." She'd gone back to her room for the black coat she now wore, leaving Laney to change into clean socks, underwear, a blue shirt. He didn't have a tie, so he'd buttoned the shirt at the collar and put his jacket back on. He'd wondered if everyone who worked for Lo/Rez stayed in that same hotel.

Laney saw the man's eyes through the transparent visor as they passed. A look of grim patience. The stilts were the kind workers wore to put up ceilings, articulated alloy sprung with steel. "What's supposed to happen when there's enough nervous tissue?"

"A new order of being. They don't talk about it. Rez was interested in them, apparently. He tried to arrange an audience with the founder."

"And?"

"The founder declined. He said that Rez made his living through the manipulation of human nervous tissue, and that that made him untouchable."

"Rez was unhappy?"

"Not according to Blackwell. Blackwell said it seemed to cheer him up a little."

"He's not cheerful, ordinarily?" Laney sidestepped to avoid a bicycle someone was wheeling in the opposite direction.

"Let's say that the things that bother Rez aren't the things that bother most people."

Laney noticed a dark green van edging along beside them. Its wraparound windows were mirrored, its neon license plates framed with animated tubes of mini-Vegas twinklers. "I think we're being followed," he said.

"We'd better be. I wanted the kind with the weird chrome curb-feelers that make them look like silverfish, but I had to settle for custom license-plate trim. Where you go, it goes. And parking, around here, is probably more of a challenge than anything you'll be expected to do tonight. Now," she said, "down here."

Steep, narrow stairs, walled with an alarming pink mosaic of glistening tonsil-like nodules. Laney hesitated, then saw a sign, the letters made up of hundreds of tiny pastel oblongs: LE CHICLE. Stepping down, he lost sight of the van.

A chewing-gum theme-bar, he thought, and then: I'm getting too used to this. But he still avoided touching the wall of chewed gum as he followed her down.

Into powdery pinks and grays, but these impersonating the unchewed product, wall-wide slabs of it, hung with archaic signage from the nation of his birth. Screen-printed steel. Framed and ancient cardboard, cunningly lit. Icons of gum. Bazooka Joe featured centrally, a figure unknown to Laney but surely no more displaced.

"Come here often?" Laney asked, as they took stools with bulbous cushions in a particularly lurid bubble-gum pink. The bar was laminated with thousands of rectangular chewing-gum wrappers.

''Yes,'' she said, ''but mainly because it's unpopular. And it's non-smoking, which is still kind of special here.''

''What's 'Black Black'?'' Laney asked, looking at a framed poster depicting a stylized 1940s automobile hurtling through the faint suggestion of city streets. Aside from ''Black Black,'' it was lettered in a sort of Art Deco Japanese.

''Gum. You can still buy it,'' she said. ''The cab drivers all chew it. Lots of caffeine.''

''In gum?''

''They sell pick-me-ups here full of liquid nicotine.''

''I think I'll have a beer instead.''

When the waitress, in tiny silver shorts and a prehensile pink angora top, had taken their orders, Arleigh opened her purse and removed a notebook. ''These are linear topographies of some of the structures you accessed earlier today.'' She passed Laney the notebook. ''They're in a format called Realtree 7.2.''

Laney clicked through a series of images: abstract geometrics arranged in vanishing linear perspective. ''I don't know how to read them,'' he said.

She poured her sake. ''You really were trained by DatAmerica?''

''I was trained by a bunch of Frenchmen who liked to play tennis.''

''Realtree's from DatAmerica. The best quantitative analysis software they've got.'' She closed the notebook, put it back in her purse.

Laney poured his beer. ''Ever hear of something called TIDAL?''

'' 'Tidal'?''

''Acronym. Maybe.''

''No.'' She lifted the china cup and blew, like a child cooling tea.

''It was another DatAmerica tool, or the start of one. I don't think it reached the market. But that was how I learned to find the nodal points.''

''Okay,'' she said. ''What *are* the nodal points?''

Laney looked at the bubbles on the surface of his beer. ''It's like seeing things in clouds,'' Laney said. ''Except the things you see are really there.''

She put her sake down. ''Yamazaki promised me you weren't crazy.''

''It's not crazy. It's something to do with how I process low-level, broad-spectrum input. Something to do with pattern-recognition.''

''And Slitscan hired you on the basis of that?''

''They hired me when I demonstrated that it works. But I can't do that with the kind of data you showed me today.''

''Why not?''

Laney raised his beer. ''Because it's like trying to have a drink with a bank. It's not a person. It doesn't drink. There's no place for it to *sit.*'' He drank. ''Rez doesn't generate patterns I can read, because everything he does is at one remove. It's like looking in an annual report for the personal habits of the chairman of the board. It's not going to be there. From the outside, it just looks like that Realtree stuff. If I enter a specific area, I don't get any sense of how the data there relates to the rest of it, see? It's got to be *relational.*" He drummed his fingers on the laminated gum wrappers. "Somewhere in Ireland. Guesthouse with a beach view. Nobody there. Records of how it was kept stocked: stuff for the bathroom, toothpaste, shaving foam . . ."

"I've been there," she said. "That's on an estate he bought from an older musician, an Irishman. It's beautiful. Like Italy, in a way."

"You think he'll take this idoru back there, when they get hitched?"

"Nobody has any idea what he's talking about when he says he wants to 'marry' her."

"Then an apartment in Stockholm. Huge. Great big stoves in each room, made of glazed ceramic bricks."

"I don't know that one. He has places all over, and some of them are kept very quiet. There's another country place in the south of France, a house in London, apartments in New York, Paris, Barcelona. . . . I was working out of the Catalan office, reformatting all their stuff and Spain's as well, when this idoru thing hit. I've been here ever since."

"But you know him? You knew him before?"

"He's the navel of the world I work in, Laney. That has a way of making people unknowable."

"What about Lo?"

"Quiet. Very. Bright. Very." She frowned at her sake. "I don't think any of it's ever really gotten to Lo. He seems to regard their entire career as some freak event unrelated to anything else."

"Including his partner deciding to marry a software agent?"

"Lo told me a story once, about a job he'd had. He worked for a soup vendor in Hong Kong, a wagon on the sidewalk. He said the wagon had been in business for over fifty years, and their secret was that they'd never cleaned the kettle. In fact, they'd never stopped cooking the soup. It was the same seafood soup they'd been selling for fifty years, but it was never the same, because they added fresh ingredients every day, depending on what was available. He said that was what his career as musician felt like, and he liked that about it. Blackwell says if Rez were more like Lo, he'd still be in prison."

"Why?"

"Blackwell was serving a nine-year sentence, in an Australian maximum-security prison, when Rez talked his way in. To give a concert. Just Rez. Lo and the others thought it was too dangerous. They'd been warned that it could turn into a hostage-taking situation. The prison authorities refused to take any responsibility, and they wanted it in writing. Rez signed anything they put in front of him. His security people resigned on the spot. He went in with two guitars, a wireless mike, and a very basic amplification system. During the concert, a riot broke out. Apparently it was orchestrated by a group of Italian prisoners from Melbourne. Five of them took Rez into the prison laundry, which they'd chosen because it was windowless and easily defended. They informed Rez they were going to kill him if they couldn't negotiate their release in exchange for his. They discussed cutting off at least one of his fingers to demonstrate that they meant business. Or possibly some more intimate part, though that may simply have been to make him more anxious. Which it did.'' She signaled the pink angora waitress for more sake. ''Blackwell, who'd evidently been extremely irritated at the interruption of the concert, which he'd been enjoying enormously, appeared in the laundry approximately forty minutes after Rez was taken prisoner. Neither Rez nor the Italians saw him arrive, and the Italians definitely hadn't been expecting him.'' She paused. ''He killed three of them, with a tomahawk. Put the end of it into their heads: one, two, three, Rez says, like that. No fuss whatever.''

''A tomahawk?''

''Sort of narrow-bladed hatchet, with a spike opposite the blade. Extends the reach, imparts terrific force, and with practice can be thrown with considerable accuracy. Blackwell swears by it. The other two fled, although they both seem to have died in the aftermath of the riot. Personally, I'm sure Blackwell or his 'mates' killed them, because he was never charged with the murder of the other three. The sole surviving witness was Rez, whom Blackwell escorted to the barricade the guards had erected in the exercise yard.'' Her sake arrived. ''It took Rez's lawyers three months to get Blackwell's sentence reversed on a technicality. They've been together ever since.''

''What was Blackwell in for?''

''Murder,'' she said. ''Do you know what a standover man is?''

''No.''

''It's a peculiarly Australian concept. I'm tempted to think it could only have grown out of a culture comprised initially of convicts, but my Australian friends don't buy that. The standover man is a loner, a predator who preys on other, more prosperous criminals, often extremely dangerous ones. He captures them and 'stands over' them. To extort money.''

''What's that mean?''

''He tortures them until they tell him where their money is. And these are often fairly serious operators, with people paid to take care of them, specifically to prevent this sort of thing . . .''

''Tortures them?''

'' 'Toe-cutter' is a related term. When they tell him what he needs to know, he kills them.''

And Blackwell was suddenly and noiselessly and simply *there,* very black, and matte, in an enormous waxed-cotton drover's coat. Behind him the faded American advertising and the grays and pinks of gum. His fretted scalp concealed by the waxed-cotton crown of a broad black hat.

"Arleigh, dear, you wouldn't take the name in vain, would you?"

But he smiled at her.

"I'm explaining your earlier career to Mr. Laney, Blackwell. I'd only just gotten up to the massage parlor, and now you've ruined it."

"Never mind. Dinner's been moved up, at the request of his Rozzer. I'm here to take you. Change of venue as well. Hope you don't mind."

"Where?" Arleigh asked, as if not yet prepared to move.

"The Western World," said Blackwell.

"And me in my good shoes," she said.

Gomi Boy

The trains more crowded now, standing room only, everyone pressed in tight, and somehow the eye-contact rules were different here, but she wasn't sure how. Her bag with the Sandbenders was jammed up against Masahiko's back. He was looking at the control-face again, holding it up the way a commuter would hold a strategically folded newspaper.

On their way back to Mitsuko's father's restaurant, and then she didn't know what. She'd done the thing that Hiromi hadn't wanted her to do. And gotten nothing for it but a vaguely unpleasant idea of Rez as someone capable of being boring. And where did it leave her? She'd gone ahead and used Kelsey's cash-card, to pay for the train, and now another train back. And Zona had said somebody was looking for her;

they could track her when she used the cashcard. Maybe there was a way to cash it in, but she doubted it.

None of this had gone the way she'd tried to imagine it, back in Seattle, but then you couldn't be expected to imagine anyone like Maryalice, could you? Or Eddie, or even Hiromi.

Masahiko frowned at the control-face. Chia saw the dots and squiggles changing.

That thing Maryalice had stuck in her bag. Right here under her arm. She should've left it at Mitsuko's. Or thrown it away, but then what would she say if Eddie or Maryalice showed up? What if it was full of drugs?

In Singapore they hung people, right in the mall, for that. Her father didn't like it and he said that was one of the reasons he never invited her there. They put it on television, too, so that it was really hard to avoid seeing it, and he didn't want her to see it. Now she wondered how far Singapore was from Tokyo? She wished she could go there and keep her eyes closed until she was in her father's apartment, and never turn the tv on, just be there with him and smell his shaving smell and put her face against his scratchy wool shirt, except she guessed you didn't wear those in Singapore because it was hot there. She'd keep her eyes closed anyway, and listen to him talk about his work, about the arbitrage engines shuttling back and forth through the world's markets like invisible dragons, fast as light, shaving fragments of advantage for traders like her father . . .

Masahiko turned, accidentally knocking her bag aside, as the train stopped at a station—not theirs. A woman with a yellow shopping bag said something in Japanese. Masahiko took Chia's wrist and pulled her toward the open door.

"This isn't where we get off—"

"Come! Come!" Out onto the platform. A different smell here; something chemical and sharp. The walls not so clean, somehow. A broken tile in the ceramic ceiling.

"What's the matter? Why are we getting off?"

He pulled her into the corner formed by the tiled wall and a huge vending machine. "Someone is at the restaurant, waiting for you." He looked down at her wrist, as if amazed to find that he was holding it, and instantly released her.

"How do you know?"

"Walled City. There have been inquiries, in the last hour."

"Who?"

"Russians."

"Russians?"

"There are many from the Kombinat here, since the earthquake. They forge relationships with the gumi."

"What's gumi?"

"Mafia, you call it. Yakuza. My father has arrangement with local gumi. Necessary, in order to operate restaurant. Gumi representatives spoke about you to my father."

"Your neighborhood mafia is Russian?" Behind his head, on the side of the machine, the animated logo of something called Apple Shires.

"No. Yamaguchi-gumi franchise. My father knows these men. They tell my father Russians ask about you, and this is not good. They cannot guarantee usual safety. Russians not reliable."

"I don't know any Russians," Chia said.

"We go now."

"Where?"

He led her along the crowded platform, its pavement wet from hundreds of furled umbrellas. It must be raining now, she thought. Toward an escalator.

"When Walled City saw attention was being paid to our addresses, my sister's and mine, a friend was sent to remove my computer . . ."

"Why?"

"Because I have responsibility. For Walled City. Distributed processing."

"You've got a MUD in your computer?"

"Walled City is not anywhere," he said, as they stepped onto the escalator. "My friend has my computer. And he knows about men who are waiting for you."

Masahiko said his friend was called Gomi Boy.

He was very small, and wore an enormous, balloon-bottomed pair of padded fatigue pants covered with at least a dozen pockets. These were held up with three-inch-wide Day-Glo orange suspenders, over a ratty cotton sweater with the cuffs rolled back. His shoes were pink, and looked like the shoes babies wore, but bigger. He was perched on an angular aluminum chair now and the baby shoes didn't quite touch the floor. His hair looked as though it had been sculpted with a spatula, gleaming swirls and dips, like your hand might stick there if you touched it. It was the way they painted J. D. Shapely's hair on those murals in Pioneer Square, and Chia knew from school that that had something to do with that whole Elvis thing, though she couldn't remember exactly what.

He was talking with Masahiko in Japanese, over the crashing sound-surf of this gaming arcade. Chia wished she was wearing a translator, but she'd have to open her bag, find one, turn the Sandbenders on. And Gomi Boy looked like he'd be just as happy knowing she couldn't understand him.

He was drinking a can of something called Pocari Sweat, and smoking a cigarette. Chia watched the blue smoke settling out in layers in the air, lit by the glare of the games. There was cancer in that, and they'd arrest you in Seattle if you did it. Gomi Boy's cigarette looked like it had been made in a factory: a perfect white tube with a brown tip he put to his lips. Chia had seen those in old movies, sometimes, the ones they hadn't gone through yet to digitally erase them, but the only other cigarettes she'd seen were the twisted-up paper ones they sold on the street in Seattle, or you could buy a little baggie of the tobacco stuff and the white squares of paper to roll it up in. Meshbacks in school did it.

The rain was still coming down. Through the arcade's streaming window she could make out another arcade, across the street, one of the ones with the machines the silver balls poured through. The neon and the rain and the silver balls ran all together, and she wondered what Masahiko and Gomi Boy were talking about.

Gomi Boy had Masahiko's computer in a plaid plastic carry-bag with quilted pink International Biohazard symbols on the sides. It was sitting on the little table beside the can of Pocari Sweat. What was a Pocari? She imagined a kind of wild pig, with bristles, turned-up tusks, like she'd seen on the Nature Channel.

Gomi Boy sucked on his cigarette, making the end glow. He squinted through the smoke at Masahiko and said something. Masahiko shrugged. There was a fresh mini-can of microwaved espresso in front of him, and Chia had another Coke Lite. In Tokyo there was nowhere to sit down unless you bought something, and it was quicker to buy a drink than something to eat. And it cost less. Except she wasn't paying for these. Gomi Boy was, because he and Masahiko didn't want her to use Kelsey's cashcard.

Gomi Boy spoke again. "He wishes to talk with you," Masahiko said.

Chia bent over, unzipped her bag, found the ear-clips. She only had the two, so she handed one to Gomi Boy, put the other on herself, and hit power. He put his on. "I am from Walled City," he said. "You understand?"

"A MUD, right? Multi user domain."

"Not in the sense you mean, but approximately, yes. Why are you in Tokyo?"

"To gather information about Rez's plan to marry the idoru, Rei Toci."

Gomi Boy nodded. Being an otaku was about caring a lot about information; he understood being a fan. "Do you have dealings with the Combine?" Chia knew he had said *Kombinat,* and the translator had covered it. He meant that mafia government in Russia.

"No," Chia said.

"And you came to be at Masahiko's because . . . ?"

"Mitsuko's the social secretary of the Tokyo chapter of the Lo/Rez group I belong to in Seattle."

"How many times did you port, from the restaurant?"

"Three times." The Silke-Marie Kolb outfit. The meeting. Zona Rosa. "I paid for presentation software, Mitsuko and I did the meeting, I linked home."

"You paid for the software with your cashcard?"

"Yes." She looked from Gomi Boy to Masahiko. Between and behind them, the rain. The endless racketing cascade of the little silver balls, through the glass across the street. Players hunched there on integral stools, manipulating the flood of metal. Masahiko's expression told her nothing at all.

"Masahiko's computer maintains certain aspects of Walled City," Gomi Boy said. "Contingency plans were in place for its removal to safety. When it became obvious that both Masahiko's and his sister's user addresses were attracting unusual attention, I was sent to secure his machine. We frequently exchange hardware. I am a dealer in second-hand equipment. That is why I am called Gomi Boy. I have my own keys to Masahiko's room. His father knows I am allowed to enter. His father does not care. I came and took the computer. Nearby is a small civic recreation area. The restaurant is visible from it. Seeing Oakland Overbombers, I crossed the street and spoke with them."

"Seeing what?"

"A skateboard group. They are named for the California soccer club. I asked them if there had been unusual activity. They told me they had seen a very large vehicle, an hour before . . ."

—A Graceland.

"A Daihatsu Graceland. There are fewer here than in America, I think."

Chia nodded. Her stomach did that cold flip-thing again. She thought she might throw up.

Gomi Boy leaned sideways with his cigarette, which was short now, and mashed the lit end into a little chrome bowl that was fastened to the side of a game console. Chia wondered what this was actually used for, and why he did that, but she supposed he had to put it somewhere or it would burn his fingers. "The Graceland parked near the restaurant. Two men got out . . ."

"What did they look like?"

"Gumi representatives."

"Japanese?"

"Yes. They went into the restaurant. The Graceland waited. After fifteen minutes, they returned, got into the Graceland, and left. Masahiko's father appeared. He looked in all directions, studying the street. He took his phone from his pocket and spoke with someone. He went back into the restaurant." Gomi Boy looked at the carry-bag. "I did not want to remain in the recreation area with Masahiko's computer. I told the leader of the Overbombers I would give him a better telephone, later, if he would remain there and phone me if more activity occurred. The Overbombers do nothing anyway, so he agreed. I left. He phoned twenty minutes later to report a gray Honda van. The driver is Japanese, but the other three are foreigners. He thinks they are Russian."

"Why?"

"Because they are very large, and dress in a style he associates with the Combine. They are still there."

"How do you know?"

"If they leave, he must call me. He wants his new phone."

"Can I port from here? I have to talk to Air Magellan right away about changing my reservations. *I want to go home.*'' And leave Maryalice's package in that trash cannister she could see behind Gomi Boy.

''You must not port,'' Masahiko said. ''You must not use the cashcard. If you do, they will find you.''

''But what else am I supposed to *do?*'' she said, startled by her own voice, which sounded like someone else's. ''I just want to go *home!*''

''Let me see the card,'' Gomi Boy said. It was in her parka, with her passport and her ticket home. She took it out and handed it to him. He opened a pocket on his fatigue pants and took out a small rectangular device that seemed to be held together with multiple layers of fraying silver tape. He swiped Chia's card along a slot and peered into a peephole reader like the one on a fax-beeper. ''This is nontransferable and cannot be used to obtain cash. It is also very easy to trace.''

''My friend's pretty sure they've got the number anyway,'' Chia said, thinking of Zona.

Gomi Boy began to tap the edge of the cashcard on the rim of his can of Pocari Sweat. ''There is a place where you can use this and not be traced,'' he said. Tap tap. ''Where Masahiko could access Walled City.'' Tap tap. ''Where you could phone home.''

''Where's that?''

''A love hotel.'' Tap. ''Do you know what that is?''

''No,'' Chia said.

Tap.

23

Here at the Western World

Emerging from Le Chicle's pink mosaic gullet into the start of rain, Laney saw that the stilt-walking New Logic disciple was still at his post, his animated sandwich-board illuminated against the evening. As Blackwell held the door of a mini-limo for Arleigh, Laney looked back at the scrolling numerals and wondered how much the planet's combined weight of human nervous tissue had increased while they'd been in the bar.

Laney got in after her, noticing those Catalan suns again, the three of them, decreasing in size down her inner calf. Blackwell thunked the door behind him, then opened the front, should've-been driver's side door and seemed to pour himself into the car, a movement that simultaneously suggested the sliding of a ball of mercury and the settling of hundreds of pounds of liquid concrete. The car waddled and swayed as its shocks adjusted to accommodate his weight.

Laney saw how the brim of Blackwell's black-waxed hat drooped low in back, but not far enough to conceal a crisscrossing of fine red welts decorating the back of his neck.

Their driver, to judge by the back of his head, might have been the same one who'd driven them to Akihabara. He pulled out into the mirror-image traffic. The rain was running and pooling, tugging reflected neon out of the perpendicular and spreading it in wriggly lines across sidewalk and pavement.

Arleigh McCrae was wearing perfume, and it made Laney wish that Blackwell wasn't there, and that they were on their way somewhere other than wherever it was they were going now, and in another city, and that quite a lot of the last seven months of Laney's life hadn't happened at all, or had happened differently, or maybe even as far back as DatAmerica and the Frenchmen, but as it became more complicated, it became depressing.

"I'm not sure you're going to enjoy this place," she said.

"How's that?"

"You don't seem like the type."

"Why not?"

"I could be wrong. Lots of people do enjoy it. I suppose if you take it as a very elaborate joke . . ."

"What is it?"

"A club. Restaurant. An *environment.* If we turned up there without Blackwell, I doubt they'd let us in. Or even admit it's there."

Laney was remembering the Japanese restaurant in Brentwood, the one Kathy Torrance had taken him to. Not Japanese Japanese. Owned and operated. Its theme an imaginary Eastern European country. Decorated with folk art from that country, and everyone who worked there wore native garb from that country, or else a sort of metallic-gray prison outfit and these big black shoes. The men who worked there all had these haircuts, shaved high on the sides, and the women had big double braids, rolled up like wheels of cheese. Laney's entrée had had all kinds of different little sausages in it, the smallest he'd ever seen, and some kind of pickled cabbage on the side, and it hadn't tasted like it had come from anywhere in particular, but maybe that was the point. And then they'd gone back to her apartment, decorated like a sort of deluxe version of the Cage at Slitscan. And that hadn't worked out either, and sometimes he wondered whether that had made her even angrier, when he'd gone over to Out of Control.

"Laney?"

"Sorry. . . . This place—Rez likes it?"

Past ambient forests of black umbrellas, waiting to cross at an intersection.

"I think he just likes to brood there," she said.

• • •

The Western World occupied the top two floors of an office building that hadn't quite survived the quake. Yamazaki might have said that it represented a response to trauma and subsequent reconstruction. In the days (some said hours) immediately following the disaster, an impromptu bar and disco had come into being in the former offices of a firm that had brokered shares in golf-club memberships. The building, declared structurally unsound, had been sealed by emergency workers at the ground floor, but it was still possible to enter through the ruined sublevels. Anyone willing to climb eleven flights of mildly fissured concrete stairs found the Western World, a bizarrely atypical (but some said mysteriously crucial) response to the upheaval that had, then, so recently killed eighty-six thousand of the region's thirty-six million inhabitants. A Belgian journalist, struggling to describe the scene, had said that it resembled a cross between a permanent mass wake, an ongoing grad night for at least a dozen subcultures unheard of before the disaster, the black market cafes of occupied Paris, and Goya's idea of a dance party (assuming Goya had been Japanese and smoked freebase methamphetamine, which along with endless quantities of alcohol was the early Western World's substance of choice). It was, the Belgian said, as though the city, in its convulsion and grief, had spontaneously and necessarily generated this hidden pocket universe of the soul, its few unbroken windows painted over with black rubber aquarium paint. There would be no view of the ruptured city. As the reconstruction began around it, it had already become a benchmark in Tokyo's psychic history, an open secret, an urban legend.

But now, Arleigh was explaining, as they climbed the first of those eleven flights of stairs, it was very definitely a commercial operation, the damaged building owing its continued survival to the unlicensed penthouse club that was its sole occupant. If in fact it continued to be unlicensed, and she had her doubts about that. "There isn't a lot of slack here," she said, climbing, "not for things like that. Everybody knows the Western World's here. I think there's a very quiet agreement, somewhere, to allow them to operate the place as though it were still unlicensed. Because that's what people want to pay for."

"Who owns the building?" Laney asked, watching Blackwell float up the stairs in front of them, his arms, in the matte black sleeves of the drover's coat, like sides of beef dressed for a funeral. The stairwell was lit with irregular loops of faintly bioluminescent cable.

"Rumor has it, one of the two groups who can't quite agree on who owns our hotel."

"Mafia?"

"Local equivalent, but only very approximately equivalent. Real estate was baroque, here, before the quake; now it's more like occult."

Laney, glancing down as they passed one of the glowing loops, noticed, on the treads of the stairs, hardened trickles of something that resembled greenish amber. "There's stuff on the stairs," he said.

"Urine," Arleigh said.

"Urine?"

"Solidified, biologically neutral urine."

Laney took the next few steps in silence. His calves were starting to ache. Urine?

"The plumbing didn't work, after the quake," she said. "They couldn't use the toilets. People just started going, down the stairs. Pretty horrible, by all accounts, although some people actually get nostalgic about it."

"It's solid?"

"There's a product here, a powder, looks like instant soup. Some kind of enzyme. They sell it mainly to mothers with young kids. The kid has to pee, you can't get them to a toilet in time, they pee in a paper cup, an empty juice box. You drop in the contents of a handy, purse-sized sachet of this stuff, zap, it's a solid. Neutral, odorless, completely hygienic. Pop it in the trash, it's landfill."

They passed another loop of light and Laney saw miniature stalactites suspended from the edges of a step. "They used that stuff . . ."

"Lots of it. Constantly. Eventually they had to start sawing off the build-up . . ."

"They still . . . ?"

"Of course not. But they kept the Grotto."

Another flight. Another loop of ghostly undersea light.

"What did they do about the solids?" he asked.

"I'd rather not know."

Winded, his ankles sore, Laney emerged from the Grotto. Into a black-walled and indeterminate space defined by blue light and the uprights of gilded girders. After chemically frozen frescoes of piss, the Western World disappointed. A gutted office block dressed with mismatched couches and nondescript bars. Something looming in the middle foreground. He blinked. A tank. American, he thought, and old.

"How did they get that up here?" he asked Arleigh, who was passing her black coat to someone. And why hadn't the floor collapsed?

"It's resin," she said. "Membrane sculpture. Stereo lithography. Otaku thing: they bring them in in sections and glue them together."

Blackwell had given up his drover's coat, exposing a garment that resembled a suit jacket but seemed to have been woven from slightly tarnished aluminum. Whatever this fabric was, there was enough of it there for a double bedspread. He moved forward, through the maze of couches and low tables, with that same effortless determination, Laney and Arleigh drawn along in his wake.

"That's a Sherman tank," Laney said, remembering a CD-ROM from Gainesville, one about the history of armored vehicles. Arleigh didn't seem to have heard him. But then she'd probably never played with

CD-ROMs, either. Time in a Federal Orphanage had a way of acquainting you with dead media platforms.

If Arleigh were right, and the Western World were being kept on as a kind of tourist attraction, Laney wondered what the crowd would have been like in the early days, when the sidewalks below were buried in six feet of broken glass.

These people on the couches, now, hunched over the low tables that supported their drinks, seemed unlike any crowd he'd seen so far in Tokyo. There was a definite edged-out quality there, and prolonged eye-contact might have been interesting in some cases, dangerous in others. Distinct impression that the room's combined mass of human nervous tissue would have been found to be freighted with the odd few colorants. Or else these people were somehow preselected for a certain combination of facial immobility and intensity of glance?

"Laney," Blackwell said, dropping a hand on Laney's shoulder and twirling him into the gaze of a pair of long green eyes, "this is Rez. Rez, Colin Laney. He's working with Arleigh."

"Welcome to the Western World," smiling, and then the eyes slid past him to Arleigh. "Evenin', Miz MacCrae."

Laney noticed something then that he knew from his encounters with celebs at Slitscan: that binary flicker in his mind between image and reality, between the mediated face and the face there in front of you. He'd noticed how it always seemed to speed up, that alternation, until the two somehow merged, the resulting composite becoming your new idea of the person. (Someone at Slitscan had told him that it had been clinically proven that celebrity-recognition was handled by one particular area in the brain, but he'd never been sure whether or not they were joking.)

Those had been tame celebrities, the ones Kathy had already had her way with. In the building (but never the Cage) to have various aspects of their public lives scripted, per whatever agreements were already in place. But Rez wasn't tame, and was a much bigger deal in his own way, although Laney had only been aware of his later career because Kathy had hated him so.

Rez had his arm around Arleigh now, gesturing with the other into the relative darkness beyond the Sherman tank, saying something Laney couldn't hear.

"Mr. Laney, good evening." It was Yamazaki, in a green plaid sportscoat that sat oddly on his narrow shoulders. He blinked rapidly.

"Yamazaki."

"You have met Rez, yes? Good, very good. A table is prepared, to dine." Yamazaki put two fingers inside the oversized, buttoned collar of his cheap-looking white dress shirt and tugged, as though it were far too tight. "I understand initial attempts to identify nodal points did not meet with success." He swallowed.

"I can't pull a personal fix out of something textured like corporate data. He's just not *there.*"

Rez was moving in the direction of whatever lay beyond the tank.

"Come," Yamazaki said, then lowered his voice. "Something extraordinary. She is here. She dines with Rez. Rei Toei."

The idoru.

24

Hotel Di

In this tiny cab now with Masahiko and Gomi Boy, Masahiko up front, on what should've been the driver's side, Gomi Boy beside her in the back. Gomi Boy had so many pockets in his fatigue pants, and so many things in them, that he had trouble getting comfortable. Chia had never been in a car this small, let alone a cab. Masahiko's knees were folded up, almost against his chest. The driver had white cotton gloves and a hat like the hats cab drivers wore in 1940s movies. There were little covers made of starched white lace fixed to all the headrests with special clips.

She guessed it was such a small cab because Gomi Boy was going to be paying, cash money, and he made it clear he didn't have a lot of that.

Somehow they had ascended out of the rain into

this crazy, impressive, but old-fashioned-looking multilevel expressway, its steel bones ragged with bandages of Kevlar, and were whipping past the middle floors of tall buildings—maybe that Shinjuku again, because there went that Tin Toy Building, she thought, glimpsed through a gap, but far away and from another direction—and here, gone so fast she was never sure she'd seen him, through one window like all the rest, was a naked man, crosslegged on an office desk, his mouth open as wide as possible, as if in a silent scream.

Then she began to notice other buildings, through sheets of rain, and these were illuminated to a degree excessive even by local standards, like Nissan County attractions in a television ad, isolated theme-park elements thrusting up out of a strata of more featureless structures, unmarked and unlit. Each bright building with its towering sign: HOTEL KING MIDAS with its twinkling crown and scepter, FREEDOM SHOWER BANFF with blue-green mountains flanking a waterfall of golden light. At least six more in rapid succession, then Gomi Boy said something in Japanese. The driver's shiny black bill dipped in response.

They swung onto an off-ramp, slowing. From the ramp's curve, in the flat, ugly flare of sodium floods, she saw a rainy, nowhere intersection, no cars in sight, where pale coarse grass lay wet and dishevelled up a short steep slope. No place at all, like it could as easily have been on the outskirts of Seattle, the outskirts of anywhere, and the homesickness made her gasp.

Gomi Boy shot her a sidewise glance, engaged in the excavation of something from another of his pockets, this one apparently *inside* his pants. From somewhere well below the level of his crotch he fished up a wallet-sized fold of paper money, secured with a wide black elastic band. In the passing glare of another road light Chia saw him snap the elastic back and peel off three bills. Bigger than American money, and on one she made out the comfortingly familiar logo of a company whose name she'd known all her life. He tucked the three bills into the sleeve of his sweater and set about replacing the rest wherever it was he kept it.

"There soon," he said, withdrawing his hand and refastening his suspenders.

"Where soon?"

They took a right and stopped, all around them a strange white fairy glow, falling with the rain to oil-stained concrete neatly painted with two big white arrows, side by side, pointing in opposite directions. The one pointing in the direction they were headed indicated a square opening in a featureless, white-painted concrete wall. Five-inch-wide ribbons of shiny pink plastic hung from its upper edge to the concrete below, concealing whatever was behind and reminding Chia of streamers at a school dance. Gomi Boy gave the driver the three bills. He sat patiently, waiting for change.

Her legs cramping, Chia reached for the door handle, but Masahiko quickly reached across from the front, stopping her. "Driver must open," he said. "If you open, mechanism breaks, very expensive." The driver gave Gomi Boy change. Chia thought Gomi Boy would tip him, but he didn't. The driver reached down and did something, out of sight, that made the door beside Chia open.

She climbed out into the rain, dragging her bag after her, and looked up at the source of the white glow: a building like a wedding cake, HOTEL DI spelled out in white neon script edged with clear twinkling bulbs. Masahiko beside her now, urging her toward the pink ribbons. She heard the cab pull away behind her. "Come." Gomi Boy with the plaid bag, ducking through the wet ribbons.

Into an almost empty parking area, two small cars, one gray, one dark green, their license plates concealed by rectangles of smooth black plastic. A glass door sliding aside as Gomi Boy approached.

A disembodied voice said something in Japanese. Gomi Boy answered. "Give him your card," Masahiko said. Chia took out the card and handed it to Gomi Boy, who seemed to be asking the voice a series of questions. Chia looked around. Pale blues, pink, light gray. A very small space that managed to suggest a hotel lobby without actually offering a place to sit down. Pictures cycling past on wallscreens: interiors of very strange-looking rooms. The voice answering Gomi Boy's questions.

"He asks for a room with optimal porting capacity," Masahiko said quietly.

Gomi Boy and the voice seemed to reach agreement. He slotted Chia's card above something that looked like a small pink water fountain. The voice thanked him. A narrow hatch opened and a key slid down into the pink bowl. Gomi Boy picked it up and handed it to Masahiko. Chia's card emerged from the slot; Gomi Boy pulled it out and passed it to Chia. He handed Masahiko the plaid bag, turned, and walked out, the glass door hissing open for him.

"He isn't coming with us?"

"Only two people allowed in room. He is busy elsewhere. Come." Masahiko pointed toward an elevator that opened as they approached.

"What kind of hotel did you say this is?" Chia got into the elevator. He stepped in behind her and the door closed.

He cleared his throat. "Love hotel," he said.

"What's that?" Going up.

"Private rooms. For sex. Pay by the hour."

"Oh," Chia said, as though that explained everything. The elevator stopped and the door opened. He got out and she followed him along a narrow corridor lit with ankle-high light-strips. He stopped in front of a door and inserted the key they'd been given. As he opened the door, lights came on inside.

"Have you been to one of these before?" she asked, and felt herself blush. She hadn't meant it that way.

"No," he said. He closed the door behind her and examined the locks. He pushed two buttons. "But people who come here sometimes wish to port. There is a reposting service that makes it very hard to trace. Also for phoning, very secure."

Chia was looking at the round pink furry bed. It seemed to be upholstered in what they made stuffed animals out of. The wall-to-wall was shaggy and white as snow, the combination reminding her of a particularly nasty-looking sugar snack called a Ring-Ding.

Velcro made that ripping sound. She turned to see Masahiko removing his nylon gaiters. He took off his black workshoes (the toe was out, in one of his thin gray socks) and slid his feet into white paper sandals. Chia looked down at her own wet shoes on the white shag and decided she'd better do the same. "Why does this place *look* the way it does?" she asked, kneeling to undo her laces.

Masahiko shrugged. Chia noticed that the quilted International Biohazard symbol on the plaid bag was almost exactly the color of the fur on the bed.

Spotting what was obviously the bathroom through an open door, she carried her own bag in there and closed the door behind her. The walls were upholstered with something black and shiny, and the floor was checkered with black and white tiles. Complicated mood-lighting came on and she was surrounded by ambient birdsong. This bathroom was nearly as big as the bedroom, with a bath like a miniature black swimming pool and something else that Chia only gradually recognized as a toilet. Remembering the one back in Eddie's office, she put her bag down and approached the thing with extreme caution. It was black, and chrome, and had arms and a back, sort of like a chair at the stylist's. There was a display cycling, on a little screen beside it, with fragments of English embedded in the Japanese. Chia watched as "(A) Pleasure" and "(B) Super Pleasure" slid past. "Uh-uh," she said.

After studying the seat and the ominous black bowl, she lowered her pants, positioned herself strategically over the toilet, squatted carefully, and urinated without sitting down. She'd let someone else flush that one, she decided, while she washed her hands at the basin, but then she heard it flush itself.

There was a glossy pink paper bag beside the basin with the words "Teen Teen Toiletry Bag" printed on it in swirly white script. It was sealed at the top with a silver stick-on bow. She removed the bow and looked inside. Lots of different little give-away cosmetics and at least a dozen different kinds of condoms, everything packaged to look more or less like candy.

There was a shiny black cabinet to the left of the mirror above the basin, the only thing in the room that looked Japanese in that old-fashioned way. She opened it; a light came on inside, revealing three glass shelves arranged with shrink-wrapped plastic models of guy's dicks, all different sizes of them, molded in weird colors. Other objects she didn't recognize at all: knobby balls, something that looked like a baby's pacifier, miniature inner-tubes with long rubbery whiskers. In the middle of it all stood a little black-haired doll in a pretty kimono made of bright paper and gold cloth. But when she tried to pick it up, the wig and the kimono came off in one piece, revealing yet another shrink-wrapped replica, this one with delicately painted eyes and a Cupid's-bow mouth. When she tried to put the wig and kimono back on, it fell over, knocking over everything on its shelf, so she closed the cabinet. Then she washed her hands again.

Back in the Ring-Ding room, Masahiko was cabling his computer to a black console on a shelf full of entertainment gear. Chia put her bag on the bed. Something chimed softly, twice, and then the surface of the bed began to ripple, slow osmotic waves centering in on the bag, which began to rise slightly, and fall . . .

"Ick," she said, and pulled the bag off the bed, which chimed again and began to subside.

Masahiko glanced in her direction, but went back to whatever he was doing with the equipment on the shelf.

Chia found that the room had a window, but it was hidden behind some kind of softscreen. She tried the clips that held the screen in place until she got the one that let her slide the screen aside on hidden tracks. The window looked out on a chainlinked parking lot beside a low, beige building sided with corrugated plastic. There were three trucks parked there, the first vehicles she'd seen in Japan that weren't new or particularly clean. A wet-looking gray cat emerged from beneath one of the trucks and sprang into the shadow beneath another. It was still raining.

"Good," she heard Masahiko say, evidently satisfied. "We go to Walled City."

The Idoru

"How do you mean, she's 'here'?" Laney asked Yamazaki, as they rounded the rear of the Sherman tank. Clots of dry clay clung to the segments of its massive steel treads.

"Mr. Kuwayama is here," Yamazaki whispered. "He represents her—"

Laney saw that several people were already seated at a low table.

Two men. A woman. The woman must be Rei Toei.

If he'd anticipated her at all, it had been as some industrial-strength synthesis of Japan's last three dozen top female media faces. That was usually the way in Hollywood, and the formula tended to be even more rigid, in the case of software agents—*eigen-*

heads, their features algorithmically derived from some human mean of proven popularity.

She was nothing like that.

Her black hair, rough-cut and shining, brushed pale bare shoulders as she turned her head. She had no eyebrows, and both her lids and lashes seemed to have been dusted with something white, leaving her dark pupils in stark contrast.

And now her eyes met his.

He seemed to cross a line. In the very structure of her face, in geometries of underlying bone, lay coded histories of dynastic flight, privation, terrible migrations. He saw stone tombs in steep alpine meadows, their lintels traced with snow. A line of shaggy pack ponies, their breath white with cold, followed a trail above a canyon. The curves of the river below were strokes of distant silver. Iron harness bells clanked in the blue dusk.

Laney shivered. In his mouth a taste of rotten metal.

The eyes of the idoru, envoy of some imaginary country, met his.

''We're here.'' Arleigh beside him, hand at his elbow. She was indicating two places at the table. ''Are you all right?'' she asked, under her breath. ''Take your shoes off.''

Laney looked at Blackwell, who was staring at the idoru, something like pain in his face, but the expression vanished, sucked away behind the mask of his scars.

Laney did as he was told, kneeling and removing his shoes, moving as if he were drunk, or dreaming, though he knew he was neither, and the idoru smiled, lit from within.

"Laney?"

The table was set above a depression in the floor. Laney seated himself, arranging his feet beneath the table and gripping his cushion with both hands. "What?"

"Are you okay?"

"Okay?"

"You looked . . . blind."

Rez was taking his place now at the head of the table, the idoru to his right, someone else—Laney saw that it was Lo, the guitarist—to his left. Next to the idoru sat a dignified older man with rimless glasses, gray hair brushed back from his smooth forehead. He wore a very simple, very expensive-looking suit of some lusterless black material, and a high-collared white shirt that buttoned in a complicated way. When this man turned to address Rei Toei, Laney quite clearly saw the light of her face reflect for an instant in the almost circular lenses.

Arleigh's sharp intake of breath. She'd seen it too.

A hologram. Something generated, animated, projected. He felt his grip relax slightly, on the edges of the cushion.

But then he remembered the stone tombs, the river, the ponies with their iron bells.

Nodal.

• • •

Laney had once asked Gerrard Delouvrier, the most patient of the tennis-playing Frenchmen of TIDAL, why it was that he, Laney, had been chosen as the first (and, as it would happen, the only) recipient of the peculiar ability they sought to impart to him. He hadn't applied for the job, he said, and had no reason to believe the position had even been advertised. He had applied, he told Delouvrier, to be a trainee service rep.

Delouvrier, with short, prematurely gray hair and a suntable tan, leaned back in his articulated workstation chair and stretched his legs. He seemed to be studying his crepe-soled suede shoes. Then he looked out the window, to rectangular beige buildings, anonymous landscaping, February snow. "Do you not see? How we do not teach you? We watch. We wish to learn from you."

They were in a DatAmerica research park in Iowa. There was an indoor court for Delouvrier and his colleagues, but they complained constantly about its surface.

"But why me?"

Delouvrier's eyes looked tired. "We wish to be kind to the orphans? We are an unexpected warmth at the heart of DatAmerica?" He rubbed his eyes. "No. Something was done to you, Laney. In our way, perhaps, we seek to redress that. Is that a word, 'redress'?"

"No," Laney said.

"Do not question good fortune. You are here with us, doing work that matters. It is winter in this Iowa, true, but the work goes on." He was looking at Laney now. "You are our only proof," he said.

"Of what?"

Delouvrier closed his eyes. "There was a man, a blind man, who mastered echo-location. Clicks with the tongue, you understand?" Eyes closed, he demonstrated. "Like a bat. Fantastic." He opened his eyes. "He could perceive his immediate environment in great detail. Ride a bicycle in traffic. Always making the *tik, tik*. The ability was his, was absolutely real. And he could never explain it, never teach it to another . . ." He wove his long fingers together and cracked his knuckles. "We must hope that this is not the case with you."

Don't think of a purple cow. Or was it a brown one? Laney couldn't remember. Don't look at the idoru's face. She is not flesh; she is information. She is the tip of an iceberg, no, an Antarctica, of information. Looking at her face would trigger it again: she was some unthinkable volume of information. She induced the nodal vision in some unprecedented way; she induced it as narrative.

He could watch her hands. Watch the way she ate.

The meal was elaborate, many small courses served on individual rectangular plates. Each time a plate was placed before Rei Toei, and always within the field of whatever projected her, it was simultaneously veiled with a flawless copy, holo food on a holo plate.

Even the movement of her chopsticks brought on peripheral flickers of nodal vision. Because the chopsticks were information too, but nothing as dense as her features, her gaze. As each "empty" plate was removed, the untouched serving would reappear.

But when the flickering began, Laney would concentrate on his own meal, his clumsiness with his own chopsticks, conversation around the table. Kuwayama, the man with the rimless glasses, was answering something Rez had asked, though Laney hadn't been able to catch the question itself. "—the result of an array of elaborate constructs that we refer to as 'desiring machines.' " Rez's green eyes, bright and attentive. "Not in any literal sense," Kuwayama continued, "but please envision *aggregates of subjective desire.* It was decided that the modular array would ideally constitute an architecture of articulated longing . . ." The man's voice was beautifully modulated, his English accented in a way that Laney found impossible to place.

Rez smiled then, his eyes going to the face of the idoru. As did Laney's as well, automatically.

He fell through her eyes. He was staring up at a looming cliff face that seemed to consist entirely of small rectangular balconies, none set at quite the same level or depth. Orange sunset off a tilted, steel-framed window. Oilslick colors crawling in the sky.

He closed his eyes, looked down, opened them. A fresh plate there, more food.

"You're really into your meal," Arleigh said.

A concentrated effort with the chopsticks and he managed to capture and swallow something that was like a one-inch cube of cold chutney omelet. "Wonderful. Don't want any of that fugu though. Blowfish with the neurotoxins? Heard about that?"

"You've already had seconds," she said. "Remember the big plate of raw fish arranged like the petals of a chrysanthemum?"

"You're kidding," Laney said.

"Lips and tongue feel faintly numb? That's it."

Laney ran his tongue across his lips. Was she kidding? Yamazaki, seated to his left, leaned close. "There may be a way around the problem you face with Rez's data. You are aware of Lo/Rez global fan activity?"

"Of what?"

"Many fans. They report each sighting of Rez, Lo, other musicians involved. There is much incidental detail."

Laney knew from his day's video education that Lo/Rez were theoretically a duo, but that there were always at least two other "members," usually more. And Rez had been adamant from the start about his dislike of drum machines; the current drummer, "Blind" Willy Jude, seated opposite Yamazaki, had been with them for years. He'd been turning his enormous black glasses in the idoru's direction throughout the meal; now he seemed to sense Laney's glance. The black glasses, video units, swung around. "Man," Jude said, "Rozzer's sittin' down there makin' eyes at a big aluminum thermos bottle."

"You can't see her?"

"Holos are hard, man," the drummer said, touching his glasses with a fingertip. "Take my kids to Nissan County, I'll call ahead, get 'em tweaked around a little. Then I can see 'em. But this lady's on a funny frequency or something. All I can see's the projector and this kinda, kinda ectoplastic, right? Glow, like."

The man seated between Jude and Mr. Kuwayama, whose name was Ozaki, bobbed apologetically in Jude's direction. "We regret this very much. We regret deeply. A slight adjustment is required, but it cannot be done at this time."

"Hey," Jude said, "no big problem. I seen her already. I get all the music channels with these. That one where she's a Mongol princess or something, up in the mountains . . ."

Laney lost a chopstick.

"The most recent single," Ozaki said.

"Yeah," Jude said, "that's pretty good. She wears that gold mask? Okay shit." He popped a section of maki into his mouth and chewed.

Hak Nam

Chia and Masahiko sat facing one another on the white carpet. Thc room's only chair was a fragile-looking thing with twisted wire legs and a heart-shaped seat upholstered in pink metal-flake plastic. Neither of them wanted to sit on the bed. Chia had her Sandbenders across her knees and was working her fingers into her tip-sets. Masahiko's computer was on the carpet in front of him; he'd put its control-face back on and peeled a very compact pair of tip-sets out of the back of the cube, along with two small black oval cups on fine lengths of optical cable. Another length of the cable ran from his computer to a small open hatch at the back of the Sandbenders.

''Okay,'' Chia said, settling the last of her tips, ''let's go. I've got to get hold of somebody . . .''

"Yes," he said. He picked up the black cups, one in either hand, and placed them over his eyes. When he let go, they stayed there. It looked uncomfortable.

Chia reached up and pulled her own glasses down, over her eyes. "What do I—"

Something at the core of things moved simultaneously in mutually impossible directions. It wasn't even like porting. Software conflict? Faint impression of light through a fluttering of rags.

And then the thing before her: building or biomass or cliff face looming there, in countless unplanned strata, nothing about it even or regular. Accreted patchwork of shallow random balconies, thousands of small windows throwing back blank silver rectangles of fog. Stretching either way to the periphery of vision, and on the high, uneven crest of that ragged facade, a black fur of twisted pipe, antennas sagging under vine growth of cable. And past this scribbled border a sky where colors crawled like gasoline on water.

"Hak Nam," he said, beside her.

"What is it?"

" 'City of darkness.' Between the walls of the world."

She remembered the scarf she'd seen, in his room behind the kitchen, its intricate map of something chaotic and compacted, tiny irregular segments of red and black and yellow. And then they were moving forward, toward a narrow opening. "It's a MUD, right?" Something like a larger, permanent version of the site the Tokyo chapter had erected for the meeting, or the tropical forest Kelsey and Zona had put up. But people played games in MUDs; they made up characters for themselves and pretended. Little kids did it, and lonely people.

"No," he said, "not a game." They were inside now, smoothly accelerating, and the squirming density of the thing was continual visual impact, an optical drumming. "Tai Chang Street." Walls scrawled and crawling with scrolling messages, spectral doorways passing like cards in a shuffled deck.

And they were not alone: others there, ghost-figures whipping past, and everywhere the sense of eyes . . .

Fractal filth, bit-rot, the corridor of their passage tented with crazy swoops of faintly flickering lines of some kind. "Alms House Backstreet." A sharp turn. Another. Then they were ascending a maze of twisting stairwells, still accelerating, and Chia took a deep breath and closed her eyes. Retinal fireworks bursting there, but the pressure was gone.

When she opened her eyes, they were in a much cleaner but no larger version of his room behind the kitchen in the restaurant. No empty ramen bowls, no piles of clothing. He was beside her on the sleeping ledge, staring at the shifting patterns on his computer's control-face. Beside it on the work-surface, her Sandbenders. The texture-mapping was rudimentary, everything a little too smooth and glossy. She looked at him, curious to see how he'd present. A basic scan job, maybe a year out of date: his hair was shorter. He wore the same black tunic.

On the wall behind the computers was an animated version of the printed scarf, its red, black, and yellow bits pulsing slightly. A bright green line traced a route in from the perimeter; where it ended, bright green, concentric rings radiated from one particular yellow square.

She looked back at him, but he was still staring at the control-face.

Something chimed. She glanced at the door, which was mapped in a particularly phoney-looking wood-grain effect, and saw a small white rectangle slide under the door. And keep sliding, straight toward her, across the floor, to vanish under the sleeping ledge. She looked down in time to see it rise, at exactly the same rate, up the edge of the striped mattress and over, coming to a halt when it was in optimum position to be read. It was in that same font they'd used at Whiskey Clone, or one just like it. It said "Ku Klux Klan Kollectibles," and then some letters and numbers that didn't look like any kind of address she knew.

Another chime. She looked at the door in time to see a gray blur scoot from under it. Flat, whirling, fast. It was on the white rectangle now, something like the shadow of a crab or spider, two-dimensional and multi-legged. It swallowed it, shot for the door.

"I have completed responsibility to Walled City," Masahiko said, turning from the control-face.

"What were those things?" Chia asked him.

"What things?"

"Like a business card. Crawled under the door. Then another thing, like a gray cut-out crab, that ate it."

"An advertisement," he decided, "and a sub-program that offered criticism."

"It didn't offer criticism; it ate it."

"Perhaps the person who wrote the sub-program dislikes advertising. Many do. Or dislikes the advertiser. Political, aesthetic, personal reasons, all are possible."

Chia looked around at the reproduction of his tiny room. "Why don't you have a bigger site?" Instantly worried that it was because he was Japanese, and maybe they were just used to that. But still it was about the smallest virtual space she could remember having been in, and it wasn't like a bigger one cost more, not unless you were like Zona and wanted yourself a whole country.

"The Walled City is a concept of scale. Very important. Scale *is* place, yes? Thirty-three thousand people inhabited original. Two-point-seven hectares. As many as fourteen stories."

None of which made any sense to Chia. "I have to port, okay?"

"Of course," he said, and gestured toward her Sandbenders.

She was braced for that two-directions-at-once thing, but it didn't happen. The bit-mapped fish were swimming around in the glass coffee table. She looked out the window at the crayon trees and wondered where the Mumphalumpagus was. She hadn't seen it for a while. It was something her father had made for her when she was a baby, a big pink dinosaur with goofy eyelashes.

She checked the table for mail, but there was nothing new.

She could phone from here. Call her mother. Sure.

—Hi, I'm in Tokyo. In a "love hotel." People are after me because somebody put something in my bag. So, uh, what do you think I should do?

She tried porting to Kelsey's address instead, but all she got was that annoying marble anteroom and the voice, not Kelsey's, that said that Kelsey Van Troyer wasn't in at the moment. Chia exited without leaving a message. The next address she tried was Zona's, but Zona's provider was down. That happened a lot, in Mexico, and particularly in Mexico City, where Zona lived. She decided to try Zona's secret place, because it was on a mainframe in Arizona and it was never down. She knew Zona didn't like people just showing up there, because Zona didn't want the company that had built the original website, and then forgotten about it, to discover that Zona had gotten in and set up her own country.

She asked the Sandbenders where she was porting from now and it said Helsinki, Finland. So that reporting capability at the hotel was working, at least.

Just before twilight at Zona's, like always. Chia

scanned the floor of a dry swimming pool, looking for Zona's lizards, but she didn't see them. Usually they were right there, waiting for you, but not this time. "Zona?"

Chia looked up, wondering if she'd see those spooky condor-things that Zona kept. The sky was beautiful but empty. Originally that sky had been the most important part of this place, and no expense had been spared. Serious sky: deep and clean and a crazy Mexican shade like pale turquoise. They'd brought people here to sell them airplanes, corporate jets, when the jets were still in the design phase. There'd been a white concrete landing strip, but Zona had folded it up into a canyon and mapped over it. All the local color was Zona's stuff: the cooking fires and the dead pools and the broken walls. She'd imported landscape files, maybe even real stuff she knew from somewhere in Mexico. "Zona?"

Something rattled, up the nearest ridge, like pebbles on a sheet of metal.

—It's okay. One of the lizards. She's just not here now.

A twig snapped. Closer.

—Don't fuck around, Zona.

But she exited.

The bit-mapped fish swam back and forth.

That had been very creepy. She wasn't sure why, exactly, but it had been. Still was, kind of. She looked at the door to her bedroom and found herself wondering what she'd find there if she gestured for it. The bed, her *Lo Rez Skyline* poster, the agent of Lo greeting her in his mindless friendly way. But what if she found something else? Something waiting. Like she could still hear that rattle, up the slope. Or what if she went to the wire-framed door where her mother's room would have been? What if she opened it and her mother's room was there after all, and not her mother, waiting, but something else?

She was creeping herself out, that was all. She looked at her stack of Lo/Rez albums beside the lithographed lunch box, her virtual Venice beside that. Even her Music Master would seem like company now. She opened it, watching the Piazza decompress like some incredibly intricate paper pop-up book on fast-forward, facades and colonnades springing up around her, with the hour before a winter's dawn for backlight.

Turning from the water, where the prows of black gondolas bobbed like marks in some lost system of musical notation, she lifted her finger and shot forward into the maze, thinking as she did that this place had been as strange, in its way, as Masahiko's Walled City, and what was that all supposed to be about anyway?

And it was only as she crossed her third bridge that she noticed that he wasn't there.

—Hey.

She stopped. A shop window displayed the masks of Carnival, the really ancient ones. Black, penis-nosed leather, empty eye-holes. A mirror draped with yellowed crepe.

Checking the Sandbenders to make sure she hadn't turned him off. She hadn't.

Chia closed her eyes and counted to three. Made herself feel the carpeted floor she sat on in the Hotel Di. She opened her eyes.

At the end of the narrow Venetian street, down the tilted, stepped cobbles, where it opened out into a small square or plaza, an unfamiliar figure stood beside the central fountain.

She pulled the goggles off without bothering to close Venice.

Masahiko sat opposite her, his legs crossed, the black cups sucked up against his eyes. His lips were moving, silently, and his hands, on his knees, in their black tip-sets, traced tiny finger-patterns in the air.

Maryalice was sitting on the furry pink bed with an unlit cigarette in her mouth. She had a little square gray gun in her hand, and Chia saw how the freshly glossed red of her nails contrasted with the pearly plastic of the handle.

"Started again," Maryalice said, around the cigarette. She pulled the trigger, causing a small golden flame to spring up from the muzzle, and used it to light her cigarette. "Tokyo. I'll tell you. Does it every time."

That Physical Thing

Laney was at a black rubber urinal in the Men's when he noticed the Russian combing his hair in the mirror.

At least it looked like black rubber, with sort of floppy edges. They obviously had the plumbing working, but he wondered what they'd say if you asked to make your own contribution to the Grotto? On his way here he'd noticed that one of the bars was topped with a slab of something murky green and translucent, lit from below, and he'd hoped they hadn't made that from what they'd sawn out of the stairwell.

Dinner was over and he'd probably had too much sake with it. He and Arleigh and Yamazaki had watched Rez meeting this new version of the idoru, the one Willy Jude saw as a big silver thermos. And Blackwell was having to get used to that, because

Laney guessed that the bodyguard hadn't had any idea she'd be here, not until he'd walked in and Rez had told him.

Arleigh had talked with Lo through most of it, mainly about real estate. Different properties he owned around the world. Laney had listened to more of Yamazaki's ideas about accessing this teenage fan-club stuff, and there might actually be something to that, but they'd have to try it to find out. Blackwell hadn't said two words to anybody, drinking lager instead of sake and packing his food away as though he were trying to plug something, some gap in security that could be taken care of if you stuffed it methodically with enough sashimi. The Australian was an ace with chopsticks; he could probably stick one in your eye at fifty paces. But the main show had been Rez and the idoru, and to a lesser extent Kuwayama, who'd carried on long conversations with them both. The other one, Ozaki, seemed to be the guy they brought along in case someone had to change the batteries in the silver thermos. And Willy Jude was amiable enough, but in about as content-free a way as possible.

Techs were supposed to be an easy source of whatever passed for gossip in a given company, so Laney had tried a few openings in that direction, but Ozaki hadn't said any more than he'd had to. And since Laney couldn't get Rei Toei within his field of vision without starting to slide over into nodal mode, he'd had to conduct his evening's eavesdropping with whatever pick-up visuals were available. Arleigh wasn't too bad for that. There was something about the line of her jaw that he particularly liked, and kept coming back to.

Laney zipped up and went to wash his hands, the basin made of that same floppy-looking black stuff, and noticed that the Russian was still combing his hair. Laney had no way of knowing if the man was literally Russian or not, but he thought of him that way because of the black patent paratrooper boots with contrasting white stitching, the pants with the black silk ribbon down the side, and the white leather evening jacket. Either Russian or one of those related jobs, but very definitely Kombinat-inflected, that mutant commie-mafioso thing.

The Russian was combing his hair with a total concentration that made Laney think of a fly grooming itself with its front feet. He was very large, and had a large head, though it was mainly in the vertical, quite tall from the eyebrows up, seeming to taper very slightly toward the crown. For all the attention being given to the combing, the man didn't actually have much hair, not on top anyway, and Laney had thought these guys all went in for implants. Rydell had told him Kombinat types were all over Tokyo. Rydell had seen a documentary about it, how they were so singularly and surrealistically brutal that nobody wanted to mess with them. Then Rydell had started to tell him about two Russians, San Francisco cops of some kind, who he'd had some sort of run-in with, but Laney had to take a meeting with Rice Daniels and a make-up artist, and never heard the end of it.

Laney checked to see that he didn't have anything stuck in his teeth from dinner.

As he went out, the Russian was still combing.

He saw Yamazaki, blinking and looking lost. "It's back there," he said.

"What is?"

"The can."

" 'Can'?"

"Men's. The toilet."

"But I was looking for you."

"You found me."

"I observed, as we ate, that you avoided looking directly at the idoru."

"Right."

"I surmise that density of information is sufficient to allow nodal apprehension . . ."

"You got it."

Yamazaki nodded. "Ah. But this would not be the case with one of her videos, or even with a 'live' performance."

"Why not?" Laney had started back in the direction of their table.

"Bandwidth," Yamazaki said. "The version here tonight is high-bandwidth prototype."

"Are we compensated for beta-testing?"

"Can you describe the nature of nodal apprehension, please?"

"Like memories," Laney said, "or clips from a

movie. But something the drummer said made me think I was just seeing her latest video.''

Someone shoved Laney out of the way, from behind, and he fell across the nearest table, breaking a glass. He felt the glass shatter under him and found himself staring straight down, for a second, into the taut gray latex lap of a woman who screamed explosively just before the table gave way. Something, probably her knee, clipped him hard in the side of the head.

He managed to get to his knees, holding his head, and found himself recalling an experiment they'd done in Science, back in Gainesville. Surface tension. You sprinkled pepper over the water in a glass. Brought the tip of a needle close to the film of pepper. Watched it spring back from the needle like a live thing. And he saw that happening here, his head ringing, but instead of pepper it was the crowd in the Western World, and he knew that the needle must be pointed at Rez's table.

The back of a white leather evening jacket. . . . But then he saw the Sherman tank come unmoored on the shoulders of the recoiling crowd, spinning toward him, huge and weightless, and the lights went out.

The crowd had been screaming anyway, but the dark twisted the communal pitch up into something that had Laney covering his ears. Or trying to, because someone stumbled into him and he went over, backward, instinctively curling into a tight fetal knot and clamping his hands across the back of his neck.

''Hey,'' said a voice, very close to his ear, ''get on up. You gonna get stepped on.'' It was Willy Jude. ''I can see.'' A hand around his wrist. ''Got infrared.''

Laney let the drummer pull him to his feet. ''What is it? What's happening?''

''Dunno, but come on. Gonna get worse—'' As if on cue, a terrible squeal of raw animal pain cut through the frenzied crowd-noise. ''Blackwell got one,'' Willy Jude said, and Laney felt the drummer's hand grip his belt. He stumbled as he was pulled along. Someone ran into him, shouted in Japanese. After that he kept his hands up, trying to protect his face, and went where the drummer pulled him.

Suddenly they were in a cove or pocket of relative quiet. ''Where are we?'' Laney asked.

''This way . . .'' Something clipped Laney across the shins. ''Stool,'' Willy Jude said. ''Sorry.'' Glass snapped beneath Laney's shoes.

A curve of greenish light, broken cursive hanging in the dark. Another few steps and he saw the Grotto. Willy Jude let go of his belt. ''You can see here, right? That bioluminescent stuff?''

''Yeah,'' Laney said. ''Thanks.''

''It doesn't register on my glasses. I get infrared off warm bodies, but I can't make out the steps. Walk me down.'' He took Laney's hand. They started down the stairs together. A black-clad trio of Japanese shot past them, leaving a high-heeled pump on the encrusted stairs, and vanished around the landing. Laney kicked the shoe out of Willy Jude's way and kept going.

When they rounded the corner at the landing, Arleigh was there, a green champagne bottle cocked over her shoulder. There was a smear of blood at the corner of her mouth, darker than her lipstick. When she saw Laney, she lowered the bottle. "Where were you?" she said.

"The Men's," Laney said.

"You missed the show."

"What happened?"

"Damn it," she said, "my coat's up there."

"Keep moving, keep moving," Willy Jude said.

More stairs, more landings, the rippling walls of the Grotto giving way to concrete. People kept rushing down, past them, knots and singles, taking the stairs too fast. Laney rubbed his ribs where he'd come down on the glass. It hurt, but somehow he hadn't been cut.

"They looked like Kombinat," Arleigh said. "Big ugly guys, bad outfits. I couldn't tell if they were after Rez or the idoru. Like they just thought they could walk in and do it."

"Do what?"

"Don't know," she said. "Kuwayama had at least a dozen of his own security people at the two closest tables. And Blackwell probably prays for a scene like that every night before he goes to bed. He reached into his jacket, then the lights went out."

"He put 'em out," Willy Jude said. "Some kinda

remote. He can see better in the dark than I can with these infrareds. Dunno how that is, but he can.''

``How'd you get out?'' Laney asked Arleigh.

``Flashlight. In my purse.''

``Laney-san . . .''

Looking back to see Yamazaki, one sleeve of his green plaid coat pulled free at the shoulder, his glasses missing a lens. Arleigh had taken a phone from her purse and was cursing softly as she tried to get it to work.

Yamazaki caught up with them at the next landing. The four of them continued down together, Laney still holding the blind drummer's hand.

When they reached the street, the Western World's sullen crew of doorpeople were nowhere in sight. A single policeman with a plastic rain-cover on his cap was muttering frantically into a microphone clipped to the front of his rain-cape. He was walking in tight circles as he did this, gesturing dramatically with a white baton at nothing in particular. Several kinds of alien siren were converging on the Western World, and Laney thought he could hear a helicopter.

Willy Jude dropped Laney's hand and adjusted his video-goggles to the street's light-level. ``Where's my car?''

Arleigh lowered her phone, which apparently was working now. ``You'd better come with us, Willy. Some kind of tactical unit is on the way . . .''

``Nothing like it,'' Rez said, and Laney turned, to see the singer emerging from the Western World, brushing something white from his dark jacket. "That physical thing. Too much time in the virtual, we forget that, don't we? You're Leyner?" Extending his hand.

"Laney," Laney said, as Arleigh's dark green van pulled up beside them.

28

A Matter of Credit

Maryalice opened a curved drawer that was built into the pink bed's headboard. She was wearing a black skirt-suit with big red Ashleigh Modine Carter–style sequin roses on the lapels. She took out a little blue glass dish and balanced it on her knee. "I hate these places," she said. "There's lots of ways to make sex ugly, but it's kind of hard to make it look this ridiculous." She knocked the gray end off her cigarette, into the blue saucer. "How old are you, anyway?"

"Fourteen," Chia said.

"About what I told 'em. You're fourteen, fifteen, for real, and no way you were on to me. I was on to *you,* right? It was my move. I planted on you. But they don't believe me. Say you're some kind of operator, say I'm just stupid, say that Rez guy sent you to SeaTac to get the stuff. Say you're a set-up and I'm crazy to believe a kid couldn't do that.'' She sucked on the cigarette, squinting. ''Where is it?'' She looked down at Chia's bag, open on the white carpet. ''There?''

''I didn't mean to take it. I didn't know it was there.''

''I know that,'' Maryalice said. ''What I told 'em. I meant to get it back off you at the club.''

''I don't understand any of this,'' Chia said. ''It just scares me.''

''Sometimes I bring stuff back for Eddie. Party favors for the club. It's illegal, but it's not all *that* illegal, you know? Not hard stuff, really. But this time he was doing something else on the side, something with the Russians, and I didn't like it. That's what scares me, that stuff. Like it's alive.''

''What stuff?''

''That. Assemblers, they're called.''

Chia looked at her bag. ''That thing in my bag is a nanotech assembler?''

''More like what you start with. Kind of an egg, or a little factory. You plug that thing into another machine that programs 'em, and they start building themselves out of whatever's handy. And when there's enough of 'em, they start building whatever it was you wanted them to. There's some kind of law against selling that stuff to the Kombinat, so they want it bad. But Eddie worked out a way to do it. I met these two creepy German guys in the SeaTac

Hyatt. They'd flown in there from wherever, I figured maybe Africa.'' She mashed the lit end of the cigarette into the little blue dish, making it smell even worse. ''They didn't want to give it to me, because they were expecting Eddie. Lot of back and forth on the phone. Finally they did. I was supposed to put it in the suitcase with the other stuff, but it made me nervous. Made me wanna self-medicate.'' She looked around the room. She put the blue dish with the crushed cigarette on a square black side table and did something that made the front of it open. It was a refrigerator, filled with little bottles. Maryalice bent over, peering in there. The pistol-shaped lighter slid off the pink bed. ''No tequila,'' Maryalice said. ''You tell me why anybody'd name a vodka 'Come Back Salmon' . . .'' Removing a little square bottle with a fish on its side. ''Japanese would, though.'' She looked down at the lighter. ''Like a Russian would make a cigarette lighter that looks like a pistol.''

Chia saw that Maryalice didn't have her hair-extensions in anymore. ''When they were taking DNA samples, in SeaTac,'' Chia said, ''you stuck the end of your extension in there . . .''

Maryalice cracked the seal on the little bottle, opened it, drained it in a single gulp, and shivered. ''Those extensions are all my own hair,'' she said. ''Grew 'em out when I was on sort of a health diet, understand? They catch people doing recreationals, when they take those hair samples. Some recreationals, they stay in your hair a long time.'' Maryalice put the empty bottle down beside the blue dish. ''What's he doing?'' Pointing at Masahiko.

''Porting,'' Chia said, unable to think of a quick way to explain the Walled City.

''I can see that. You came here 'cause these places'll re-post, right?''

''But you found us anyway.''

''I got connections with a cab company. I figured it was worth a try. But the Russians'll think of it, too, if they haven't already.''

''But how'd you get in? It was all locked.''

''I know my way around these places, honey. I know my way entirely too well.''

Masahiko removed the black cups that covered his eyes, saw Maryalice, looked down at the cups, then back up at Chia.

''Maryalice,'' Chia said.

Gomi Boy presented like a life-size anime of himself, huge eyes and even taller hair. ''Who drank the vodka?'' he asked.

''Maryalice,'' Chia said.

''Who's Maryalice?''

''She's in the room at the hotel,'' Chia said.

''That was the equivalent of twenty minutes porting,'' Gomi Boy said. ''How can there be someone in your room at the Hotel Di?''

''It's complicated,'' Chia said. They were back in Masahiko's room in the Walled City. They'd just clicked back, none of that maze-running like the first time. Past an icon reminding her she'd left her Venice open, but too late for that. Maybe once you were in here, you got back fast. But Masahiko'd said they had to, quick, there was trouble. Maryalice had said she didn't mind, but Chia didn't like it at all that Maryalice was in the room with them while they were porting.

"Your cashcard is good for twenty-six more minutes of room-time," Gomi Boy said. "Unless your friend hits the mini-bar again. Do you have an account in Seattle?"

"No," Chia said, "just my mother . . ."

"We've already looked at that," Masahiko said. "Your mother's credit would not sustain rental of the room plus porting charges. Your father—"

"My *father?*"

"Has an expense account with his employer in Singapore, a merchant bank—"

"How do you know that?"

Gomi Boy shrugged. "Walled City. We find things out. There are people here who know things."

"You can't tap into my father's account," Chia said. "It's for his job."

"Twenty-five minutes remaining," Masahiko said.

Chia pulled her goggles off. Maryalice was taking another miniature bottle from the little fridge. "Don't open that!"

Maryalice gave a guilty little shriek and dropped the bottle. "Just maybe some rice crackers," she said.

"Nothing," Chia said. "It's too expensive! We're running out of money!"

"Oh," Maryalice said, blinking. "Right. I don't have any, though. Eddie's cut my cards off, for sure, and the first time I plug one, he'll know exactly where I am."

Masahiko spoke to Chia without removing the eyecups. "We have your father's expense account on line . . ."

Maryalice smiled. "What we like to hear, right?"

Chia was pulling off her tip-sets. "You'll have to take it to them," she said to Maryalice, "the nano-thing. I'll give it to you now, you take it to them, give it to them, tell them it was all a mistake." She scooted on her hands and knees over to where her bag sat open on the floor. She dug for the thing, found it, held it out to Maryalice in what was left of the blue and yellow bag from the SeaTac duty-free. The dark gray plastic and the rows of little holes made it look like some kind of deformed designer pepper grinder. "Take it. Explain to them. Tell them it was just a mistake."

Maryalice cringed. "Put it back, okay?" She swallowed. "See, the problem isn't whether or not there's been a mistake. The problem's they'll kill us now anyway, because we know about it. And Eddie, he'll let 'em. 'Cause he has to. And 'cause he's just sort of generally fed up with me, the ungrateful little greasy shithead motherfucker . . ." Maryalice shook her head sadly. "It's about the end of our relationship, you ask me."

"Account accessed," Masahiko said. "Join us here now, please. You have another visitor."

Her Bad Side

Arleigh's van smelled of long-chain monomers and warm electronics. The rear scats had been removed to make room for the collection of black consoles, cabled together and wedged into place with creaking wads of bubble-pack.

Rez rode up front, beside the driver, the ponytailed Japanese Californian from Akihabara. Laney squatted on a console, between Arleigh and Yamazaki, with Willy Jude and the red-haired tech behind them. Laney's ribs hurt, where he'd come down on the table, and that seemed to be getting worse. He'd discovered that the top of his left sock was sticky with blood, but he wasn't sure where it had come from or even if it was his own.

Arleigh had her phone pressed to her ear. "Option

eight,'' she said, evidently to the driver, who touched the pad beside the dashboard map. Laney glimpsed Tokyo grid-segments whipping past on the screen. ''We're taking Rez back with us.''

''Take me to the Imperial,'' Rez said.

''Blackwell's orders,'' Arleigh said.

''Let me talk to him.'' Reaching back for the phone.

They swung left, into a wider street, their lights picking out a small crowd speedwalking away from the Western World, all of them trying to look as though they just happened to be there, out for a brisk stroll. The neighborhood was nondescript and generically urban and, aside from the guilty-looking speedwalkers, quite deserted.

''Keithy,'' Rez said, ''I want to go back to the hotel.'' The terrible white daystar of a police helicopter swept over them, carbon-black shadows speeding away across concrete. Rez was listening to the phone. They passed an all-night noodle wagon, its interior ghostly behind curtains of yellowed plastic. Images flicking past on a small screen behind the counter. Arleigh nudged Laney's knee, pointed past Rez's shoulder. A trio of white armored cars shot through the approaching intersection, blue lights flashing on their rectangular turrets, and vanished without a sound. Rez turned, handing the phone back to her. ''Keithy's being his para self. He wants me to go to your hotel and wait for him.''

Arleigh took the phone. "Does he know what it was about?"

"Autograph-hunters?" Rez started to turn back around in his seat.

"What happened to the idoru?" Laney asked.

Rez peered at him. "If you kidnapped that new platform—and I thought it was wonderful—what exactly would you have?"

"I don't know."

"Rei's only reality is the realm of ongoing serial creation," Rez said. "Entirely *process;* infinitely more than the combined sum of her various selves. The platforms sink beneath her, one after another, as she grows denser and more complex . . ." The long green eyes seemed to grow dreamy, in the light of passing storefronts, and then the singer turned away.

Laney watched Arleigh dab at the cut corner of her mouth with a tissue.

"Laney-san . . ." Yamazaki, a whisper. Putting something into his hand. A cabled set of eyephones. "We have global fan-activity database . . ."

His ribs hurt. Was his leg bleeding? "Later, okay?"

Arleigh's suite was at least twice as large as Laney's room. It had its own miniature sitting room, separated from the bedroom and bath with gilded French doors. The four chairs in the sitting room had very tall, very narrow backs, each one tapering to a rendition of the elf hat, done in sandblasted steel. These chairs were quite amazingly uncomfortable, and Laney was hunched forward on one now, in considerable pain, hugging his bruised ribs. The blood in his sock had turned out to be his own, from a skinned patch on his left shin. He'd plastered it over with micropore from the professional-looking first-aid kit in Arleigh's bathroom. He doubted there was anything there for his ribs, but he was wondering if some kind of elastic bandage might help.

Yamazaki was on the chair to his right, reattaching the sleeve of his plaid jacket with bright gold safety pins from an Evil Elf Hat emergency sewing kit. Laney had never actually seen anyone use a hotel room's emergency sewing kit for anything. Yamazaki had removed his damaged glasses and was working with the jacket held close to his face. This made him look older, and somehow calmer. To Yamazaki's right, the red-haired technician, who was called Shannon, was sitting up very straight and reading a complimentary style magazine.

Rez was sprawled on the bed, propped up on the maximum available number of pillows, and Willy Jude sat at its foot, channel-surfing with his video units. The panic at the Western World apparently hadn't made the news yet, although the drummer said he'd caught an oblique reference on one of the clubbing channels.

Arleigh was standing by the window, pressing an ice cube in a white washcloth against her swollen lip.

"Did he give you any idea of when he might turn up?" Rez, from the bed.

"No," Arleigh said, "but he made it clear he wanted you to wait."

Rez sighed.

"Let the people take care of you, Rez," Willy Jude said. "It's what they're paid for."

Laney had taken it for granted that all of them were expected to wait, along with Rez, for Blackwell. Now he decided to try to return to his room. All they could do was stop him.

Blackwell opened the door from the corridor, pocketing something black, something that definitely wasn't your standard-issue hotel key. There was a pale X of micropore across his right cheek, the longest arm reaching the tip of his chin.

"Evening, Keithy," Rez said.

"You really mustn't piss off like that," the bodyguard said. "Those Russians are a serious crew. Massive triers, those boys. Wouldn't do if they got hold of you, Rozzer. Not at all. You wouldn't like it."

"Kuwayama and the platform?"

"Have to tell you, Rez." Blackwell stood at the foot of the bed. "I've seen you go with women I wouldn't take to a shit-fight on a dark night, but at least they were human. Hear what I'm saying?"

"I do, Keithy," the singer said. "I know how you feel about her. But you'll come around. It's the way of things, Keithy. The new way. New world."

"I don't know anything about that. My old dad was

a Painter and Docker; had a docky's brief. Broke his heart I turned out the sort of crim I did. Died before you'd got me out of B Division. Would've liked him to see me assume responsibility, Rez. For you. For your safety. But now I don't know. Might not impress him so. Might tell me I'm just minding a fool with a bloated sense of himself."

Rez came up off the bed, surprising Laney with his speed, a performer's grace, and then he was in front of Blackwell, his hands on the huge shoulders. "But you don't think that, do you, Keithy? You didn't in Pentridge. Not when you came for me. And not when I came back for you."

Blackwell's eyes glistened. He was about to say something, but Yamazaki suddenly stood up, blinking, and put his green plaid sportscoat on. He craned his neck, peering nearsightedly at the pins he'd used to mend it, then seemed to realize that everyone in the suite was looking at him. He coughed nervously and sat back down.

A silence followed. "Out of line, I was, Rozzer," Blackwell said, breaking it.

Rez clapped the bodyguard's shoulder, releasing him. "Stressed. I know." Rez smiled. "Kuwayama? The platform?"

"Had his own team there."

"And our crashers?"

"That's a bit odd," Blackwell said. "Kombinat, Rez. Say we've stolen something of theirs. Or at least that's all the one I questioned knew."

Rez looked puzzled, but seemed to put whatever it was out of his mind. "Take me back to the hotel," he said.

Blackwell checked his huge steel watch. "We're still sweeping there. Another twenty minutes and I'll check with them."

Laney took this as his opportunity, standing up and stepping past Blackwell to the door. "I'm going to take a hot shower," he said. "Cracked my ribs up there." No one said anything. "Call if you need me." Then he opened the door, stepped out, closed it behind him, and limped in what he hoped was the direction of the elevator.

It was. In it, he leaned against the mirrored wall and touched the button for his floor.

It said something in a soothing tone, Japanese.

The door closed. He shut his eyes.

He opened his eyes as the door opened. Stepped out, turned the wrong way, then the right way. Fishing for his wallet, where he'd put his key. Still there. Bath, hot shower, these concepts more theoretical as he approached his room. Sleep. That was it. Undress and lie down and not be conscious.

He swiped the key down the slot. Nothing. Again. Click.

Kathy Torrance, sitting on the edge of his bed. She smiled at him. Pointed at the moving figures on the screen. One of whom was Laney, naked, with a larger erection than he recalled ever having had. The girl vaguely familiar, but whoever she was, he didn't remember doing that with her.

"Don't just stand there," Kathy said. "You have to see this."

"That's not me," Laney said.

"I know," she said, delighted. "He's *way* too big. And I'd *love* to see you try to prove it."

The Etruscan

Chia worked the tips back on, regoggled, let Masahiko take her to his room. That same instant transition, the virtual Venice icon strobing. . . . Gomi Boy was there, and someone else, though at first she couldn't see him. Just this glass tumbler on the work-surface that hadn't been there before, mapped to a higher resolution than the rest of the room: filthy, chipped at the rim, something crusted at the bottom.

"That woman," Gomi Boy began, but someone coughed. A strange dry rattle.

"You *are* an interesting young woman," said a voice unlike any Chia had heard, a weird, attenuated rasp that might have been compiled from a library of faint, dry, random sounds. So that a word's long vowel might be wires in the wind, or the click of a consonant, the rattle of a dead leaf against a window. "*Young* woman," it said again, and then there was something indescribable, which she guessed was meant as laughter.

"This is the Etruscan," Masahiko said. "The Etruscan accessed your father's expense account for us. He is most skilled."

Something there for a second. Skull-like. Above the dirty glass. The mouth drawn and petulant. "It was nothing, really . . ."

She told herself it was all presentation. Like when Zona presented, you could never quite focus on her. This was like that, but more extreme. And a lot of work put into the audio. But she didn't like it.

"You brought me here to meet him?" she asked Masahiko.

"Oh, no," said the Etruscan, the *Oh* a polyphonic chorale, "I just wanted a look, dear." The thing like laughter.

"The woman," Gomi Boy said. "Did you arrange for her to meet you, at Hotel Di?"

"No," Chia said. "She checked the taxi cabs, so you aren't as smart as you think."

"Well put." The *put* the sound of a single pebble falling into a dry marble fountain. Chia focused on the glass. A huge centipede lay curled at its bottom, a thing the color of dead cuticle. She saw that it had tiny, pink hands—

The glass was gone.

"Sorry," Masahiko said. "He wished only to meet you."

"Who is the woman in Hotel Di?" Gomi Boy's anime eyes were bright and eager, but his tone was hard.

"Maryalice," Chia said. "Her boyfriend's with those Russians. The thing they're after's in my bag there."

"What thing?"

"Maryalice says it's a nano-assembler."

"Unlikely," Gomi Boy said.

"Tell it to the Russians."

"But you have contraband? In the room?"

"I've got something they want."

Gomi Boy grimaced, vanished.

"Where'd he go?"

"This changes the situation," Masahiko said. "You did not tell us you have contraband."

"You didn't ask! You didn't ask why they were looking for me . . ."

Masahiko shrugged, calm as ever. "We were not certain that it was you they were interested in. The Kombinat would be very eager for the skills of someone like the Etruscan, for instance. Many people know of Hak Nam, but few know how to enter. We reacted to protect the integrity of the city."

"But your computer's in the hotel room. They can just come there and get it."

"It no longer matters," he said. "I am no longer engaged in processing. My duties are assumed by others. Gomi Boy is concerned now for his safety outside, you understand? Penalties for possession of contraband are harsh. He is particularly vulnerable, because he deals in second-hand equipment.''

''I don't think it's the police you want to worry about, right now. I think we want to *call* the police. Maryalice says those Russians'll kill us, if they find us.''

''The police would not be a good idea. The Etruscan has accessed your father's account in Singapore. That is a crime.''

''I think I'd rather get arrested than killed.''

Masahiko considered that. ''Come with me,'' he said. ''Your visitor is waiting.''

''Not the centipede,'' Chia said. ''Forget it.''

''No,'' he said, ''not the Etruscan. Come.''

And they were out of his room, fast-forward through the maze of Hak Nam, up twisted stairwells and through corridors, the strange, compacted world flickering past. . . . ''What *is* this place? A communal site, right? But what are you so worried about? Why's it all a secret?''

''Walled City is of the net, but not on it. There are no laws here, only agreements.''

''You can't be on the net and *not* be on the net,'' Chia said, as they shot up a final flight of stairs.

''Distributed processing,'' he said. ''Interstitial. It began with a shared killfile—''

''Zona!'' There across this uneven roofscape, overgrown with strangeness.

"Touch nothing. Some are traps. I come to you." Zona, presenting in that quick, fragmentary way, moved forward.

To Chia's right, a kind of ancient car lay tilted in a drift of random textures, something like a Christmas tree growing from its unbroken windshield. Beyond that . . .

She guessed that the rooftops of the Walled City were its dumping ground, but the things abandoned there were like objects out of a dream, bit-mapped fantasies discarded by their creators, their jumbled shapes and textures baffling the eye, the attempt to sort and decipher them inducing a kind of vertigo. Some were moving.

Then a movement high in the gasoline sky caught her eye. Zona's bird-things?

"I went to your site," Chia said. "You weren't there, something—"

"I know. Did you see it?" As Zona passed the Christmas tree, its round, silver ornaments displayed black eye-holes, each pair turning to follow her.

"No. I thought I heard it."

"I do not know what it is." Zona's presentation was even quicker and more jumpy than usual. "I came here for advice. They told me that you had been to my site, and that now you were here . . ."

"You know this place?"

"Someone here helped me establish my site. It is impossible to come here without an invitation, you understand? My name is on a list. Although I cannot go below, into the city itself, unaccompanied.''

''Zona, I'm in so much trouble now! We're hiding in this horrible hotel, and Maryalice is there—''

''This bitch who made you her mule, yes? She is where?''

''In the room at this hotel. She said she broke up with her boyfriend, and it's his, the nano-thing—''

''The what?''

''She says it's some kind of nano-assembler thing.''

Zona Rosa's features snapped into focus as her heavy eyebrows shot up. ''Nanotechnology?''

''This is in your bag?'' Masahiko asked.

''Wrapped in plastic.''

''One moment.'' He vanished.

''Who is that?'' Zona asked.

''Masahiko. Mitsuko's brother. He lives here.''

''Where did he go?''

''Back to the hotel we're porting from.''

''This shit you are in, it is crazy,'' Zona said.

''Please, Zona, help me! I don't think I'll ever get home!''

Masahiko reappeared, the thing in his hand minus the duty-free bag. ''I scanned it,'' he said. ''Immediate identification as Rodel-van Erp primary biomolecular programming module C-slash-7A. This is a lab prototype. We are unable to determine its exact legal status, but the production model, C-slash-9E, is Class 1 nanotechnology, proscribed under international law. Japanese law, conviction of illegal possession of Class 1 device carries automatic life sentence."

"Life?" Chia said.

"Same for thermonuclear device," he said, apologetically, "poison gas, biological weapon." He held up the scanned object for Zona's inspection.

Zona looked at it. "Fuck your mother," she said, her tone one of somber respect.

The Way Things Work

"See how things work, Laney? 'What goes around, comes around'? 'You can run, but you can't hide'? Know those expressions, Laney? How some things get to be clichés because they touch on certain truths, Laney? Talk to me, Laney."

Laney lowered himself into one of the miniature armchairs, hugging his ribs.

"You look like shit, Laney. Where have you been?"

"The Western World," he said. He didn't like watching himself do those things on the screen, but he found he couldn't look away. He knew that wasn't him, there. They'd mapped his face onto someone else. But it was his face. He remembered hearing something someone had said about mirrors, a long time ago, that they were somehow unnatural and dangerous.

"So you're trying your hand at the Orient now?"

She hadn't understood, he thought, which meant she didn't know where he'd been, earlier. Which meant they hadn't been watching him here. "That's that guy," he said, "that Hillman. From the day I met you. My job interview. He was a porno extra."

"Don't you think he's being awfully rough with her?"

"Who is she, Kathy?"

"Think back. If you can remember Clinton Hillman, Laney . . ."

Laney shook his head.

"Think actor, Laney. Think Alison Shires . . ."

"His daughter," Laney said, no doubt at all.

"I definitely think that's too rough. That borders on rape, Laney. Assault. I think we could make a case for assault."

"Why would she do that? How could you get her to do that?" Turning from the screen to Kathy. "I mean, unless it really is rape."

"Let's hear the soundtrack, Laney. See what you're saying, there. Cast some light on motive . . ."

"Don't," he said. "I don't want to hear it."

"You're talking about her father the whole time, Laney. I mean, obsession is one thing, but just droning on about him that way, right through a white-knuckle skull-fuck—"

He almost fell, coming up out of the chair. He

couldn't find the manual controls. Wires back there. He pulled out the first three he found. Third did it.

"Put it on the Lo/Rez tab, Laney? Rock and roll lifestyle? Aren't you supposed to throw them out the window, though?"

"What's it about, Kathy? You want to just tell me now?"

She smiled at him. Exactly the smile he remembered from his job interview. "May I call you Colin?"

"Kathy: fuck you."

She laughed. "We may have come full circle, Laney."

"How's that?"

"Think of this as a job interview."

"I've got a job."

"We're offering you another, Laney. You can moonlight."

Laney made it back to the chair. Lowered himself in as slowly as possible. The pain made him gasp.

"What's wrong?"

"Ribs. Hurt." He found a way to settle back that seemed to help.

"Were you in a fight? Is that blood?"

"I went to a club."

"This is Tokyo, Laney. They don't have fights in clubs."

"That was really her, the daughter?"

"It certainly is. And she'll be more than happy to talk about it on Slitscan, Laney. Seduced into sadistic sex games by a stalker obsessed with her famous, her loving dad. Who has come around, by the way. Who is one of ours now.''

''Why? Why would she do that? Because he told her to?''

''Because,'' Kathy said, looking at him as though she were concerned that he might have sustained brain damage as well, ''she's an aspiring actress in her own right, Laney.'' She looked at him hopefully, as though he might suddenly start to process. ''The big break.''

''*That* is going to be her big break?''

''A break,'' Kathy Torrance said, ''is a break. And you know something? I'm trying, I'm trying really hard, to give *you* one instead. Right now. And it wouldn't be the first, would it?''

The phone began to ring. ''You'd better take this,'' she said, passing him the white slab of cedar.

''Yes?''

''The fan-activity data-base.'' It was Yamazaki. ''You must access it now.''

''Where are you?''

''In hotel garage. With van.''

''Look, I'm in kind of rough shape, here. Can it wait?''

''Wait?'' Yamazaki sounded horrified.

Laney looked at Kathy Torrance. She was wearing something black and not quite short enough to show her tattoo. Her hair was shorter now. ''I'll be down when I can. Keep it open for me.'' He hung up before Yamazaki could reply.

''What was that about?''

''Shiatsu.''

''You're lying.''

''What do you want, Kathy? What's the deal?''

''Him. I want him. I want a way in. I want to know what he's doing. I want to know what he thinks he's doing, trying to screw a piece of Japanese software.''

''Marry,'' Laney said.

Her smile vanished. ''You don't correct me, Laney.''

''You want me to spy on him.''

''Research.''

''Balls.''

''You wish.''

''If I got anything you could use, you'd want me to set him up.''

The smile returned. ''Let's not get ahead of ourselves.''

''And I get?''

''A life. A life in which you haven't been branded an obsessive stalker who preyed on the attractive daughter of the object of your obsession. A life in which it isn't public knowledge that a series of disastrous pharmaceutical trials permanently and hideously rewired you. Fair enough?''

''What about her? The daughter. She do all that with the Hillman guy for nothing?''

"Your call, Laney. Work for us, get me what I need, she's shit out of luck."

"That easy? She'd go along with that? After what she had to do?"

"If she wants even the remotest hope of having a career eventually—yes."

Laney looked at her. "That isn't me. It's a morph. If I could prove it was a morph, I could sue you."

"Really? You could afford that, could you? It takes years. And even then, you might not win. We've got a lot of money and talent to throw at problems like that, Laney. We do it all the time." The door chimed. "That'll be mine," she said. She got up, went to the door, touched the security screen. Laney glimpsed part of a man's face. She opened the door. It was Rice Daniels, minus his trademark sunglasses. "Rice is with us now, Laney," she said. "He's been a terrific help with your backgrounder."

"Out of Control didn't work out?" Laney asked Daniels.

Daniels showed Laney a lot of very white teeth. "I'm sure we could work together, Laney. I hope you don't have any issues around what happened."

"Issues," Laney said.

Kathy walked back, handed Laney a blank white card with a pencilled number. "Call me. Before nine tomorrow. Leave a message. Yes or no."

"You're giving me a choice?"

"It's more fun that way. I want you to *think* about it." She reached down and flicked the collar of Laney's shirt. "Stitch-count," she said. Turned and walked out, Daniels pulling the door shut behind them.

Laney sat there, staring at the closed door, until the phone began to ring.

It was Yamazaki.

The Uninvited

"We must *attack,*" said Zona Rosa, punctuating it with a quick shift to Aztec death's-head mode. They were with Masahiko and Gomi Boy now, back in Masahiko's room in the Walled City, away from the hypnotic chaos of the crawling roofscape.

"Attack?" Gomi Boy's huge eyes bulged as brightly as ever, but his voice betrayed his tension. "Who will you attack?"

"We will find a way to carry the fight to the enemy," Zona Rosa said, gravely. "Passivity is death."

Something that looked to Chia like a bright orange drink coaster came gliding in under Masahiko's door and across the floor, but the shadow-thing gobbled it before she could get a closer look.

"*You,*" said Gomi Boy to Zona Rosa, "are in

Mexico City. *You* are not physically or legally endangered by *any* of this!''

''Physically?'' said Zona Rosa, snapping back into a furious version of her previous presentation. ''You want *physically,* son of a bitch? I'll fucking kill you, physically! You think I can't do that? You think you live on Mars or something? I fly here Aeronaves direct with my girls, we find you, we cut your Japanese balls off! You think I can't do that?'' The saw-toothed, dragon-handled switchblade was out now, quivering, in front of Gomi Boy's face.

''Zona, *please,*'' Chia begged. ''He hasn't done anything so far but help me! Don't!''

Zona snorted. The blade reversed, vanishing. ''You don't push me,'' she said to Gomi Boy. ''My friend, she is in some bad shit, and I have some ghost-bastard *thing* on my site . . .''

''It's in the software on my Sandbenders, too,'' Chia said. ''I saw it in Venice.''

''You *saw* it?'' The fractured images cycling faster.

''I saw *some*thing—''

''What? You saw *what?*''

''Someone. By the fountain at the end of a street. It might have been a woman. I was scared. I bailed. I left my Venice open—''

''Show me,'' Zona said. ''In my site I could not see it. My lizards could not see it either, but they grew agitated. The birds flew lower, but could find nothing. Show me this thing!''

''But Zona—''

"Now!" Zona said. "It is part of this shit you are in. It must be."

"My God," Zona said, staring up at St. Mark's. "Who wrote this?"

"It's a city in Italy," Chia said. "It used to be a country. They invented banking. That's St. Mark's. There's a module where you can see what they do at Easter, when the Patriarch brings out all these bones and things, set into gold, parts of saints."

Zona Rosa crossed herself. "Like Mexico . . . this is where the water comes up to the bottoms of the doors, and the streets, they are water?"

"I think a lot of this is *under* water now," Chia said.

"Why is it dark?"

"I keep it that way . . ." Chia looked away, searching the shadows beneath archways. "That Walled City, Zona, what *is* that?"

"They say it began as a shared killfile. You know what a killfile is?"

"No."

"It is an old expression. A way to avoid incoming messages. With the killfile in place, it was like those messages never existed. They never reached you. This was when the net was new, understand?"

Chia knew that when her mother was born, there had been no net at all, or almost none, but as her teachers in school were fond of pointing out, that was hard to imagine. "How could that become a city? And why's it all squashed in like that?"

"Someone had the idea to turn the killfile inside out. This is not really how it happened, you understand, but this is how the story is told: that the people who founded Hak Nam were angry, because the net had been very free, you could do what you wanted, but then the governments and the companies, they had different ideas of what you could, what you couldn't do. So these people, they found a way to unravel something. A little place, a piece, like cloth. They made something like a killfile of *everything,* everything they didn't like, and they turned that inside out." Zona's hands moved like a conjurer's. "And they pushed it through, to the other side . . ."

"The other side of *what?*"

"This is not how they did it," Zona said impatiently, "this is the *story.* How they did it, I don't know. But that is the story, how they tell it. They went there to get away from the laws. To have no laws, like when the net was new."

"But why'd they make it look like that?"

"That I know," Zona said. "The woman who came to help me build my country, she told me. There was a place near an airport, Kowloon, when Hong Kong wasn't China, but there had been a mistake, a long time ago, and that place, very small, many people, it still belonged to China. So there was no law there. An outlaw place. And more and more people crowded in; they built it up, higher. No rules, just building, just people living. Police wouldn't go there. Drugs and whores and gambling. But people living, too. Factories, restaurants. A city. No laws."

"Is it still there?"

"No," Zona said, "they tore it down before it all became China again. They made a park with concrete. But these people, the ones they say made a hole in the net, they found the data. The history of it. Maps. Pictures. They built it again."

"Why?"

"Don't ask me. Ask them. They are all crazy." Zona was scanning the Piazza. "This place makes me cold . . ." Chia considered bringing the sun up, but then Zona pointed. "Who is that?"

Chia watched her Music Master, or something that looked like him, stroll toward them from the shadows of the stone arches where the cafes were, a dark greatcoat flapping to reveal a lining the color of polished lead.

"I've got a software agent that looks like that," Chia said, "but he isn't supposed to be there unless I cross a bridge. And I couldn't find him, when I was here before."

"This is not the one you saw?"

"No," Chia said.

An aura bristled around Zona, who grew taller as the spikey cloud of light increased in resolution. Shifting, overlapping planes like ghosts of broken glass. Iridescent insects whirling there.

As the figure in the greatcoat drew toward them

across the Piazza's patchworked stone, snow resolved behind it; it left footprints.

Zona's aura bristled with gathering menace, a thunderhead of flickering darkness forming above the shattered sheets of light. There was a sound that reminded Chia of one of those blue-light bug-zappers popping a particularly juicy one, and then vast wings cut the air, so close: Zona's Colombian condors, things from the data-havens. And gone. Zona spat a stream of Spanish that overwhelmed translation, a long and liquid curse.

Behind the advancing figure of her Music Master, Chia saw the facades of the great square vanish entirely behind curtains of snow.

Zona's switchblade seemed the size of a chainsaw now, its toothed spine rippling, alive. The golden dragons from the plastic handles chased their fire-maned double tails around her brown fist, through miniature clouds of Chinese embroidery. "I'll take you *out*," Zona said, as if savoring each word.

Chia saw the world of snow that had swallowed her Venice abruptly contract, shrinking, following the line of footprints, and the features of the Music Master became those of Rei Toei, the idoru.

"You already have," said the idoru.

Topology

Arleigh was waiting for him by the elevator, on the fifth and lowest of the hotel's parking levels. She'd changed back into the work clothes he'd first seen her in. Despite the patch of micropore on her swollen lip, the jeans and nylon bomber jacket made her look wide-awake and competent, two things Laney felt he might never be again.

"You look terrible," she said.

The ceiling here was very low, and flocked with something drab and wooly, to reduce noise. Lines of bioluminescent cable were bracketed to it, and the unmoving air was heavy with the sugary smell of exhausted gasohol. Spotless ranks of small Japanese cars glittered like bright wet candy. "Yamazaki seemed to feel it was urgent," Laney said.

"If you don't do it now," she said, "we don't know how long it'll take to get it all up and running again."

"So we'll do it."

"You don't look like you should even be walking."

He started walking, unsteadily, as if by way of demonstration. "Where's Rez?"

"Blackwell's taken him back to his hotel. The sweep team didn't find anything. This way." She led him along a line of surgically clean grills and bumpers. He saw the green van parked with its front to the wall, its hatch and doors open. It was fenced behind orange plastic barricades, and surrounded by the black modules. Shannon, the red-haired tech, was doing something to a red and black cube centered on a folding plastic table.

"What's that?" Laney asked.

"Espresso," he said, his hand inside the housing, "but I think the gasket's warped."

"Sit here, Laney," Arleigh said, indicating the van's front passenger seat. "It reclines."

Laney climbed up into the seat. "Don't try it," he said. "You might not be able to wake me up."

Yamazaki appeared, over Arleigh's shoulder, blinking. "You will access the Lo/Rez data as before, Laney-san, but you will simultaneously access the fan-activity base. Depth of field. Dimensionality. The fan-activity data providing the degree of personalization you require. Parallax, yes?"

Arleigh handed Laney the eyephones. ''Have a look,'' she said. ''If it doesn't work, to hell with it.'' Yamazaki flinched. ''Either way, we'll go and find you the hotel doctor, after.''

Laney settled his neck against the seat's headrest and put the 'phones on.

Nothing. He closed his eyes. Heard the 'phones power up. Opened his eyes to those same faces of data he'd seen earlier, in Akihabara. Characterless. Institutional in their regularity.

''Here comes the fan club,'' he heard Arleigh say, and the barren faces were suddenly translucent, networked depths of postings and commentary revealed there in baffling organic complexity.

''Something's—'' he started to say, but then he was back in the apartment in Stockholm, with the huge ceramic stoves. But it was a place this time, not just a million tidily filed factoids. Shadows of flames danced behind the narrow mica panes of the stove's ornate iron door.

Candlelight. The floors were wooden planks, each one as broad as Laney's shoulders, spread with the soft tones of old carpets. Something directed his point of view into the next room, past a leather sofa spread with more and smaller rugs, and showed him the black window beyond the open drapes, where snowflakes, very large and ornate, fell with a deliberate gravity past the frosted panes.

''Getting anything?'' Arleigh. Somewhere far away.

He didn't answer, watching as his view reversed. To be maneuvered down a central hallway, where a tall oval mirror showed no reflection as he passed. He thought of CD-ROMs he'd explored in the orphanage: haunted castles, monstrously infested spacecraft abandoned in orbit. . . . Click here. Click there. And somehow he'd always felt that he never found the central marvel, the thing that would have made the hunt worthwhile. Because it wasn't there, he'd finally decided; it never quite was, and so he'd lost interest in those games.

But the central marvel here—click on bedroom—was Rei Toei. Propped on white pillows at the head of a sea of white, her head and gowned shoulders showing above eyelet lace and the glow of fine cottons.

"You were our guest tonight," she said. "I wasn't able to speak with you. I am sorry. It ended badly, and you were injured."

He looked at her, waiting for the mountain valleys and the bells, but she only looked back, nothing came, and he remembered what Yamazaki had said about bandwidth.

A stab of pain in his side. "How do you know? That I was injured?"

"The preliminary Lo/Rez security report. Technician Paul Shannon states that you appeared to have been injured."

"Why are you here?" ("Laney," he heard Arleigh say, "are you okay?")

"I found it," the idoru said. "Isn't it wonderful? But he has not been here since the renovations were completed. So, really, he's never been here. But you've been here before, haven't you? I think that's how I found it." She smiled. She was very beautiful here, floating in this whiteness. He hadn't been able to really look at her in the Western World.

"I accessed it earlier," he said, "but it wasn't like this."

"But then it . . . rounded out, didn't it? It became so much better. Because one of the artisans who reassembled the stoves had made a record of it all, when it was done. Just for herself, for her friends, but you see what it's done. It was in the data from the fan club." She gazed in delight at a single taper, banded horizontally in cream and indigo, that burned in a candlestick of burnished brass. Beside it on the bedside table were a book and an orange. "I feel very close to him, here."

"I'd feel closer to him if you'd put me back, outside."

"In the street? It's snowing. And I'm not certain the street is there."

"In the general data-construct. Please. So I can do my job . . ."

"Oh," she said, and smiled at him, and he was staring into the tangled depths of the data-faces.

"Laney?" Arleigh said, touching his shoulder. "Who are you talking to?"

"The idoru," Laney said.

"In nodal manifestation?" Yamazaki.

"No. She was there in the data, I don't know how. She was in a model of his place in Stockholm. Said she got there because I'd cruised it before. Then I asked her to put me back out here . . ."

"Out where?" Arleigh asked.

"Where I can see," Laney said, staring down into intricately overgrown canyons, dense with branchings that reminded him of Arleigh's Realtree 7.2, but organic somehow, every segment thickly patched with commentary. "Yamazaki was right. The fan stuff seems to do it."

He heard Gerrard Delouvrier, back in the TIDAL labs, urge him *not* to focus. *What you do, it is opposite of the concentration, but we will learn to direct it.*

Drift. Down through deltas of former girlfriends, degrees of confirmation of girlfriendhood, personal sightings of Rez or Lo together with whichever woman in whatever public place, each account illuminated with the importance the event had held for whoever had posted it. This being for Laney the most peculiar aspect of this data, the perspective in which these two loomed. Human in every detail but then not so. Everything scrupulously, fanatically accurate, probably, but always assembled around the hollow armature of celebrity. He could *see* celebrity here, not like Kathy's idea of a primal substance, but as a paradoxical quality inherent in the substance of the world. He saw that the quantity of data accumulated here by the band's fans was much greater than everything the band themselves had ever generated. And their actual art, the music and the videos, was the merest fragment of that.

"But this is my favorite," Laney heard the idoru say, and then he was watching Rez mount a low stage in a crowded club of some kind, everything psychedelic Korean pinks, hypersaturated tints like cartoon versions of the flesh of tropical melons. "It is what we feel." Rez raised a microphone and began to speak of new modes of being, of something he called "the alchemical marriage."

And somewhere Arleigh's hand was on his arm, her voice tense. "Laney? Sorry. We need you back here now. Mr. Kuwayama is here."

34

Casino

Chia looked out between the dusty slats, to the street where it was raining. The idoru had done that. Chia had never made it rain, in Venice, but she didn't mind the way it looked. It seemed to fit. It was like Seattle.

The idoru said this apartment was called a casino. Chia had seen casinos on television and they hadn't looked anything like this. This was a few small rooms with flaking plaster walls, and big old-fashioned furniture with gold lion-feet. Everything worked up with fractals so you could almost smell it. It would've smelled dusty, she thought, and also like perfume. Chia hadn't been to many of these modules, the insides of her Venice, because they were all sort of creepy. They didn't give her the feeling she got in the streets.

Zona's head, on the lion-footed table, made that bug-zap sound. She'd reduced herself to that, Zona: this little blue neon miniature of her Aztec skull, about the size of a small apple. Because Chia had told her to shut up and put the switchblade away. And that had pissed her off, and maybe hurt her feelings, but Chia hadn't known what else to do. Chia had wanted to hear what the idoru had had to say, and Zona's I'm-dangerous act totally got in the way. And that was all it was, just acting out, because people couldn't really hurt each other when they were ported. Not physically, anyway. And that had always been a problem, with Zona. That whole swelling-up thunderhead macho thing. Kelsey and the others would make fun of it, but Zona was fierce enough, verbally, that they'd only do it behind her back. Chia had never known what to make of it; it was like Zona's personality wasn't together, around acting like that.

Now Zona wasn't talking, just making the bug-zap sound every so often, to remind Chia she was still there and still pissed off.

The idoru was talking, though, telling Chia the old Venetian meaning of the word *casino,* not some giant sort of mall place where people went to gamble and watch shows, but something that sounded more like what Masahiko had said about love hotels. Like people had houses where they lived, but these casinos, these secret little apartments, hidden around town, were where they went to be with other people. But they hadn't been too comfortable there, not to judge by this one, even though the idoru kept adding more and more candles. The idoru said she loved candles.

The idoru had the Music Master's haircut now; it made her look like a girl pretending to be a boy. She seemed to like his greatcoat, too, because she kept turning on her heel—his heel—to twirl the hem out. "I've seen so many new places," she said, smiling at Chia, "so many different people and things."

—So have I, but . . .

"He told me it would be this way, but I had no idea, really." Twirl. "Having seen all this, I'm so much *more* . . . Does it feel like that for you, when you travel?"

The death's-head emitted a burst of blue light and a sound like a short, sharp fart. "Zona!" Chia hissed. Then all in a rush, to the idoru, "I haven't traveled much and so far I don't think I like it, but we just came here to see what you were, because we didn't know, because you're in my software, and maybe in Zona's site, too, and that bothers her because it's supposed to be private."

"The country with the beautiful sky?"

"Yeah," Chia said. "You aren't really supposed to be able to go there unless she asks you."

"I didn't know. I'm sorry." The idoru looked sad. "I thought I could go anywhere—except where you come from."

"Seattle?"

"The hive of dreams," said the idoru, "windows heaped against the sky. I can see the pictures, but there is no path. I know you've come from there, but its *there* . . . isn't there!''

''The Walled City?'' It had to be, because that was where she and Zona were coming from now. ''We're only ported through. Zona's in Mexico City and I'm in this hotel, okay? And we really better go back now, 'cause I don't know what's happening—''

The blue skull expanded and went Zonaform, grim and sullen. ''Finally you say something worthwhile. Why do you speak with this thing? She is nothing, only a more expensive version of this toy of yours she's stolen and taken over. Now that I have seen her, I can only think that Rēz is crazy, pathetically deluded . . .''

''But he isn't crazy,'' the idoru said. ''It is what we *feel* together. He has told me that we will not be understood, not at first, and there will be resistance, hostility. But we mean no harm, and he believes that in the end only good can come from our union.''

''You synthetic bitch,'' Zona said. ''You think we don't see what you're doing? You aren't real! You aren't as real as this imitation of a drowned city! You're a made-up thing, and you want to suck what's real out of him!'' Chia saw the thunderhead, the aura, starting to build. ''This girl crossed the ocean to find you out, and now her life is in danger, and she is too stupid to see that you are the cause!''

The idoru looked at Chia. ''Your life?''

Chia had to swallow. ''Maybe,'' she said. ''I don't know. I'm scared.''

And the idoru was gone, draining from Chia's Music Master like a color that had no name. He stood there in the light of twenty candles, his expression unreadable. "I'm sorry," he said, "but what exactly was it we were discussing?"

"We weren't," said Chia, then her goggles were lifted away, taking the Music Master and the room in Venice and Zona with them, and two of the fingers of the hand that held the goggles was ringed with gold, each ring linked to a gold watch's massive bracelet with its own fine length of chain. Pale eyes looked into hers.

Eddie smiled.

Chia drew her breath in to scream, and another hand, not Eddie's, but large and white, smelling of metallic perfume, covered her mouth and nose. And a hand on her shoulder, pressing down, as Eddie stepped back, letting the goggles fall to the white carpet.

Holding her gaze, Eddie raised one finger to his lips, smiled, and said "Shhhh." Then stepped aside, turning away, so that Chia saw Masahiko sitting there on the floor, the black cups over his eyes, his fingers moving in their tip-sets.

Eddie took something black from his pocket and reached Masahiko in two silent, exaggerated steps. He did something to the black thing and bent down with it. She saw it touch Masahiko's neck.

Masahiko's muscles all seemed to jerk at once, his legs straightening, throwing him sideways, where he lay on the white carpet, twitching, his mouth open. One of the black cups had come off. The other still covered his right eye.

Eddie turned back, looking at her.

"Where is it?" he said.

The Testbed of Futurity

Shannon offered Laney a tall foam cup with half an inch of very hot, very black coffee in it. Beyond him, past the orange barricades, was a long white Land-Rover with integral crash-bars and green-tinted windows. Kuwayama waited there, in a dark gray suit, his rimless glasses glinting in the greenish light from the cable overhead. A black-suited driver stood beside him.

"What's he want?" Laney asked Arleigh, tasting Shannon's espresso. It left grit on his tongue.

"We don't know," said Arleigh. "But apparently Rez told him where to find us."

"Rez?"

"That's what he said."

Yamazaki appeared at Laney's elbow. His glasses

had either been repaired or replaced, but two of the pins holding the sleeve of his green jacket had come undone. "Mr. Kuwayama is Rei Toei's creator, in a sense. He is the founder and chief executive officer of Famous Aspect, her corporate entity. He was the initiator of her project. He asks to speak with you."

"I thought it was so urgent that I access the combined data for you."

"It is, yes," said Yamazaki, "but I think you should speak with Kuwayama now, please."

Laney followed him through the black modules and past the barricades, and watched as the two exchanged bows. "This is Mr. Colin Laney," Yamazaki said, "our special researcher." Then, to Laney: "Michio Kuwayama, Chief Executive Officer of Famous Aspect."

No one would have guessed that Kuwayama had so recently been up there in the dark at the Western World, the crowd heaving and screaming around him. How had he gotten out, Laney wondered, and wouldn't the idoru have been lit up like a Christmas tree? Blood had seeped down into Laney's shoe; it was sticky between his toes. How much had the combined weight of all the human nervous tissue on the planet increased since he and Arleigh had left the bubble-gum bar with Blackwell? He felt like he'd acquired more himself, all of it uncomfortable. "I'm sorry," he said. "I don't have a card."

"It doesn't matter," Kuwayama said, in his precise, oddly accented English. He shook Laney's hand.

''I know that you are very busy. We appreciate your taking the time to meet with us.'' The plural caused Laney to glance at the driver, who wore the kind of shoes that Rydell had worn at the Chateau, flexible-looking black lace-ups with cleated, rubbery soles, but it didn't seem as though the driver was the other half of that ''we.'' ''Now,'' Kuwayama said to Yamazaki, ''if you will excuse us . . .'' Yamazaki bowed quickly and walked back toward the van, where Arleigh, pretending to be doing something to the espresso machine, was watching out of the corner of her eye. The driver opened the Land-Rover's rear door for Laney, who got in. Kuwayama got in from the other side. When the door closed behind him, they were alone.

Something that looked like a large silver thermos bottle was mounted between the two seats, in a rack with padded clamps.

''Yamazaki tells us that you had band-width difficulties during the dinner,'' Kuwayama said.

''That's true,'' Laney said.

''We have adjusted the band-width . . .'' And the idoru appeared between them, smiling. Laney saw that the illusion even provided a seat for her, melding the two buckets in which he and Kuwayama sat into a third.

''Did you find what you were looking for, when you left me in Stockholm, Mr. Laney?''

He looked into her eyes. What sort of computing power did it take to create something like this, something that looked back at you? He remembered phrases from Kuwayama's conversation with Rez: desiring machines, aggregates of subjective desire, an architecture of articulated longing. . . . "I started to," he said.

"And what was it that you saw, that made you unable to look at me, during our dinner?"

"Snow," Laney said, and was startled to feel himself begin to blush. "Mountains. . . . But I think it was only a video you've made."

"We don't 'make' Rei's videos," Kuwayama said, "not in the usual sense. They emerge directly from her ongoing experience of the world. They are her dreams, if you will."

"You dream as well, don't you, Mr. Laney?" the idoru said. "That is your talent. Yamazaki says it is like seeing faces in the clouds, except that the faces are really there. I cannot see the faces in clouds, but Kuwayama-san tells me that one day I will. It is a matter of plectics."

Yamazaki says? "I don't understand it," Laney said. "It's just something I can do."

"An extraordinary talent," Kuwayama said. "We are most fortunate. And we are fortunate as well in Mr. Yamazaki, who, though hired by Mr. Blackwell, has an open mind."

"Mr. Blackwell is not too pleased about Rez and . . ." Nodding toward her. "Mr. Blackwell might be unhappy that I'm talking with you."

"Blackwell loves Rez in his own way," she said.

"It is concern that he feels. But he does not understand that our union has already taken place. Our 'marriage' will be gradual, ongoing. We wish simply to grow together. When Blackwell and the others can see that our union is best for both of us, all will be well. And you can do that for us, Mr. Laney."

"I can?"

"Yamazaki has explained what you are attempting with the data from the Lo/Rez fan archives," Kuwayama said. "But that data says nothing, or very little, about Rei. We propose the addition of a third level of information: we will add Rei to the mix, and the pattern that emerges will be a portrait of their union."

But you're just information yourself, Laney thought, looking at her. Lots of it, running through God knows how many machines. But the dark eyes looked back at him, filled with something for all the world like hope. "Will you do it, Mr. Laney? Will you help us?"

"Look," Laney said, "I only work here. I'll do it if Yamazaki tells me to. If he takes the responsibility. But I want you to tell me something, okay?"

"What is it that you wish to know?" asked Kuwayama.

"What is all this *about?*" The question surprised Laney, who hadn't quite known what it was he was about to ask.

Kuwayama's mild eyes regarded him through the rimless lenses. "It is about futurity, Mr. Laney."

"Futurity?"

"Do you know that our word for 'nature' is of quite recent coinage? It is scarcely a hundred years old. We have never developed a sinister view of technology, Mr. Laney. It is an aspect of the natural, of oneness. Through our efforts, oneness perfects itself." Kuwayama smiled. "And popular culture," he said, "is the testbed of our futurity."

Arleigh made a better espresso than Shannon. Laney, squatting in the back of the green van, on popping shreds of bubble-pack, watched Yamazaki over the rim of a foam cup with a fresh double shot. "What do you think you're doing, Yamazaki? You want us both to wind up wearing smaller shoes, or what? Blackwell likes to nail people's hands to tables, and you're making deals with the idoru and her boss?" Laney had insisted that they climb in back here for privacy. Yamazaki squatted opposite him, blinking.

"I am not the one making deals," Yamazaki said. "Rez and Rei Toei are in almost constant contact now, and recent improvements allow her new degrees of freedom. Rez let her into the data, all that you first tried to access. He did this without informing Blackwell." He shrugged. "Now she accesses the fan data as well. And what they propose may well allow us to bring this to a conclusion. Blackwell is more than ever convinced there is some conspiracy. The attack in the nightclub . . ."

"Which was about?"

"I do not know. An attempted kidnapping? They wished to harm Rez? To abduct the idoru's peripheral? It was handled with amazing clumsiness, but Blackwell says that is the earmark of the Kombinat. . . . Is that the word, 'earmark'?"

"I don't know," Laney said.

" 'Hallmark'?"

"You don't think Blackwell's going to cut our toes off, if we do this?"

"No. We are employed by a Lo/Rez shell corporation—"

"Paragon-Asia?"

"—but Blackwell is employed by the Lo/Rez Partnership. If Rez tells us to do something, we must do it."

"Even if Blackwell thinks it endangers Rez's security?"

Yamazaki shrugged. Past his shoulder, through the van's rear window, Laney could see Shannon trundling the gray module they'd unloaded from the rear of Kuwayama's Land-Rover. It was twice the size of the black ones that Arleigh used.

He watched Shannon push it past the orange barricades.

Maryalice

''Not yelling, please,'' said the one who held her, and then he took his hand away from her mouth.

''Where is it?'' Eddie's pale eyes.

''There,'' Chia said, pointing. She could see the ragged edge of blue and yellow plastic sticking up out of her open bag. Then she saw that Maryalice was asleep on the pink bed, curled up with her high-heeled shoes still on, clutching a pillow to her face. The top of the little fridge was covered with empty, miniature bottles.

Eddie took a black-and-gold pen from his coat pocket and went to the bag. He bent over it and used his pen as a probe, moving the plastic aside so he could see. ''It's here,'' he said.

''Is there?'' The other hand was still holding Chia's

shoulder down, where she sat on the carpet.

"This is it," Eddie said.

"Stay putting." The hand left her shoulder and the man, who must've been kneeling behind her, got up and joined Eddie, peering into Chia's bag. He was taller, and wore a tan suit and fancy Western boots. Big bones in his face, his hair a lighter blond than Eddie's, a reddish, crescent-shaped birthmark high on his right cheekbone. "How you are being sure?"

"Jesus, Yevgeni . . ."

The man in the tan suit straightened up, looked at Maryalice, bent to pull the pillow away from her face. "How is your woman sleeping on bed in this room, Eddie?"

Eddie saw that it was Maryalice. "Fuck," he said.

"You are telling us girl and your woman, is 'incidental.' You are telling us they meet on plane, is only *accident.* Is *accident* your woman is here? We do not *like* accident."

Eddie looked from Maryalice to the man—he must be Russian—to Chia. "What the *fuck* is this bitch doing here?" Like it had to be Chia's fault.

"She found us," Chia said. "She said she knew somebody at the cab company."

"No," said the Russian, "*we* know somebody at cab company. Is too much incident."

"We've got it, okay?" Eddie said. "Why do you want to complicate things?"

The Russian rubbed his cheek, as though the birthmark might come off on his hand. "Please consider," he said. "We are giving you isotope. You want to know is isotope, you can test. You are giving us this." He poked the sharp toe of his cowboy boot into the side of Chia's bag. "How are we sure?"

"Yevgeni," Eddie said, very calmly, "you must know that deals like this require a certain basis of trust."

The Russian considered that. "No," he said, "basis not good. Our people trace this girl to big rocker band. What is she working for, Eddie? Tonight we send people to talk to them, they fall on us like fucking wolfs. One man I am still losing."

"I don't work for Lo/Rez!" Chia said. "I'm just in the club! Maryalice put that thing in my bag when I was asleep on the plane!"

Masahiko groaned, sighed, and seemed to go back under. Eddie still had the stungun in his hand. "You ready for another jolt?" he asked Masahiko, supertense and angry.

"Eddie," Maryalice said from the bed, "you ungrateful piece of shit . . ." Sitting up on the edge of the bed with her cigarette lighter held in both hands, pointing it straight at Eddie.

Eddie stiffened. You could see something run through him, freezing him there.

"Some basis," said the Russian.

"Jesus, Maryalice," Eddie said. "Where'd you get that? You got any idea how illegal that is, here?"

"Off a Russian boy," she said. "Exit-holes the size of grapefruit . . ." Maryalice didn't sound drunk, exactly, but something about the look in her reddened eyes told Chia she was. Some very scary kind of drunk. "You think you can just use people up, Eddie? Use 'em up and throw 'em away?" She used the toe of one shoe to get the other off, then used her toe to get the first shoe off. She stood up in her stocking feet, swaying just a little bit, but the gun-shaped lighter stayed straight out from her shoulders, the way cops did it on television.

Eddie still had the stungun in his hand. "Make him throw that black thing away, Maryalice!" Chia urged.

"Drop it," Maryalice said, and it seemed to give her pleasure to say it, something she'd been hearing people say on shows all her life, and now she was getting to say it herself, and mean it. Eddie dropped it. "Now kick it away."

That's the other half of the line, Chia thought.

The stungun wound up a few feet from Chia's knee, beside her goggles, which were upside down on the carpet, still cabled to her Sandbenders. She could see the twin flat rectangles on the opaque lens-faces, simple video units; if Zona went to Chia's systems software and activated those, now, she'd get a bug's-eye view of Maryalice's stocking feet, Eddie's shoes, the Russian's cowboy boots, and maybe the side of Masahiko's head.

"Ungrateful," Maryalice said. "Ungrateful shit. Get in that bathroom." She came around so the lighter was pointing at Eddie and the Russian, but with the open bathroom door behind them.

"I know you're upset—"

"Shit. Shit goes in the toilet, Eddie. Get in the bathroom."

Eddie took a step backward, his palms up in what he probably thought looked like an appeal to reasonableness and understanding. The Russian took a step back too.

"Seven fucking *years,*" Maryalice said. "Seven. You weren't shit when I met you. God. You and that uppity-mobile talk. You make me sick. Who paid the fucking rent? Who bought the meals? Who bought you your fucking clothes, you vain piece of shit? You and your uppity-mobile and your image and you gotta have a *smaller* fucking phone than the next guy because I'm telling you, honey, you sure as *fuck* don't have a bigger dick!" Maryalice's hands were shaking now, but really just enough to make the lighter look even more dangerous.

"Maryalice," Eddie said, "you know I know everything you've done for me, everything you've contributed to my career. It doesn't leave my mind for a minute, baby, believe me, it never does, and all of this is a misunderstanding, baby, just a rough patch on the highway of life, and if you will only just put down that fucking gun and have a nice drink like a civilized person—"

"Shut the fuck *up!*" Maryalice screamed, at the top of her lungs, the words all run together.

Eddie's mouth snapped shut like a puppet's.

"Seven fucking years," Maryalice said, making it

sound like some children's charm, "seven fucking years and two of 'em here, Eddie, two of 'em here, and flying back and fucking forth for you, Eddie, and coming back. And it's always *light,* here . . ." Tears came, streaking Maryalice's makeup. "Everywhere. Couldn't sleep for all the light, like a fog over the city. . . . Get in the bathroom." Maryalice taking a step forward, Eddie and the Russian taking one back.

Chia reached over and picked up the stungun, she wasn't sure why. It had a pair of blunt chrome fangs on one end, a red, ridged stud on one edge. She was surprised at how little it weighed. She remembered the ones the boys at her school had made from those disposable flash-cameras.

"And it always finds me, that light," Maryalice said. "Always. No matter what I drink, what I take on top of that. It finds me and it wakes me up. It's like powder, blows in under the door. Nothing to do about it. Gets in your eyes. And all that brightness, falling . . ." Eddie was half back through the doorway now, the Russian behind him, actually in the bathroom, and Chia didn't like that because she couldn't see the Russian's hands. She heard the ambient birdsong start as the bathroom sensed the Russian. "And you put me there, Eddie. That Shinjuku. You put me where that light could get me, and I could never get away."

And then Maryalice pulled the trigger.

Eddie screamed, a weird shrill sound bouncing off

the black and white tiles. That must've covered the click of the lighter, which hadn't even produced a flame.

Maryalice didn't panic.

She held her aim and calmly pulled the trigger again.

She got a light, that time, but Eddie, with a howl of rage, swatted the lighter aside, grabbed Maryalice by the throat, and started pounding her in the face with his fist, the howl resolving into "Bitch! Bitch! Bitch!" in sync with each blow.

And that was when Chia, without really thinking about it, came up from where she'd been sitting for so long that, she found, her legs were asleep, and didn't work, so that she had to turn her lunge into a roll, and roll again, before she could jam the chrome tips of the stungun against Eddie's ankle and push the red stud.

She wasn't sure it would work on an ankle, or through his sock. But it did. Maybe because Eddie wore those really thin socks.

But it got Maryalice, too, so that they seemed to jerk together, toppling into each other's arms.

And the dark blur that flew past Chia then was Masahiko, who pulled the door shut on the Russian, grabbed the knob with both hands and jumped up, jamming one paper-slippered foot against the wall, the other against the door, and hung there. "Run," he said, his arms and legs straining. Then his hands slipped off the round chrome knob and he landed on his ass.

Chia saw the knob start to turn.

She put the fangs of the stungun against the doorknob and pushed the stud. And kept pushing it.

Work Experience

Laney sat in the van's front passenger seat again, the 'phones on his lap, waiting for Arleigh to connect Kuwayama's gray module. He looked through the windshield at the concrete wall. His side didn't hurt quite as much now, but the meeting with Kuwayama and the idoru, and then his huddle in the van with Yamazaki, had left him more confused than ever. If Rez and Rei Toei were making decisions in tandem, and if Yamazaki had decided to go along with them, where did that leave him? He couldn't see that Blackwell was going to wake up to find some innate wonderfulness in the idea of Rez and Rei together. As far as Blackwell was concerned, Rez was still just trying to marry a software agent—whatever that might turn out to mean.

But Laney knew now that the idoru was more complex, more powerful, than any Hollywood synthespian. Particularly if Kuwayama were telling the truth about the videos being her "dreams." All he knew about artificial intelligence came from work he'd done on a Slitscan episode documenting the unhappy personal life of one of the field's leading researchers, but he knew that true AI was assumed never to have been achieved, and that current attempts to achieve it were supposed to be in directions quite opposite the creation of software that was good at acting like beautiful young women.

If there were going to be genuine AI, the argument ran, it was most likely to evolve in ways that had least to do with pretending to be human. Laney remembered screening a lecture in which the Slitscan episode's subject had suggested that AI might be created accidentally, and that people might not initially recognize it for what it was.

Arleigh opened the door on the driver's side and got in. "Sorry this is taking so long," she said.

"You weren't expecting it," Laney said.

"It isn't the software, it's an optical valve. A cable-tip. They use a different gauge, one the French use." She curled her hands around the top of the wheel and rested her chin on them. "So we're dealing with these huge volumes of information, no problem, but we don't have the right cable to pour it through."

"Can you fix it?"

"Shannon's got one in his room. Probably on a

porno outfit, but he won't admit it.'' She looked at him sideways. ''Shannon's got a friend on the security team. His friend says that Blackwell 'questioned' one of the men who tried to grab Rez tonight.''

''That's who they were after? Rez?''

''Seems like it. They're Kombinat, and they claim Rez has hijacked something of theirs.''

''Hijacked what?''

''He didn't know.'' She closed her eyes.

''What do you think happened to him, the one Blackwell questioned?''

''I don't know.'' She opened her eyes, straightened up. ''But somehow I don't think we'll find out.''

''Can he do that? Torture people? Kill them?''

She looked at Laney. ''Well,'' she said, finally, ''he does have a certain advantage, making us think he might. It's an established fact that he did that in his previous line of work. You know what scares me most about Blackwell?''

''What?''

''Sometimes I find myself getting used to him.''

Shannon rapped on the door beside her. Held up a length of cable.

''Ready when you are,'' she said to Laney, opening the door and sliding from behind the wheel.

Laney looked through the tinted windshield at the concrete wall and remembered policing the steps outside the Municipal Court in Gainesville with Shaquille and Kenny, two others from the orphanage. Shaquille had gone on to the drug-testing program with Laney, but Kenny had been transferred to another facility, near Denver. Laney had no idea what had become of either of them, but it had been Shaquille who'd pointed out to Laney that when the injection had the real stuff in it, your mouth filled with a taste like corroded metal, aluminum or something. Pl-*ceeb*-o, Shaquille had said, don't *taste.* And it was true. You could tell right away.

The three of them had had Work Experience there, five or six times, picking up the offerings people left before their day in court. These were considered to be a health hazard, and were usually carefully hidden, and you often found them by the smell, or the buzzing of flies. Parts of chickens, usually, tied up with colored yarn. What Shaquille said was the head of a goat, once. Shaquille said the people who left these things were drug dealers, and they did it because it was their religion. Laney and the others wore pale green latex gloves with orange Kevlar thimbles on the tips that gave you heat rash. They put the offerings in a white snap-top bucket with peeling Biohazard stickers. Shaquille had claimed to know the names of some of the gods these things were offered up to, but Laney hadn't been fooled. The names Shaquille made up, like O'Gunn and Sam Eddy, were obviously just that, and even Shaquille, dropping a white ball of chicken feathers into the bucket, had said an extra lawyer or two was probably a better investment. "But they do it while they waitin'. Hedge they bet." Laney had actually preferred this to Work Experiences at fast-food franchises, even though it meant they got body-searched for drugs when they got back.

He'd told Yamazaki and Blackwell about knowing that Alison Shires was going to try to commit suicide, and now they must think he could see the future. But he knew he couldn't. That would be like those chicken parts the dealers hid around the courthouse steps changing what was going to happen. What would happen in the future came out of what was happening now. Laney knew he couldn't predict it, and something about the experience of the nodal points made him suspect that nobody could. The nodal points seemed to form when something might be about to change. Then he saw a place where change was most likely, if something triggered it. Maybe something as small as Alison Shires buying the blades for a box-cutter. But if an earthquake had come, that night, and pitched her apartment down into Fountain Avenue. . . . Or if she'd lost the pack of blades. . . . But if she'd used credit to buy that Wednesday Night Special, which she couldn't do because it was illegal, and required cash, then it would've been obvious to anybody what she might be on the verge of doing.

Arleigh opened the passenger door. "You okay?"

"Sure," Laney said, picking up the eyephones.

"Sure?"

"Let's do it." He looked at the 'phones.

"It's up to you." She touched his arm. "We'll get you a doctor, after, okay?"

"Thanks," Laney said, and put the 'phones on, the taste flooding his mouth—

The Lo/Rez data, translucent and intricately interpenetrated by the archives of the band's fan-base, was crawling with new textures, maps that resolved, when he focused on them, into—

Shaquille, in his federal-issue sweats, showing Laney the goat's head. It had been skinned, and nails had been driven into it, and Shaquille had pried open the jaw to show where the missing tongue had been replaced with a blood-soaked piece of brown paper with writing on it. That would be the name of the prosecutor, Shaquille had explained.

Laney shut his eyes, but the image remained.

He opened them on the idoru, her features rimmed with fur. She was looking at him. She wore some kind of embroidered, fur-lined hat, with earflaps, and snow was swirling around her, but then she flattened, dwindling into the texture-maps that ran down through the reef of data, and he let himself go, go with that, and he felt himself pass through the core of it, the very center, and out the other side.

"Wait—" he said, and there seemed to be a lag before he heard his own voice.

"Perspective," the idoru said. "Yamazaki's parallax." Something seemed to turn him around, so that he looked directly at the data, but from some new angle, and from a great distance. And all around it, there was . . . nothing at all.

But through the data, like some infinitely more

complex version of Arleigh's Realtree, ran two vaguely parallel armatures. Rez and the idoru. They were sculpted in duration, Rez's beginning, at the far end of it all, as something very minor, the first hints of his career. And growing, as it progressed, to something braided, multi-stranded. . . . But then it began to get smaller again, Laney saw, the strands loosening. . . . And that would be the point, he thought, where the singer began to become the thing that Kathy hated, the one who took up celebrity space just because he was a celebrity, because he was of a certain order of magnitude . . .

The idoru's data began somewhere after that, and it began as something smoothly formed, deliberate, but lacking complexity. But at the points where it had swerved closest to Rez's data, he saw that it had begun to acquire a sort of complexity. Or randomness, he thought. The human thing. That's how she learns.

And both these armatures, these sculptures in time, were nodal, and grew more so toward the point, the present, where they intertwined . . .

He stood beside the idoru on the beach he'd seen recorded on the binoculars in the bedroom of the guesthouse in Ireland. Brownish-green sea flecked with whitecaps, stiff wind catching at the earflaps of her hat. He couldn't feel that wind, but he could hear it, so loud now that he had trouble hearing her over it. "Can you see them?" she shouted.

"See what?"

"The faces in the clouds! The nodal points! I can

see nothing! You must indicate them to me!''

And she was gone, the sea with her, Laney staring into the data again, where the digitized histories of Rez and Rei Toei mingled, on the verge of something else. If he had tried, in Los Angeles, would the box-cutter blade have emerged from Alison Shires' nodal point?

He tried.

He was looking out across a fuzzy, indistinct white plain. Not snow. To where a pair of vast and very ornate brown-on-brown Western boots swung past against a cliff-like backdrop of violent pink. Then the image was gone, replaced by the rotating form of a three-dimensional object, though Laney had no idea what it was supposed to be. With no clues as to scale, it looked vaguely like a Los Angeles bus with the wheels removed.

''Suite 17,'' the idoru said. ''Hotel Di.''

''Die?'' Bus vanished, apparently taking boots with it.

''What is a 'love hotel'?''

''What?''

''Love. Hotel.''

''Where people go to make love—I think . . .''

''What is 'Rodel-van Erp primary biomolecular programming module C-slash-7A'?''

''I don't know,'' Laney said.

''But you have just shown it to me! It *is* our union, our intersection, that from which the rest must unfold!''

"Wait," Laney said, "wait, you've got *another* one here; they sort of overlap—" The trying made his side hurt, but there were hills in the distance, twisted trees, the low roofline of a wooden house—

But the idoru was gone, and the house, its fabric eaten from within, was shimmering, folding. And then a glimpse of something towering, mismatched windows and a twisting, moire sky.

Then Arleigh pulled the 'phones off. "Stop screaming," she said. Yamazaki was beside her. "Stop it, Laney."

He took a long, shuddering breath, braced his palms against the padded cowling of the dash, and closed his eyes. He felt Arleigh's hand against his neck.

"We have to go there," he said.

"Go where?"

"Suite 17. . . . We'll be late, for the wedding . . ."

Star

When the stungun quit making that zapping sound, Chia dropped it. The doorknob wasn't turning. No sound from the bathroom but the faint recorded cries of tropical birds. She whipped around. Masahiko was trying to get his computer into the plaid carrier-bag. She dived for her Sandbenders, grabbed it up, still trailing her goggles, and turned to the pink bed. Her bag was beside it on the floor, with the blue and yellow SeaTac plastic showing. She pulled that out, the thing still in it, and tossed it on the bed. She bent to shove her Sandbenders into her bag, but glanced back at the bathroom door when she thought she heard something.

The knob was turning again.

The Russian opened the door. When he let go of

the knob, she saw that his hand was inside something that looked like a Day-Glo pink hand-puppet. One of the sex toys from the black cabinet. He was using it as insulation. He peeled it off his fingers and tossed it back over his shoulder. The bird sounds faded as he stepped out.

Masahiko, who'd been trying to get one of his feet into one of his black shoes, was looking at the Russian too. He still had a paper slipper on the other foot.

"You are going?" the Russian said.

"It's on the bed," Chia said. "We didn't have anything to *do* with it."

The Russian noticed the stungun on the carpet, beside the pointed toe of his boot. He raised the boot and brought his heel down. Chia heard the plastic case crack. "Artemi, my friend of Novokuznetskaya, is doing himself great indignity with this." He prodded the fragments of the stungun with his toe. "Is wearing very tight jeans, Artemi, leather, is fashion. Putting in front pocket, trigger is pressing accident. Artemi is shocking his manhood." The Russian showed Chia his large, uneven teeth. "Still we are laughing, yes?"

"Please," Chia said. "We just want to *go.*"

The Russian stepped past Eddie and Maryalice, who lay tangled on the carpet. "You are accident like Artemi to his manhood, yes? You are only happening to this owner of fine nightclub." He indicated the unconscious Eddie. "Who is smuggler and other things, very complicated, but *you,* you are only accident?"

"That's right," Chia said.

"You are of Lo/Rez." It sounded like *Lor-ess.* He stepped closer to Chia and looked down into the bag. "You are knowing what this is."

"No," Chia lied. "I'm not."

The Russian looked at her. "We are not liking accident, ever. Not *allowing* accident." His hands came up, then, and she saw that the back of the third joint of each of his fingers was pink with those dots, each one the size of the end of a pencil eraser. She'd seen those at her last school and knew they meant a laser had recently been used to remove a tattoo.

She looked up at his face. He looked like someone who was about to do something that he might not want to do, but that he knew he had to.

But then she saw his eyes slide past her, narrowing, and she turned in time to see the door to the corridor swing inward. A man wider than the doorway seemed to flow into the room. There was a big X of flesh-colored tape across one side of his face, and he was wearing a coat the color of dull metal. Chia saw one huge, scarred hand slip into his coat; the other held something black that ended in a mag-strip tab.

"Yob tvoyu mat," said the Russian, soft syllables of surprise.

The stranger's hand emerged, holding something that looked to Chia like a very large pair of chrome-plated scissors, but then unfolded, with a series of small sharp clicks, and apparently of its own accord, into a kind of glittering, skeletal axe, its leading edge hawklike and lethal, the head behind it tapering like an icepick.

"My *mother?*" said the stranger, who sounded somehow delighted. "Did you say my *mother?*" His face was shiny with scar tissue. More scars criss-crossed his shaven, stubbled skull.

"Ah, no," the Russian said, lifting his hands so that the palms showed. "Figuring of speech, only."

Another man stepped in, around the man with the axe, and this one had dark hair and wore a loose black suit. The headband of a monocle-rig crossed his forehead, the unit covering his right eye. The eye she could see was wide and bright and green, but still it took a second before she recognized him.

Then she had to sit down on the pink bed.

"Where is it?" this man who looked like Rez asked. (Except he looked thicker, somehow, his cheeks unhollowed.)

Neither the Russian nor the man with the axe answered. The man with the axe closed the door behind him with his heel.

The green eye and the video-monocle looked at Chia. "Do you know where it is?"

"What?"

"The biomech primer module, or whatever it is you call it. . . ." He paused, touching the phone in his right ear, listening. "Excuse me: 'Rodel-van Erp primary biomolecular programming module C-slash-7A.' *I love you.*"

Chia stared.

''Rei Toei,'' he explained, touching the headband, and she knew that it had to be him.

''It's here. In this bag.''

He reached into the blue and yellow plastic and drew the thing out, turning it over in his hands. ''This? This is our future, the medium of our marriage?''

''Excuse, please,'' the Russian said, ''but you must know this is belonging to me.'' He sounded genuinely sorry.

Rez looked up, the nanotech unit held casually in his hands. ''It's yours?'' Rez tilted his head, like a bird, curious. ''Where did you get it?''

The Russian coughed. ''An exchange. This gentleman on floor.''

Rez saw Eddie and Maryalice. ''Are they dead?''

''Volted, yes? Being most-time nonlethal. Your girl on bed.''

Rez looked at Chia. ''Who are you?''

''Chia Pet McKenzie,'' she said automatically. ''I'm from Seattle. I'm . . . I'm in your fan club.'' She felt her face burning.

The brow above the green eye went up. He seemed to be listening to something. ''Oh,'' he said, and paused. ''She did? Really? That's wonderful.'' He smiled at Chia. ''Rei says you've been totally central to everything, and that we have a great deal to thank you for.''

Chia swallowed. ''She does?''

But Rez had turned to the Russian. ''We have to

have this.'' He raised the nanotech unit. ''We'll negotiate now. Name your price.''

''Rozzer,'' the man at the door said, ''you can't *do* that. This bastard's Kombinat.''

Chia saw the green eye close, as if Rez were making a conscious effort to calm himself. When it opened, he said: ''But they're the *government,* aren't they, Blackwell? We've *negotiated* with governments before.''

''It's for the *legals,*'' the scarred man said, but now there was an edge of worry in his voice.

The Russian seemed to hear it too. He slowly lowered his hands.

''What were you planning to *do* with this?'' Rez asked him.

The Russian looked down at the thing in Rez's hands, as if considering, then raised his eyes. A muscle was jumping, in his cheek. He seemed to come to a decision. ''We are developing ambitious public works project,'' he said.

''Oh, Jesus,'' Maryalice said from the carpet, so hoarsely that at first Chia couldn't identify the source. ''They must've *put* something in that. They *did.* I swear to *God* they did.'' And then she threw up.

Trans

Yamazaki lost his balance as the van shot up the narrow ramp, out of the hotel. Laney, holding Arleigh's phone to the dashboard map, toning the number of the Hotel Di, heard him crash down on the shredded bubble-pack. The display bleeped as Laney completed the number; grid-segments clicked across the screen. ''You okay, Yamazaki?''

''Thank you,'' Yamazaki said. ''Yes.'' Getting to his knees again, he craned around the headrest of Laney's seat. ''You have located the hotel?''

''Expressway,'' Arleigh said, glancing at the display, as they swung right, up an entrance ramp. ''Hit speed-dial three. Thanks. Gimme.'' She took the phone. ''McCrae. Yeah. Priority? *Fuck* you, Alex.

Ring me through to him.'' She listened. ''Di? Like D, I? Shit. Thanks.'' She clicked off.

''What is it?'' Laney asked, as they swung onto the expressway, the giant bland brow of an enormous articulated freight-hauler pulling up behind and then past them, quilted stainless steel flashing in Laney's peripheral vision. The van rocked with the big truck's passage.

''I tried to get Rez. Alex says he left the hotel, with Blackwell. Headed the same place we are.''

''When?''

''Just about the time you were having your screaming fit, when you had the 'phones on,'' Arleigh said. She looked grim. ''Sorry,'' she said.

Laney had had to argue with her for fifteen minutes, back there, before she'd agreed to this. She'd kept saying she wanted him to see a doctor. She'd said that she was a technician, not a researcher, not security, and that her first responsibility was to stay with the data, the modules, because anyone who got those got almost the entire Lo/Rez Partnership business plan, plus the books, plus whatever Kuwayama had entrusted them with in the gray module. She'd only given in after Yamazaki had sworn to take full responsibility for everything, and after Shannon and the man with the ponytail had promised not to leave the modules. Not even, Arleigh said, to piss. ''Go against the wall, God damn it,'' she'd said, ''and get half a dozen of Blackwell's boys down here to keep you company.''

"He knows," Laney said. "She told him it's there."

"What is there, Laney-san?" asked Yamazaki, around the headrest.

"I don't know. Whatever it is, they think it'll facilitate their marriage."

"Do *you* think so?" Arleigh asked, passing a string of bright little cars.

"I guess it must be capable of it," Laney said, as something under her seat began to clang, loudly and insistently. "But I don't think that means it'll necessarily happen. What the hell is *that?*"

"I'm exceeding the speed limit," she said. "Every vehicle in Japan is legally required to be equipped with one of these devices. You speed, it dings."

Laney turned to Yamazaki. "Is that true?"

"Of course," Yamazaki said, over the steady clanging.

"And people don't just disconnect them?"

"No," Yamazaki said, looking puzzled. "Why would they?"

Arleigh's phone rang. "McCrae. Willy?" Silence as she listened. Then Laney felt the van sway slightly. It slowed until the clanging suddenly stopped. She lowered the phone.

"What is it?" Laney asked.

"Willy Jude," she said. "He . . . He was just watching one of the clubbing channels. They said Rez is dead. They said he was dead. In a love hotel."

The Business

When nobody did anything to help Maryalice, Chia got up from the bed, squeezed past the Russian and into the bathroom, triggering the ambient bird track. The black cabinet was open, its light on, and there were Day-Glo penis-things scattered across the black and white tile floor. She took a black towel and a black washcloth from a heated chrome rack, wet the washcloth at the black and chrome basin, and went back to Maryalice. She folded the towel, put it down over the vomit on the white carpet, and handed Maryalice the washcloth.

Nobody said anything, or tried to stop her. Masahiko had sat back down on the carpet, with his computer between his feet. The scarred man, who seemed to take up as much space as anything in the room, had lowered his axe. He held it down, along a thigh wider than Chia's hips, with the spike jutting from beside his knee.

Maryalice, who'd managed to sit up now, wiped her mouth with the cloth, taking most of her lipstick with it. When Chia straightened up, a whiff of the Russian's cologne made her stomach heave.

"You're a developer, you say?" Rez still held the nanotech unit.

"You are asking many questions," the Russian said. Eddie groaned, then, and the Russian kicked him. "*Basis,*" the Russian said.

"A public works project?" Rez raised his eyebrow. "A water filtration plant, something like that?"

The Russian kept his eye on the big man's axe. "In Tallin," he said, "we soon are building exclusive mega-mall, affluent gated suburbs, plus world-class pharmaceutical manufakura. We are unfairly denied most advanced means of production, but we are desiring one hundred percent modern operation."

"Rez," the man with the axe said, "give it up. This hoon and his mates need that thing to build themselves an Estonian drug factory. Time I took you back to the hotel."

"But wouldn't they be more interested in . . . Tokyo real estate?"

The big man's eyes bulged, the scars on his forehead reddening. One of the upper arms of the micropore X had come loose, revealing a deep scratch.

"What bullshit is *that?* You don't *have* any real estate here!"

"Famous Aspect," Rez said. "Rei's management company. They invest for her."

"You are discussing nanotech exchanged for Tokyo real estate?" The Russian was looking at Rez.

"Exactly," Rez said.

"What *kind* real estate?"

"Undeveloped landfill in the Bay. An island. One of two. Off one of the old 'Toxic Necklace' sites, but that's been cleaned up since the quake."

"Wait a minute," Maryalice said, from the floor. "I know you. You were in that band, the one with the skinny Chinese, the guitar player, wore the hats. I know you. You were *huge.*"

Rez stared at her.

"I think is not good, here to discuss the business," the Russian said, rubbing his birthmark. "But I am Starkov, Yevgeni." He extended his hand, and Chia noticed the laser-scars again. Rez shook it.

Chia thought she heard the big man groan.

"I used to watch him in *Dayton,*" Maryalice said, as if that proved something.

The big man took a small phone from his pocket with his free hand, squinted at the call-display, and put it to his left ear. Which Chia now saw was missing. He listened. "Ta," he said, and lowered the phone. He moved to the window, the one Chia had found behind the wallscreen, and stood looking out.

"Better have a look at this, Rozzer," he said.

Rez joined him. She saw Rez touch the monocle. "What are they doing, Keithy? What is it?"

"It's your funeral," the big man said.

41

Candlelight and Tears

Office windows flickered past, very close, beyond the earthquake-bandaged uprights of the expressway. Taller buildings gave way to a lower sprawl, then something bright in the middle distance: HOTEL KING MIDAS. The dashboard map began to bleep.

"Third exit right," Laney said, watching the cursor. He felt her accelerate and heard the speed-limit warning kick in. Another glittering sign: FREEDOM SHOWER BANFF.

"Laney-san," Yamazaki asked, around the headrest. "Did you apprehend any suggestion of Rez's death or other misfortune?"

"No, but I wouldn't, not unless there was a degree of intentionality that would emerge from the data. Accidents, actions by anyone who isn't represented . . ."

The clanging stopped as she slowed, approaching the exit indicated on the map. "But I saw their data as streams, merging, and whatever it was merging *around* seemed to be where we're going."

Arleigh made the exit. They were on the off-ramp now, swinging through a curve, and Laney saw three young girls, their shoes clumped with mud, descending a sharp slope planted with some kind of pale rough grass. One of them seemed to be wearing a school uniform: kneesocks and a short plaid skirt. They looked unreal, in the harsh sodium light of the intersection, but then Arleigh stopped the van and Laney turned to see the road in front of them completely blocked by a silent, unmoving crowd.

"Jesus," Arleigh said. "The fans."

If there were boys in the crowd, Laney didn't see them. It was a level sea of glossy black hair, every girl facing the white building that rose there, with its white, brilliantly illuminated sign framed by something meant to represent a coronet: HOTEL DI. Arleigh powered down her window and Laney heard the distant wail of a siren.

"We'll never get through," Laney said. Most of the girls held a single candle, and the combined glow danced among the tear-streaked faces. They were so young, these girls: children. Kathy Torrance had particularly loathed that about Lo/Rez, the way their fanbase had refreshed itself over the years with a constant stream of pubescent recruits, girls who fell in love with Rez in the endless present of the net, where he could still be the twenty-year-old of his earliest hits.

"Pass me that black case," Arleigh said, and Laney heard Yamazaki scrabbling through the bubble-pack. A flat rectangular carrying case appeared between the seats. Laney took it. "Open it," she said. Laney undid the zip, exposing something flat and gray. The Lo/Rez logo on an oblong sticker. Arleigh pulled it from its case, put it on the dashboard, and ran her finger around its edge, looking for a switch. LO/REZ, mirror-reversed in large, luminous green letters, appeared on the windshield. **TOUR SUPPORT VEHICLE**. The asterisks began to flash.

Arleigh let the van roll forward a few inches. The girls directly in front turned, saw the windshield, and stepped aside. Silently, gradually, a few feet at a time, the crowd parted for the van.

Laney looked out across the black, center-parted heads of the grieving fans and saw the Russian, the one from the Western World, still in his white leather evening jacket, struggling through the crowd. The girls' heads came barely to his waist, and he looked as though he were wading through black hair and candle-glow. The expression on his face was one of confusion, almost of terror, but when he saw Laney at the window of the green van, he grimaced and changed course, heading straight for them.

Checking Out

Chia looked out and saw that the rain had stopped. Beyond the chainlink fence, the parking lot was full of small, unmoving figures holding candles. A few of them were standing on the tops of the trucks parked there, and there seemed to be more on the roof of the low building behind. Girls. Japanese girls. All of them seemed to be staring at the Hotel Di.

The big man was telling Rez that someone had announced that he'd died, that he'd been found dead in this hotel, and it was out on the net and was being treated like it had really happened.

The Russian had produced his own phone now and was talking to someone in Russian. ''Mr. Lor-ess,'' he said, lowering the phone, ''we are hearing police come. This nanotech being heavily proscribed, is serious problem.''

''Fine,'' Rez said. ''We have a car in the garage.''

Someone nudged Chia's elbow. It was Masahiko, handing her her bag. He'd put her Sandbenders in it and zipped it up; she could tell by the weight. He had his computer in the plaid bag. ''Put your shoes on now,'' he said. His were already on.

Eddie was curled into a knot on the carpet; he'd been like that since the Russian had kicked him. Now the Russian took a step toward him again and Chia saw Maryalice cringe, where she sat beside Eddie on the carpet.

''You are lucky man,'' the Russian said to Eddie. ''We are honoring our agreement. Isotope to be delivered. But we are wanting no more the business with you.''

There was a click, and another, and Chia watched as the big man with no left ear folded his axe, collapsing it smoothly into itself without looking at it. ''That thing you're holding is a heavy crime, Rozzer. Your fan-club turnout's bringing the police. Better let me be in possession.''

Rez looked at the big man. ''I'll carry it myself, Keithy.''

Chia thought she saw a sudden sadness in the big man's eyes. ''Well then,'' he said. ''Time to go.'' He slipped the folded weapon inside his jacket. ''Come on, then. You two.'' Gesturing Chia and Masahiko toward the door. Rez followed Masahiko, the Russian close behind him, but Chia saw that the room key was on top of the little fridge. She ran over and grabbed it. Then she stopped, looking down at Mary-alice.

Maryalice's mouth, with her lipstick gone, looked old and sad. It was a mouth that must've been hurt a lot, Chia thought. "Come with us," Chia said.

Maryalice looked at her.

"Come *on,*" Chia said. "The police are coming."

"I can't," Maryalice said. "I have to take care of Eddie."

"Tell your Eddie," Blackwell said, reaching Chia in two steps, "that if he whines to anyone about any of this, he'll be grabbed and his shoe size shortened."

But Maryalice didn't seem to hear, or if she did, she didn't look up, and the big man pulled Chia out of the room, closed the door, and then Chia was following the back of the Russian's tan suit down the narrow corridor, his fancy cowboy boots illuminated by the ankle-high light-strips.

Rez was stepping into the elevator with Masahiko and the Russian when the big man caught his shoulder. "You're staying with me," he said, shoving Chia into the elevator.

Masahiko pushed the button. "You are having vehicle?" the Russian asked Masahiko.

"No," Masahiko said.

The Russian grunted. His cologne was making Chia's stomach turn over. The door opened on the little lobby. The Russian pushed past her, looking around. Chia and Masahiko followed. The elevator door closed. "Looking for vehicle," the Russian said. "Come." They followed him through the sliding glass door, into the parking area, where Eddie's Graceland seemed to take up at least half the available space. Beside it was a silver-gray Japanese sedan, and Chia wondered if that was Rez's. Someone had put black plastic rectangles over the license plates of both cars.

She heard the glass door hiss open again and turned to see Rez coming out, the nanotech unit tucked beneath his arm like a football. The big man was behind him.

Then a really angry man in a shiny white tuxedo burst through the pink plastic strips that hung down across the entrance. He had a smaller man by the collar of his jacket, and the smaller man was trying to get away. Then the smaller man saw them there and shouted "Blackwell!" and actually managed to slip right out of his jacket, but the man in the white tuxedo reached out with the other hand and caught him by the belt.

The Russian was yelling in Russian now and the man in the white tuxedo seemed to see him for the first time. He let go of the other man's belt.

"We've got the van," the other man said.

The big man with the missing ear stepped up really close to the man in the white tuxedo, glared at him, and took the other man's jacket. "Okay, Rozzer," he said, turning to Rez. "You know the drill this one.

Old hat. Same as leaving that house in St. Kilda with the bastard Melbourne tabs outside, right?'' He draped the jacket over Rez's head and shoulders, slapped him encouragingly on the upper arm. He walked over to the pink strips and drew one aside, looking out. ''Fucking *hell,*'' he said. ''Right then, all of you. It's move fast, stay together, Rez in the center, and into the van. On my count of three.''

Toecutter's Breakfast

"You aren't eating," Blackwell said, after he'd cleared his second plate of links and eggs. He'd appropriated this dining room on one of the Elf Hat's executive floors, and insisted Laney join him. The view was similar to the one from Laney's room, six floors below, and sunlight was glinting from the distant parapets of the new buildings.

"Who put out the word that Rez was dead, Blackwell? The idoru?"

"Her? Why d'you think she would?" He was using the edge of a triangle of toast to squeegee his plate.

"I don't know," Laney said, "but she seems to like to do things. And they aren't necessarily that easy to understand."

"It wasn't her," Blackwell said. "We're checking

it out. Looks as though some fan of his in Mexico went berserk; used some fairly drastic sort of 'ware-weapon on the Tokyo club's central site. Took that over from a converted corporate website in the States and issued the bulletin. Called on every fan local to Tokyo to get up immediately and go to that love hotel.'' He popped the toast into his mouth, swallowed, and wiped his lips with a thick white napkin.

''But Rez was *there,*'' Laney said.

Blackwell shrugged. ''We're looking into it. We have more than enough on our hands, now. Have to dissociate Lo/Rez from this death hoax, reassure his audience. Legal's flying in from London and New York for talks with Starkov and his people. Her people too,'' he added. ''Going to be busy.''

''Who were those kids?'' Laney asked. ''The little redhead and the Japanese hippie?''

''Rez says they're okay. Have 'em here in the hotel. Arleigh's sorting it out.''

''Where's the nanotech unit?''

''You didn't say that,'' Blackwell said. ''Now don't say it again. The official truth of the night's events is currently being formulated, and that will never be a part of it. Am I understood?''

Laney nodded. He looked out at the new buildings again. Either the angle of light had changed or that parapet had shifted slightly. He looked at Blackwell. ''Is it my imagination, or has your attitude on all this undergone some kind of change? I thought you were adamantly opposed to Rez and the idoru getting together.''

Blackwell sighed. ''I was. But it's starting to look like something of a done deal now, isn't it? De facto relationship, really. I suppose I'm old-fashioned, but I'd hoped that he might eventually wind up with a bit of the ordinary. Someone to polish his gun, pick up his socks, have a baby or two. But it isn't going to happen, is it?''

''I guess not.''

''In which case,'' Blackwell said, ''I have two options. Either I leave the silly bastard to his own resources, or I stay and I do my job and try to adjust to whatever it is this is going to become. And at the end of the bloody day, Laney, regardless, I have to remember where I'd be if he hadn't come behind the walls at Pentridge to give that solo concert. Aren't you going to eat that?'' Looking at the scrambled eggs going cold on Laney's plate.

''My job's done,'' Laney said. ''It didn't work out the way you wanted it to, but I did it. Agreed?''

''No question.''

''Then I'd better go. Get me paid off, I'm out of here today.''

Blackwell looked at him with new interest. ''That fast, eh? What's your hurry? Don't find us agreeable?''

''No,'' Laney said. ''It's just that that way's better all 'round.''

''Not what Yama's saying. Rez either. Not to mention her otherness, who no doubt will voice an opinion in that regard. I'd say you were set to become the court prognosticator, Laney. Unless, of course, that whole business with the Kombinat turns out to be absolute bollocks, and it's discovered that you simply make that nodal nonsense up—which I for one would actually find quite amusing. But no, your services are very much desired now, you might even say required, and none of us would currently be happy to see you go.''

''I have to,'' Laney said. ''I'm being blackmailed.''

This brought Blackwell's lids to half-mast. He leaned slightly forward. The pink worm of scar tissue squirmed in his eyebrow. ''Are you?'' he said softly, as though Laney had just ventured to confess some unusual sexual complication. ''And may I ask who by?''

''Slitscan. Kathy Torrance. It's sort of personal, for her.''

''Tell me about it. Tell me all about it. Do.''

And Laney did, including the 5-SB trials and their record for eventually turning the participants into homicidal stalkers of celebrities. ''I didn't want to bring that up, before,'' Laney said, ''because I was afraid you might think I was at risk. That I might go that way.''

''Not that I haven't had experience with the type,'' Blackwell said. ''We have a young man in Tokyo right now who is the author of all of the songs Lo and Rez have ever written, not to mention Blue Ahmed's complete output for Chrome Koran. And he's an explosives expert. Watch him closely. But we have that capacity, you see. So the safest place for *you,* Laney, in the event you go werewolf on us, would be right *here,* at the watchful heart of our security apparatus."

Laney thought about it. It almost made sense. "But you won't want me around if Slitscan runs that footage. I won't want *myself* around. I don't have any family, nobody else for it to damage, but I'm still going to have to live with it."

"And how do you propose to do that?"

"I'll go somewhere where people don't watch that shit."

"Well," said Blackwell, "when you find that fair land, I will go there with you myself. We'll live on fruit and nuts, commune with all that's left of bloody nature. But 'til then, Laney, I'm going to have a conversation with your Kathy Torrance. I will explain certain things to her. Nothing complicated. Simple, *simple* protocols of cause and effect. And she will *never* allow Slitscan to run that footage of your doppelgänger."

"Blackwell," Laney said, "she *dislikes* me, she has her motive for revenge, but she wants, she *needs,* to destroy Rez. She's a very powerful woman in a very powerful, fully global organization. Some simple threat of *violence* on your part isn't going to stop her.

It'll only up the ante; she'll go to *her* security people—''

''No,'' said Blackwell, ''she won't, because that would be a violation of the very *personal* terms I will have established in our conversation. That's the key word here, Laney, 'personal.' 'Up close, and.' We will not meet, we will not carve out this deep and meaningful and bloody unforgettable episode of mutual face-time as representatives of our respective faceless corporations. Not at all. It's one-on-one time for your Kathy and I, and it may well prove to be as intimate, and I may hope enlightening, as any she ever had. Because I will bring a new certainty into her life, and we *all* need certainties. They help build character. And I will leave your Kathy with the deepest possible conviction that if she crosses me, she *will* die—but only after she's been made to desire that, absolutely.'' And Blackwell's smile, then, giving Laney the full benefit of his dental prosthesis, was hideous. ''Now how was it exactly you were supposed to contact her, to give her your decision?''

Laney found his wallet, produced the blank card with the pencilled number. Blackwell took it. ''Ta.'' He stood up. ''Shame to waste a good breakfast that way. Ring the hotel doctor from your room and get yourself sorted. Sleep. I'll deal with this.'' He tucked the card into the breast pocket of his aluminum jacket.

And as Blackwell left the room, Laney noticed, centered on the bodyguard's squeegeed plate and standing upright on its broad flat head, a one-and-a-half-inch galvanized roofing-nail.

Laney's ribs, an ugly patchwork of yellow, black, and blue, were sprayed with various cool liquids and tightly bound with micropore. He took the hypnotic the doctor had offered, showered at great length, climbed into bed, and was suggesting the light turn itself off when a fax was delivered.

It was addressed to C. LANEY, GUEST:

DAY MANAGER GAVE ME MY WALKING PAPERS. "FRATERNIZING." ANYWAY, I'M SECURITY HERE AT THE LUCKY DRAGON, MIDNITE ON, YOU CAN GET ME FAX, E-MAIL, PHONE'S BIZ ONLY BUT THE PEOPLE ARE OKAY. HOPE YOU'RE OKAY. FEEL RESPONSIBLE. HOPE YOU'RE ENJOYING JAPAN, WHATEVER. RYDELL

"Good night," Laney said, putting the fax on the bedside module, and fell instantly and very deeply asleep.

And stayed that way until Arleigh phoned from the lobby to suggest a drink. Nine in the evening, by the blue clock in the corner of the module-screen. Laney put on freshly ironed underwear and his other blue Malaysian button-down. He discovered that White Leather Tuxedo had sprung a few seams in his only jacket, but then the boss Russian, Starkov, hadn't let the man come with them in the van, so Laney figured they were even.

Crossing the lobby, he encountered a frantic-looking Rice Daniels, so tense that he'd reverted to the black head-clamp of his Out of Control days. "Laney! Jesus! Have *you* seen Kathy?"

"No. I've been asleep."

Daniels did a strange little jig of anxiety, rising on the toes of his brown calfskin loafers. "Look, this is *too* fucking weird, but I *swear*—I think she's been *abducted.*"

"Have you called the police?"

"We did, we did, but it's all fucking *Martian,* all these forms they tick through on their notebooks, and what *blood type* was she. . . . You don't *know* what blood type she is, do you, Laney?"

"Thin," Laney said. "Sort of straw-colored."

But Daniels didn't seem to hear. He seized Laney's shoulder and showed him teeth, a rictus intended somehow to indicate friendship. "I have real respect for you, man. How you don't have any issues."

Laney saw Arleigh wave to him from the entrance to the lounge. She was wearing something short and black.

"You take care, Rice." Shaking the man's cold hand. "She'll turn up. I'm sure of it."

And then he was walking toward Arleigh, smiling, and he saw that she was smiling back.

La Purissima

Chia was on the bed, watching television. It made her feel more normal. It was like a drug, that way. She remembered how much television her mother had watched, after her father had left.

But this was Japanese television, where girls who could have been Mitsuko, only a little younger, wearing sailor-suit dresses, were spinning huge wooden tops at a long table. They could really spin them, too; keep them up forever. It was a contest. The console could translate, but it was even more relaxing not to know what they were saying. The most relaxing parts of all were the close-ups of the tops spinning.

She'd used the translation to check out the NHK coverage of the death hoax on the net and the candlelight vigil at the Hotel Di.

She'd seen a very satisfyingly pudgy Hiromi Ogama denying she knew who had nuked her chapter's site and then issued the call to mourning from its ruins. It had not been a member of the club, Hiromi had stressed, either locally or internationally. Chia knew Hiromi was lying, because it had to have been Zona, but the Lo/Rez people would be telling her what to say. Arleigh had told Chia the whole thing had been launched out of a disused website that belonged to an aerospace company in Arizona. Which meant that Zona had blown her country, because now she wouldn't be able to go back there. (Nice as Arleigh seemed to be, Chia hadn't told her anything about Zona.)

And she'd seen the helicopter shots of the vigil, and of the baffled tactical squads facing an estimated twenty-five hundred teary-eyed girls. The injury count was low, everything fairly minor except for one girl who'd slid down a freeway embankment and broken both her ankles. The real problem had been getting everyone out of there, because a lot of them had arrived five or six to a cab, and had no way of getting home. Some had taken the family car and then abandoned it in their hurry to reach the vigil, and that had created another kind of mess. There had been a few dozen arrests, mostly for trespassing.

And she'd seen the message Rez had recorded, assuring people he was alive and well, and regretting the whole thing, which of course he'd had nothing to do with. He wasn't wearing the monocle-rig, for this, but he had on the same black suit and t-shirt. He looked thinner, though; someone had tweaked it. He'd played it light, at first, grinning, saying he'd never been to the Hotel Di and in fact had never visited a love hotel, but now maybe he should. Then he'd turned serious and said how sorry he was that people had been inconvenienced and even hurt by someone's irresponsible prank. And he'd capped it, smiling, by saying that the whole thing had been quite uniquely moving for him, because how often do you get to watch your own funeral?

And she'd seen the people who owned and managed the Hotel Di, expressing their regret. They had no idea, they said, how any of this had happened. She got the feeling that expressing regret was a big thing here, but the owners of the Di had also managed to explain how there was no on-site staff at their hotel, in the interest of the guests' greater privacy. Arleigh, watching this, had said that that was the commercial, and that she bet the place was going to be booked solid for the next two months. It was famous, now.

All in all, the coverage seemed to treat the whole thing as some kind of silly-season item that might have had serious repercussions if the police hadn't acted as calmly and as skillfully as they eventually had, bringing in electric buses from the suburbs to ferry the girls to collection-points around the city.

Arleigh was from San Francisco and she worked for Lo/Rez and knew Rez personally, and she was the one who'd driven the van out through the crowd. And then she'd lost a police helicopter by doing something completely crazy on that expressway, a kind of u-turn right over the concrete bumper-thing down the middle.

She'd brought Chia and Masahiko to this hotel, and put them in these adjoining rooms with weirdly angled corners, where they each had a private bath. She'd asked them both to please stay there, and not to port or use the phone without telling her, except for room service, and then she'd gone out.

Chia had had a shower right away. It was the best shower she'd ever had, and she felt like she never wanted to wear those clothes again as long as she lived. She didn't even want to have to look at them. She found a plastic bag you were supposed to put your clothes in to be laundered, and she put them in that and put it in the wastebasket in the bathroom. Then she'd put on all clean clothes from her bag, everything kind of wrinkled but it felt great, and she'd blow-dried her hair with the machine built into the bathroom wall. The toilet didn't talk and it only had three buttons to figure out.

Then she lay down on the bed and fell asleep, but not for long.

Arleigh kept popping in to make sure Chia was okay, and telling her news, so that Chia felt like she was part of it, whatever it was. Arleigh said Rez was back at his own hotel now, but that he'd come later to spend some time with her and thank her for all she'd done.

That made Chia feel strange. Now she'd seen him in real life, somehow that had taken over from all the other ways she'd known him before, and she felt kind of funny about him. Confused. Like all of this had pegged him in realtime for her, and she kept thinking of her mother complaining that Lo and Rez were nearly as old as she was.

And there was something else to it, too, that came from what she'd seen when she was crouched down in the back of that van, between the little Japanese guy with the sleeve of his jacket hanging down, and Masahiko: she'd looked out the window and seen the faces, as the van inched away. None of them knowing that that was Rez hunched down in there, under a jacket, but maybe sensing it somehow. And something in Chia letting her know she'd never quite be like that again. Never as comfortably a face in that crowd. Because now she knew there were rooms they never saw, or even dreamed of, where crazy things, or even just *boring* things, happened, and that was where the stars came from. And it was something like that that worried her now when she thought of Rez coming to see her. That and how he really was her mother's age.

And all of that made her wonder what she was going to tell the others, back in Seattle. How could they understand it? She thought Zona would understand. She really wanted to talk with Zona, but Arleigh had said it was better not to try to reach her now.

The longest-running top was starting to teeter, and they were cutting from that to the eyes of the girl who'd spun it.

Masahiko opened the door that connected their rooms.

The top gave a last wobble and kicked over. The girl covered her mouth with her hands, her eyes filled with the pain of defeat.

"You must come with me to Walled City now," Masahiko said.

Chia used the manual remote to turn the television off. "Arleigh asked us not to port."

"She knows," Masahiko said. "I've been there all day." He was wearing the same clothes but everything had been cleaned and pressed, and the legs of his baggy black pants looked strange with creases in them. "And on the phone with my father."

"Is he pissed off at you because those gumi guys came?"

"Arleigh McCrae asked Starkov to have someone speak with our gumi representative. They have apologized to my father. But Mitsuko was arrested near Hotel Di. That has caused him embarrassment and difficulty."

"Arrested?"

"For trespassing. She went to take part in the vigil. She climbed a fence, triggering an alarm. She could not climb back out before the police came."

"Is she okay?"

"My father has arranged her release. But he is not pleased."

"I feel like it's my fault," Chia said.

He shrugged and went back through the door.

Chia got up. Her Sandbenders was beside her bag on the luggage rack, with her goggles and tip-sets on top of it. She carried it into the other room.

It was a mess. Somehow he'd managed to turn it into something like his room at home. The sheets were tangled on the bed. Through the open bathroom door, she saw towels crumpled up on the tiled floor, a spilled bottle of shampoo on the counter beside the sink. He'd set up his computer on the desk, with his student cap beside it. There were opened mini-cans of espresso everywhere, and at least three room-service trays with half-empty ceramic bowls of ramen.

"Has anyone there seen Zona?" she asked, shoving a pillow and an open magazine aside on the foot of the bed. She sat down with her Sandbenders on her lap and started putting her tip-sets on.

She thought he gave her a strange look, then. "I don't think so," he said.

"Take me in the way you did the first time," she said. "I want to see it again."

Hak Nam. Tai Chang Street. The walls alive with shifting messages in the characters of every written language. Doorways flipping past, each one hinting at its own secret world. And this time she was more aware of the countless watching ghosts. That must be how people presented here, when you weren't in direct communication with them. A city of ghost-shadows. But this time Masahiko took another route, and they weren't climbing the twisted labyrinth of stairs but winding in at what would have been ground level in the original city, and Chia remembered the black hole, the rectangular vacancy he'd pointed out on the printed scarf in his room at the restaurant.

"I must leave you now," he said, as they burst from the maze into that vacancy. "They wish privacy."

He was gone, and at first Chia thought there was nothing there at all, only the faint grayish light filtering down from somewhere high above. When she looked up at this, it resolved into a vast, distant skylight, very far above her, but littered with a compost of strange and discarded shapes. She remembered the city's rooftops, and the things abandoned there.

"It is strange, isn't it?" The idoru stood before her in embroidered robes, the tiny bright patterns lit from within, moving. "Hollow and somber. But he insisted we meet you here."

"Who insisted? Do you know where Zona is?"

And there was a small table or four-legged stand in front of the idoru, very old, its dragon-carved legs thick with flaking, pale green paint. A single dusty glass stood centered there, something coiled inside it. Someone coughed.

“This is the heart of Hak Nam,” the Etruscan said, that same creaking voice assembled from a million samples of dry old sounds. “Traditionally a place of serious conversation.”

“Your friend is gone,” the idoru said. “I wished to tell you myself. This one,” indicating the glass, “volunteers details I do not understand.”

“But they’ve only shut down her website,” Chia said. “She’s in Mexico City, with her gang.”

“She is nowhere,” the Etruscan said.

“When you were taken from her,” the idoru said, “taken from the room in Venice, your friend went to your system software and activated the video units in your goggles. What she saw there indicated to her that you were in grave danger. As I believe you were. She must then have decided on a plan. Returning to her secret country, she linked her site with that of the Tokyo chapter of the Lo/Rez group. She ordered Ogawa, the president of the group, to post the message announcing Rez’s death at Hotel Di. She threatened her with a weapon that would shatter the Tokyo chapter’s site . . .”

“The knife,” Chia said. “It was *real?*”

“And *extremely* illegal,” the Etruscan said.

“When Ogawa refused,” the idoru said, “your friend used her weapon.”

“A serious crime,” the Etruscan said, “under the laws of every country involved.”

“She then posted her message through what remained of Ogawa’s website,” the idoru said. “It seemed official, and it had the effect of quickly surrounding Hotel Di with a sea of potential witnesses.''

''Whatever the next stage of her plan,'' the Etruscan said, ''she had exposed her presence in her website. The original owners became aware of her. She abandoned her site. They pursued her. She was forced to discard her persona.''

''What 'persona'?'' Chia felt a sinking feeling.

'' 'Zona Rosa,' '' said the Etruscan, ''was the persona of Mercedes Purissima Vargas-Gutierrez. She is twenty-six years old and the victim of an environmental syndrome occurring most frequently in the Federal District of Mexico.'' His voice was like rain on a thin metal roof now. ''Her father is an extremely successful criminal lawyer.''

''Then I can find her,'' Chia said.

''But she would not wish this,'' the idoru said. ''Mercedes Purissima is severely deformed by the syndrome, and has lived for the past five years in almost complete denial of her physical self.''

Chia was sitting there crying. Masahiko removed the black cups from his eyes and came over to the bed.

''Zona's gone,'' she said.

''I know,'' he said. He sat down beside her. ''You never finished telling me the story of the Sandbenders,'' he said. ''It was very interesting story.''

So she began to tell it to him.

45

Lucky

''Laney,'' he heard her say, her voice blurred with sleep. ''What are you doing?''

The illuminated face of the cedar telephone. ''I'm calling the Lucky Dragon, on Sunset.''

''The what?''

''Convenience store. Twenty-four hours.''

''Laney, it's three in the morning . . .''

''Have to thank Rydell, tell him the job worked out . . .''

She groaned and rolled over, pulling the pillow over her head.

Through the window he could see the translucent amber, the serried cliffs of the new buildings, reflecting the lights of the city.

46

Fables of the Reconstruction

Chia dreamed of a beach pebbled with crushed fragments of consumer electronics; crab-things scuttling low, their legs striped like antique resistors. Tokyo Bay, shrouded in fog from an old movie, a pale gray blanket meant to briefly conceal first-act terrors: sea monsters or some alien armada.

Hak Nam rose before her as she waded nearer, but with a dream's logic it grew no closer. Backwashing sea, sucking at her ankles. The Walled City is growing. Being grown. From the fabric of the beach, wrack and wreckage of the world before things changed. Unthinkable tonnage, dumped here by barge and bulk-lifter in the course of the great reconstruction. The minuscule bugs of Rodel-van Erp seethe there, lifting the iron-caged balconies that are sleeping rooms, countless unplanned windows throwing blank silver rectangles back against the fog. A thing of random human accretion, monstrous and superb, it is being reconstituted here, retranslated from its later incarnation as a realm of consensual fantasy.

The alarm's infrared stutter. Sunbright halogen illuminating the printed scarf, at its center the rectangle representing an emptiness, an address unknown: the killfile of legend. Zapping the Espressomatic to life with her remote, she curls back into the quilt's dark, waiting for the building hiss of steam. Most mornings, now, she checks into the City, hears the gossip in a favorite barbershop in Sai Shing Road. The Etruscan is there, sometimes, with Klaus and the Rooster and the other ghosts he hangs with, and they tolerate her. She's proud of that, because they'll clam up around Masahiko. Are they old, incredibly ancient, or do they just act that way? Whatever, they tend to know things first, and she's learned to value that. And the Etruscan has been hinting at a vacancy, something really small, but with a window. Looking down into what would have been Lung Chun Road.

He likes her, the Etruscan. It's weird. They say he doesn't like anybody, really, but he fixed her father's credit, even though she'd forgotten to leave the key. (She keeps the key to Suite 17 in a watered-silk cosmetics case they gave her on the JAL flight home: it's made of white plastic, molded to look like an old-fashioned mechanical key, with a mag-strip down the long part and the flat thing shaped like the crown a princess wears. She gets it out and looks at it sometimes, but it just looks like a cheap white piece of plastic.)

The Etruscan and the others spy on the Project all the time. That's what they call it. Through them, Chia knows that the idoru's island isn't finished yet. It's there but it isn't stable; something they have to do it before they build, even with nanotech, in case another earthquake comes. She wonders what the Russians will do with theirs, and sometimes she wonders about Maryalice, and Eddie, and Calvin, the guy at Whiskey Clone who got her out of there, for no reason other than he thought he should. But it seems like a long time ago, between the Walled City and school.

She figures her mother knows by now that she wasn't with Hester, but her mother's never said anything about it, except to talk to her twice about contraceptives and safe sex. And, really, she wasn't there much more than forty-eight hours, if you didn't count the travel-time, because Rez hadn't been able to make it over to thank her, and Arleigh had said that, all in all, it was better if she got home before anybody started asking any questions, but they'd send her first class on Japan Air Lines. So Arleigh had driven her back out to Narita that night, but not in her green van because she said it was a write-off. And she'd still felt so bad about Zona, and it made her feel so stupid, because she felt like her friend was dead, but her friend hadn't even really existed, and there was this other girl in Mexico City, with terrible problems, and so she wound up telling all that to Arleigh and just crying.

And Arleigh said she should just wait. Because that girl in Mexico City, more than anything else, needed to be somebody else. And it didn't matter that she hadn't *been* Zona, because she'd made Zona *up,* and that was just as real. Just wait, Arleigh said, because somebody else would turn up, somebody new, and it would be like they already knew you. And Chia had sat and thought about that, beside Arleigh in her fast little car.

—But I couldn't ever tell her I knew?

—That would spoil it.

When they'd gotten to the airport, Arleigh checked her in at JAL, found somebody to take her to the lounge (which was sort of like a cross between a bar and really fancy business office), and gave her a bag with a roadie-grade Lo/Rez tour jacket in it. The sleeves were made of transparent rayon, and the lining that showed through that looked like liquid mercury. Arleigh said it was really tacky, but maybe she had a friend who'd like it. It was from their Kombinat tour, and it had all the tour dates embroidered on the back in three different languages.

She hadn't ever worn it, and she'd never really shown it to anybody either. It was hanging in her closet, under a piece of drycleaner's plastic. She hadn't really been that active in the chapter lately. (Kelsey had dropped right out.) Chia didn't really feel that anybody in the chapter would get it, if she tried to tell them what had happened, plus there were all the bits she couldn't tell them anyway.

But mainly it was the City taking up her time, because Rez and Rei were there, shadows among the other shadows but still you could tell. Working on their Project.

Plenty there who didn't like the idea, but plenty who did. The Etruscan did. He said it was the craziest thing since they'd turned that first killfile inside out.

Sometimes Chia wondered if they all weren't just joking, because it just seemed impossible that anyone could ever do that. Build that, on an island in Tokyo Bay.

But the idoru said that that was where they wanted to live, now that they were married. So they were going to do it.

And if they do, Chia thought, hearing the hiss of the Espressomatic, I'll go there.